I0676074

The Awakening and Total Transformation of Eliot Hart

A love story

Jonathan Harries

RHINO BOOKS

Rhino Books
An imprint of Jonathan Harries Ink
PO Box 183
New York, NY 10013

Copyright © 2023 by Jonathan Harries

This book is a work of fiction. Names, characters, places, and events are either the products of the author's imagination or are used fictitiously.

All rights reserved. No part of this publication may be reproduced, distributed, or transmitted in any form or by any means, including photocopying, recording, or other electronic or mechanical methods, without the prior written permission of the publisher, except in the case of brief quotations embodied in critical reviews and certain other noncommercial uses permitted by copyright law. For permission requests and other information, write to the publisher at the address above.

www.jonathanharriesink.com

ISBN (e-book): 978-1-950628-19-3
ISBN (print): 978-1-950628-20-9

First edition

To Don Marshall, who first brought the legend of "Florida Man" to my limited attention.

Contents

The Sorites Paradox

The sorites is a paradox that results from vague predicates or terms that lack sharp boundaries or precise definitions. *Bald* is a vague predicate. So are *tall* and *rich*. A *heap* is a vague predicate, and it is from the Greek word for heap, *soros,* that the sorites paradox takes its name.

Imagine a heap of rice. If you remove one grain, is it still a heap? If you remove two, is it still a heap? When does the heap become a non-heap—and vice versa: when does a non-heap become a heap? If one grain of rice is not a heap, then adding a single grain to a non-heap will not make it a heap. At some point, however, you will add one more grain and say, "By God, that appears to a heap." But if one grain cannot make a heap, how can it be? Can one extra dollar make you rich? Can you change from being an overthinker to an under-thinker by having one less thought?

Of course, the sorites paradox can be applied to moral arguments too. When does a fetus become a person, or when is a person no longer alive? But this book does not focus on too many moral issues. It's a story about love, and while love is a term filled with vagueness, the story attempts to pinpoint the exact moment—a kiss, a squeeze, a jolt of electricity—that Eliot Hart defied the paradox, moved from over-thinking to a more spontaneous cognitive process, and knew he was in love with Cori-Anne van Cleave.

Chapter 1

Florida man denies condom filled with heroin in rectum is his

"Eliot, why are you staring at that headline?" Belinda asked, leaning over the back of his chair.

"Because it worries me," he replied, putting down his iPad.

"Well, it worries me that my partner is looking at newspaper headlines about men shoving things up their asses. Honestly, you can be very weird at times." She moved to the kitchen to pour herself a cup of coffee. Eliot looked at her and wondered why she was dressed as if she were going to a business meeting on a Sunday.

"I'm obviously not looking at it from that angle, although it might be interesting to know the angle he was at when the heroin was placed in his rectum. The article doesn't mention that. If you think about it, he couldn't have been standing unless the other party was kneeling. That to me is the key piece of information missing from this article."

"Eliot," said Belinda, sounding like his kindergarten

teacher, "I don't want to think about it. Nor do I want you to think about it. What I want is for you to stop overthinking about ridiculous things and stop underthinking about what is important."

But Eliot didn't hear her. He was totally focused on the trigonometric function involved in calculating the angle of insertion. Belinda cleared her throat loudly.

"Eliot...Eliot!"

He looked up and smiled. "The thing that concerns me about the article is that no one—neither the medics nor the police—asked the man whose bag it was. Their only issue seems to be the fact that it was filled with heroin. They've simply assumed the bag was his and aren't even bothering to investigate his claim that it wasn't."

"Of course it's his. Who else's drugs could it be? Now, why don't you stop contemplating what people stick into their posteriors and finish that paper you were supposed to have completed two days ago. Remember I'm flying to London tonight for a board meeting. Finish it before I get back."

"Why are you leaving on Sunday?"

"I realize that every day is the same for you, but for those of us still gainfully employed, today happens to be Monday."

"Oh," he said, looking at the date on his iPad, "so it is. Well...." He put the iPad down on the side table. "I have a feeling this may just be the headline I've been looking for. Don't ask me why because I can't tell you yet, but this could be the very thing I need to finally finish my paper."

"Oh, Jesus. Please tell me you're joking. No one's going to publish let alone read a paper that focuses on something that disgusting, and you can kiss the job goodbye if anyone happens to be insane enough to print it. Seriously, Eliot, you'll embarrass me and make a total fool out of yourself. I don't need that, nor do you. Now don't be a total idiot—find an alternative subject to write about. I hate to say this, but you're very annoying lately. More so than usual, and quite frankly it's becoming tiresome."

With that she tapped the top of his head as if it were the perfect substitute for a kiss, took a final swig of her coffee, and left him alone to contemplate just how this one Florida Man headline would finally put him on the home stretch to the completion of his paper on the sorites paradox.

"I've never heard of the sorites paradox," Belinda had said to him a few weeks before when he'd brought it up as a possible subject for the paper. They were sitting on the couch discussing just what he'd need to do to get the job at the local community college. More correctly, Belinda was lying on the couch telling him what to do, and Eliot was sitting up massaging her feet. In truth he was not that keen on Belinda's feet, but she'd asked—or rather, demanded—and so he was doing the best he could.

"You've probably heard of the premise before," he replied, "even if you don't know the name. Let me try to explain it as best I can." He gave her right big toe a tweak, which drew a contented *oof* from her. His best explanation did nothing to alleviate Belinda's lack of interest. She groaned once or twice to indicate her boredom, though she knew that when Eliot's mouth was open, his ears tended to close.

"One grain does not make a heap," continued Eliot, blissfully unaware that he'd lost Belinda at the mention of the word "predicates." He droned on for a while, ending only when he realized she'd fallen asleep. "Oh well," he said quietly, "that is the basic idea and probably more than you want to know."

"It's not only more than I want to know," Belinda said, opening one eye and sitting up so she could take a sip of her wine. "It sounds positively stupid and a total waste of time. Why don't you choose something that'll help the students find decent jobs? Something...useful."

But "useful" and "practical" were not in Eliot's stable of things that needed considering at that moment in time. As far as he was concerned, the sorites paradox encapsulated his entire existence. If anyone could throw new light on it, it was he, Eliot Bartholomew Hart. He'd been building up to the challenge his whole life.

On Eliot's tenth birthday his maternal grandparents gave him the complete twenty-volume set of The Book of Knowledge—the Children's Encyclopedia. He began to read volume one an hour after he'd thrown up from eating too much of his chocolate birthday cake and finished volume twenty about four weeks later. He'd sprinted through The Encyclopedia Britannica by his sixteenth birthday, adding one piece of knowledge to another. He continued his quest book by book, magazine after magazine, and then when the internet democratized information on the small screen, he knew he was set for life.

He did his undergraduate at Brown and enrolled at Princeton for a PhD in neuroscience. His thesis on *The Role of Volatile Molecules in Vanilla Extract in Ice Cream on Brain Freeze and their Impact on the Flavor Decision Factor (FDF)* was rejected. The head of the thesis review committee told him that he'd never met anyone who "put so much thought into something so irrelevant." Instead of taking it as an insult, which is what the professor intended it to be, Eliot took it as a mission.

While too much information about an object or subject, he thought, might lead to short-term confusion, too little would result in an inability to make a rational decision. The question he kept asking himself was at which point would one have enough details to make an intelligent choice. This obsession—and anyone who knew Eliot knew it to be so for him—led to a business relationship with his closest friend, who had just completed his MS in artificial intelligence and the development of a program called WhatMatters.

WhatMatters used a combination of AI and consumer behavior data to predict the key motivator for a consumer for just about any product or service. Their proposition was that were lots of *things* that marketers thought mattered about their products, but there was always *one thing* that mattered more than anything else—the *thing* that would increase the desire on the part of a consumer to learn more about the product. And that *one thing* was what WhatMatters synthesized with a 95 percent accuracy. The line they used to sell it to marketers was, "We give customers just enough to want to know more."

A year after they launched WhatMatters, Google bought it from them for $1.6 billion. That was seven months ago, and Eliot hadn't worked a day since. He'd also left $600 million on the table because he broke his agreement to stay on for two years. It didn't worry him in the least. As he explained to an absolutely flabbergasted Belinda, $200 million is more money than anyone needs—certainly more than he'd ever imagined he'd have—and in any case it was time for him to do something else.

"Then you're lucky I'm not with you for your money," said Belinda, who was an extremely successful hedge fund manager at a big global company. She didn't expound further on why she was with him because she didn't know herself and was secretly thinking of a way to tell him she was moving on. The idea that she might have been with him for his money had never entered Eliot's mind, though he did wonder sometimes what she saw in him. Sometimes he even wondered what he saw in her and when their relationship would end, but unlike her, he had nothing imminent in mind.

Belinda wasn't the first person he'd been with for an extended period of time. He'd had two other serious relationships, but both had ended because the women involved felt that he was more committed to what he did than to them. It was different with Belinda. In the beginning they'd both been so focused on their jobs that the idea of commitment hadn't even come up. As their relationship progressed it had been more about convenience than anything else, and for the most part it worked. But not the entire part.

One of the biggest roadblocks in Eliot's quest to move forward after he left WhatMatters was that he was by nature a physically lazy person. He was thrilled to go out to eat—something he did a little too much of—or to see a comedy or thriller at the local movie theater, but he rarely, and then always reluctantly, accompanied Belinda to the theater or art openings. He did work out just about every day but not the way serious people work out. His time in the gym was at a more leisurely pace than that of Belinda, a workout fanatic, who made it clear to him that he was getting slightly chubby and inordinately slothful. He took these jibes good naturedly because he couldn't imagine she'd be purposefully mean.

"You know," he said when Belinda got particularly indignant one morning when he was lounging about in his pajamas staring out the window of their 54th floor apartment in Manhattan, "when I don't appear to be doing anything obvious, then I am thinking."

"No, you're not. You're overthinking. Which you do about everything. Now stop overthinking about thinking and do something!"

The genesis of Eliot's proposed paper on the sorites paradox occurred two days after the "thinking" conversation, when Belinda decided to take matters into her own hands to get her lazy boyfriend—and potentially soon-to-be ex-boyfriend—off the couch.

At 11:00 a.m. she called Eliot from her office to inform

him that they were going to dinner with a woman she knew from one of the boards she served on and who happened to be the dean of a nearby community college that catered to people who wanted to enter a trade rather than go to a four-year college. Eliot didn't ask why he had to go to what sounded like a horrifically boring dinner but assumed it would be for the dean to ask him for a donation.

Halfway through the meal, Belinda poked Eliot in the chest and said, "Cynthia has an idea for you, and I'd really like you to consider it."

Cynthia, a large woman in her mid-sixties, sniffed and pointed her fork at Eliot. He looked at her and then down at the half-eaten shrimp dangling precariously on the end of the utensil.

"Yes," she said in a booming voice, no doubt honed on students who had no wish to hear anything remotely connected with higher education. "I told Belinda that I had an opening for someone to teach a course in critical thinking. She suggested you'd be perfect. Are you?"

"Um," replied Eliot, totally focused on the shrimp. By his calculation, using standard-formula Newtonian physics, the splat factor would occur in under a second from the moment the crustacean left the fork.

"Excuse me," said Cynthia. "Are you staring at my breasts?"

Eliot blinked and then emerged from his seafood-induced reverie when Belinda kicked him on the shin. "No, absolutely not!"

"Well, good, because we don't tolerate that sort of behavior at Greystone Community College. So, let me ask you once more: do you think you're right for this job?"

"Am I right for the...job?"

"Yes, yes. No need to repeat what I said. You are not a parrot. My initial impression of you is not a good one, but I have every faith in Belinda. If she vouches for you, and you're interested, then you'll have to write and publish a paper to present to the board before school reopens in two months."

Before Eliot could open his mouth to reply to the woman who was rapidly making him feel like a rowboat in the path of a battleship, Belinda jumped in.

"Of course he's interested. I'll make sure of it. Don't you worry, Cynthia."

But fate has a funny way of dealing with the arrogant prognostications of mere mortals. Precisely three hours before Belinda committed him to the paper, an event occurred in a city twelve hundred miles away. Though totally unrelated to his current predicament, it would have a profound impact on Eliot Hart. Far greater than anything Belinda had in mind.

In New York, the dangling shrimp plummeted from Cynthia's fork, bounced off the top of her left breast, and would have fallen onto her white Dior dress if Eliot, with a move reminiscent of an Old West gunfighter drawing his pistol, hadn't shot out his hand and caught it. In Miami, Cori-Anne van Cleave shoved a condom containing two bags of heroin between the butt cheeks of Jorge "el Clavo" Coronel Morales.

Chapter 2

Two months earlier

At thirty-six years old, Cori-Anne van Cleave still had the body of a college cheerleader—which she'd once been—and the flexibility of a twelve-year-old Russian gymnast. Ten years of teaching yoga had been kind to her physically, though recently she'd become somewhat emotionally distraught. The cause of her mental discomposition was the yoga studio of a local competitor.

Cori-Anne had a small, well-appointed yoga studio on 65th street in Miami's North Beach. She also owned a raggedy condo nearby, which she got in the divorce settlement after her ex-husband's arrest and incarceration for smuggling fifty-five pounds of cocaine from Bolivia. The cocaine had been inserted into the bellies of twenty mules that Eduardo Reyes, Cori-Anne's ex, had brought into the US "to provide donkey rides for the kids like they do on the beaches in England." As he explained to Cori-Anne the last time she visited him in jail, "I thought the customs guys would be so focused on human drug mules that they'd never suspect actual mules." Cori-Anne was less upset about her husband being a deranged idiot than she was about the poor mules, which fortunately, after passing the bags of cocaine, were adopted by a famous singer who had a ranch in Homestead where she housed rescued animals.

The issues associated with her failed marriage, however, were not what kept Cori-Anne up at night. Her anguish, as she told her friend Coachella de Ville when she met her at a beach bar one evening, had everything to do with Ram-Dann Anubis's Hard Core Yoga and Pilates Studio that had opened just two blocks from her own studio.

"He's taking all my customers," said Cori-Anne, ordering herself another large martini and staring forlornly out at the storm clouds gathering over the Atlantic. "And there's not a thing I can do about it." She'd known Coachella for almost a year. They'd met at a chiropractor's office, where they both found themselves waiting for what felt like an inordinate amount of time to see the much sought-after Dr. Forleeza, a specialist in treating common muscle strains suffered by dancers.

"Now you know why they call this a damn waiting room," said Coachella to Cori-Anne, the only other patient in the room. "'Cause all you do is damn well wait."

"And that's why they call us 'patients,'" retorted Cori-Anne with a grin.

"Why's that?" asked Coachella, looking confused.

"Oh, because you need to have a lot of patience."

For a moment Coachella stared back at Cori-Anne with a blank expression on her face.

"Uh, patients...patience," said Cori-Anne, hoping she

hadn't overestimated the brain power of the rather exotic looking woman.

Coachella let out a shriek of laughter. "I was fucking with you...of course I got it. You should see your face. Man, you thought I was a regular dumbass, didn't you?"

Before Cori-Anne could protest, Coachella stuck out her hand. "I'm DeVille Devine," she said, "but I call myself Coachella 'cause DeVille is a stupid first name. Now look. I ain't waiting another five minutes for this arrogant fucker."

"Me neither," said Cori-Anne. "I'm starving. Feel like going to lunch?" They canceled their appointments with the surprisingly sympathetic receptionist who quite frankly was surprised anyone still wanted to see the man she and the other office workers called "Dr. Forleeza, the tit-squeezer" on account of his wandering hands.

Over lunch at a small sushi restaurant, Cori-Anne decided that Coachella was unlike any person she'd ever met. There was nothing sacred, nothing off limits, and after five minutes Coachella had Cori-Anne in hysterics at the stories about the men she'd dealt with at the exotic dance club where she worked. While they were as different as pickles are from petunias in most things, they had a similar upbringing when it came to parents. Coachella was from Detroit, where her father had worked at the Detroit-Hamtramck Cadillac assembly plant. He'd named her DeVille because that was the production line he oversaw. After a serious injury left him disabled, he'd drunk himself to death, leaving Coachella's mom to raise her on her own. Coachella's mom had—like Cori-Anne's—turned to religion. After her mother's pastor wanted to "exorcise the demons that possessed Coachella's soul using his sacred staff," Coachella jumped on a Greyhound and only got off when she reached Miami. Their friendship grew stronger over time, and Cori-Anne found herself relying more and more on Coachella's tough but honest advice.

"That motherfucker ain't even Indian or Egyptian or whatever that name is supposed to be," said Coachella, taking a sip of her carrot juice. She had an hour before her first performance at Jiggles Gentleman's Club, where she worked from 7:00 p.m. until 1:00 a.m. Her rule was that she didn't drink before the job, only on it. "His real name is Danny Ramirez...used to be a full-time butt shaker at the Cock Crows all-male strip joint in South Beach. So, you tell me how he got the money to open a big-ass yoga and Pilates studio."

"I have no idea," replied Cori-Anne, scowling at two half-drunk men who'd been leering at her and Coachella ever since they walked in. "All I know is that half my customers have given notice, and I don't know what I'm going to do."

"I'll tell you how he got the place," said Coachella, sucking up the last of her carrot juice. "He's bleaching money for some Mexican cartel."

"Bleaching?"

"Laundering...you know. Most of the cartels used to put their dirty money into car washes and strip joints. The word is, with fewer and fewer strip joints opening these days, those motherfuckers are looking for new places—gyms and yoga studios."

"Well then, I'm totally screwed," said Cori-Anne,

looking even more glum. "I can't take them on. They can offer all the incentives I can't begin to afford, and the place resembles the most expensive Miami nightclub on steroids. My studio looks like something out of the last century."

"Well," said Coachella, looking at her watch, "you're right. You can't fight big money with no money. That's the truth. You're going to have to come up with something they can't do. How about hot yoga? I hear that's popular."

"I don't know. It's very gimmicky, and Miami's hot enough as it is."

"Listen, girl. Gimmicky may be what you need right now. Anyway," she looked at the time on her phone, "I gotta go, but I'll keep thinking. Hang in there, sugar." Coachella leaned over and gave Cori-Anne a hug. Then she stood up and handed a coupon for a free lap dance at Jiggles to the two drunks who'd been ogling her.

Cori-Anne paid the tab and decided to walk back to her apartment before the storm hit. She almost made it, but it wasn't her day.

She was drenched by the time she arrived at her second floor apartment, and her short black hair clung to her head like an old mop. To add to the doom and gloom, she'd left her bedroom window open, and the shag carpet between the bed and window was soaked through. But none of that mattered to Cori-Anne. She was tired from worrying about finances and half-smashed from the two large martinis, and so she fell onto her bed into a deep sleep. She woke up six hours later when she desperately needed to pee and throw up.

Her first class did not begin until eleven o'clock, and

by then a couple of aspirin and some orange juice had restored her to a semi-human condition. She pulled up the attendee list for the eleven o'clock class and saw that there were only three names on the list, down four from yesterday. Just as she began to wonder whether she should call some of her used-to-be regulars to try to persuade them to come back, her phone rang. It was her mom calling from Waterloo, Iowa. She sighed, knowing it would be yet another Groundhog Day call.

"How are you, mom?"

"I'm just great, honey. Have you allowed Jesus into your life yet?"

"Not since we last spoke, Mom."

"What are you waiting for, Cori-Anne? The longer you keep him out, the worse your life will get. And it hasn't exactly been joyous up until now."

"I'm not keeping him out. He just hasn't bothered to come calling."

"Oh dear, Cori-Anne. How many times do I have to tell you? Jesus doesn't come to you unless you go to him. Pastor Johnson says there's a wonderful church near you. They'll welcome you with full hearts and open arms."

"I'll think about it, Mom."

"You always say that, honey. But finding the Lord isn't about thinking. It's about doing. Laziness is no excuse for godlessness. By the way, you sound terrible."

"I'm fine. I just had a rough night."

"So, you're not fine. The devil operates in the darkness is what Pastor Johnson says. If you won't trust me, trust him. John 8 verse 12 says 'I am the light of the world. Whomever follows me will not walk in darkness.' Accept

Jesus, honey, and you need never fear the dark of night again."

Cori-Anne groaned. After her father died from alcohol poisoning, her mom had joined an Evangelical church. It had become her whole life, and she was determined to make her wayward daughter part of it. What she didn't know was that Cori-Anne had started practicing a form of Buddhism based on a book she'd picked up at a second-hand bookstore. Cori-Anne didn't have the heart to tell her. It would have driven her mom nuttier than the fruitcake she already was.

"I try to be a good person, Mom. I may not know every verse in the Bible, but that doesn't mean I don't know right from wrong." Her mother clicked her tongue and gave a deep sigh, and Cori-Anne knew it was time to bring the conversation to an end.

"Wow!" she exclaimed. "Look at the time. My class starts in thirty minutes. Love you." She hung up without waiting for a response. Then she filled her HydroFlask with coffee and walked out her apartment, down the stairs, and into the warm sunshine. The sun felt so good on her face that her melancholy lifted for a moment. It was no more than a temporary reprieve, and by the time she arrived at her studio, she was back in the doldrums. Her two most enthusiastic students were limbering up outside, and they greeted her with an ebullient and synchronized "hello."

Marvin and Shelley Gotlieb were in their late seventies. They'd moved to Miami from New Jersey five years before and hadn't regretted their decision for a nanosecond. Florida was all they hoped it would be. They had a circle of

16

friends, all of whom had condos close by. All were relatively independent and despite encouragement from their children had no intention of moving into one of the many retirement homes in Miami. The Gotliebs were the only ones who did any real form of exercise, but every evening the entire group of retirees strode energetically, if haltingly, along the Beach Walk, ending up by 5:30 at the Purple Ibis Diner, where they ate an early supper. There was a lot to love about Miami for the Gotliebs, but most of all they loved yoga, and their beautiful instructor, and were determined somehow or other to get the others in their group to join them at their eleven o'clock class.

"Hello, Marvin and Shelley," said Cori-Anne with less enthusiasm than she normally managed. "You're early as usual."

"How are you, my dear?" replied Shelley, attempting to stretch her quads without falling over. "Well, you know how much we love you and yoga."

"And in that order," said Marvin, letting out a discreet fart as he tried valiantly to touch his toes.

"Well, you always brighten my day," said Cori-Anne, unlocking the door and flicking on the light switch. The fluorescent tube lights crackled one or twice and flooded the room in what Cori-Anne, with perhaps a touch of exaggeration, had called "a sensuous, soothing glow" in her direct mail piece. The walls were covered in old prints she'd gotten off the internet and enlarged at the FedEx store on Collins. From a distance they looked like Indian holy men on a pilgrimage but were in fact beggars looking for a handout. Fortunately, none of her students had taken the time to examine them. There was a single wooden table against the back wall covered in a paisley shawl she'd bought at a thrift shop. It was made in China but looked as if it could have come from Kashmir. The table held a chubby bronze Buddha and an incense diffuser, which she lit with a box of matches from Coachella's strip club. She ushered the Gotliebs into the studio and put an old Ravi Shankar CD into the player on the floor under the table.

"Let's wait a few minutes for the others to come," she said as the Gotliebs unrolled their yoga mats.

"Of course, sweetie," said Marvin. "We don't have anywhere to be before our afternoon nap. Take as long as you need."

Fifteen minutes later when it was clear that the Gotliebs would collapse from their pre-class stretching, Cori-Anne gave up and started the class. By the fifth cobra pose, even the Gotliebs knew that Cori-Anne's heart was not in it.

"Cori-Anne," said Shelley, struggling up from her yoga mat, which was now covered in a thin film of sweat, "something is wrong. Why don't you tell Marv and me about it. Perhaps we can help?"

"I'm so sorry," replied Cori-Anne. "I shouldn't bring my problems into the studio. I'm going to refund you for this class."

"Are you kidding? We don't need a refund—this was a great workout!" Marvin said, holding onto his wife. "But you, my dear—you look like you could do with a little advice from Uncle Marv and Auntie Shelly. Come, we'll buy you a coffee."

Cori-Anne declined, but the Gotliebs were relentless, and

eventually she gave in. What did she have to lose, she thought, except her remaining two clients? She grabbed her sweat top and walked slowly with Marv and Shelly to a nearby Starbucks. Marv and Shelly got a table outside under an umbrella, which Marvin immediately took down. They hadn't moved to Florida for the shade as he explained to Cori-Anne when she came out with their coffees.

"So," said Marvin, once Cori-Anne had explained the situation, "this guy Ramada Inn—"

"It's Ram-Dann," Cori-Anne corrected him. "Although my friend told me his real name is Danny Ramirez."

"OK, then, this Danny *shmo*, he's taken all your clients?"

"It looks like it," Cori-Anne replied. "Except, of course, for the two of you—thank you—but honestly, I wouldn't blame you if you went. His place has so much more to offer."

"Except for you." Shelly patted Cori-Anne's cheek with her hand that was warm from the coffee.

"You're so sweet, you really are." Cori-Anne looked down at the table. "But unfortunately, that's not going to cut it. Unless I can think of something to make my place more appealing, I'm going to have to shut it down."

"Then you're in the right company. Marv here used to be in advertising. One of the best copywriters in the business," said Shelly reassuringly.

"Shelly always flatters me," Marvin said, leaning over to give his wife a kiss and spilling most of his coffee on his sweatpants, which didn't seem to faze him.

"Nonsense, don't be so modest," Shelly replied. "They called him 'Marvelous Marvin, The Wizard of Words.' He could sell steak to a vegetarian."

"That's very impressive," laughed Cori-Anne, "but I don't think this is an advertising problem."

"I agree," said Marvin. "What we need is a USP."

"What's that?" Cori-Anne asked.

"A Unique Selling Proposition," he replied proudly. "Something that'll make your class different and have that Ramadan guy grinding his teeth so hard he'll need implants. You leave it to me. It's all in here." He tapped his head with his empty coffee cup. And with that the Gotliebs shuffled off to take their nap.

At four-thirty that evening Shelly called Cori-Anne to ask her to meet them at the Blue Ibis Diner at five-thirty. Marvin, she said, had come up with a brilliant idea.

"Cori-Anne!" yelled Marvin, apparently oblivious to the other diners. "Over here, come join us, darling." He and Shelly were sitting at a large round table with four other couples whose combined age, Cori-Anne estimated, must have been close to six hundred. Their faces were tanned and lined, and they all looked as if they shopped for resort wear at the same store. The Gotliebs introduced Cori-Anne to their friends, the Minskys, the Constantinedes, the Goldbergs, and the Ludlows. All greeted her warmly and all appeared to be very excited.

"We have an idea for you," said Marvin.

"It was his idea, the horny old toad," added Tina Constantinedes, giving Marvin a salacious grin, "but we're all in."

"What?" Cori-Anne asked, feeling excited for the first time in weeks. "Tell me!"

"First, we gotta have soup," said Leo Goldberg. "We never talk about important things before soup."

After the waitress cleared their empty bowls and mopped the table in front of Leo Goldberg, who was waiting for his new dentures, Marvin told Cori-Anne the idea with animated interjections from all members of the extremely earnest septuagenarian circle.

Cori-Anne didn't know whether to jump for joy or throw up.

Chapter 3

Seven weeks later

The ominous gray smoke that drifted up from the Montecristo No.4 cigar wedged firmly between the teeth of Jorge "el Clavo" Coronel Morales made Danny Ramirez think of a funeral pyre. Don Jorge, as he insisted on being called, had flown up from Culiacán, the capital of the state of Sinaloa, that morning to find out why his latest investment wasn't laundering money as efficiently as it had done just two months before.

"Did you have a good flight, Don Jorge?" asked Danny Ramirez. There was a tremor in his voice that even the yoga breathing exercise he practiced regularly hadn't helped.

Don Jorge regarded him carefully and then slowly drew the cigar out his mouth. He was a short man and his fingers, though perfectly manicured, were proportionately stubby.

"I just bought a Gulfstream G650...do you know this plane?"

"No, Don Jorge, I don't. But I can only imagine it must be beautiful."

"Beautiful doesn't begin to describe its magnificence."

Danny opened his mouth to throw out another superlative adjective, but Don Jorge held up his hand. Danny looked at the hand and saw that while the don's fingernails were shaped and polished, his hands were rough and calloused like those of someone who'd labored hard at some stage of his life. Jorge "el Clavo" Morales had labored hard. Not in the poppy fields his family owned, but as the chief *sicario* for his uncles, who ran one of the most important drug cartels in northern Mexico. He'd acquired the nickname "el Clavo," *the nail,* because his favorite method of execution was to nail his victims to a wall. Danny closed his mouth and wiped a bead of sweat from his forehead.

Don Jorge leaned forward and patted Danny's cheek with his outstretched hand. He gave Danny an avuncular smile. "You're nervous, no?"

"Uhm, should I be nervous, Don Jorge?" He looked down, not wanting to see the truth in the don's eyes, which reminded him of black holes.

"Everyone should be nervous, Danny. It keeps you on your toes. I'm nervous...."

"You, Don Jorge? I cannot imagine that you are nervous of anything."

"Of course I am. I'm nervous that my wife will find out about my mistress...mistresses. I have more than one. I'm nervous that what I pay the border control agents in Miami to look the other way may not be enough, those thieving *criminales*. But you, Danny, what do you have to be nervous of? You're young, you're good looking. We pay you a fortune to look after our interests."

"Well, yes, about that, Don Jorge. I can explain what's happening."

"I look forward to that. I'd really like to know how some young woman with no money to back her can steal more than half your members in so short a time." The avuncular tone had vanished, and Don Jorge gave the kind of snort an enraged bull gives a matador just before goring him. He stubbed the cigar into an ashtray on Danny's desk as if he were playing a needlessly violent form of whack-a-mole.

Danny's teeth began to chatter, and his breathing became dangerously fast. It was a reaction Don Jorge had seen many times before. He'd cultivated his own one-man version of good cop, bad cop, which he found extremely effective. Scare the crap out of the person, then calm them down with a little kindness; get the needed information, and then kill them. His ability to switch from one to the other in the same sentence threw most of his victims into a tailspin and virtually guaranteed a full confession every time.

"Danny, Danny...relax. It is not you I am angry at. It's her, the young woman. So calm down and tell me what she did to achieve such success." He poured Danny a small shot of the special añejo tequila he kept in a flask in his coat pocket for just such occasions. It was rough and raw and guaranteed to burn on the way down. "Here, drink this. You'll feel better, I promise."

Danny rarely drank alcohol, but he held his breath and swallowed the deep amber liquor in one sip. It was if he'd swallowed barbed wire. He spluttered and coughed until the don gave him a hefty clap on the back. He nodded, trying to appear grateful.

"Thank you, Don Jorge. That has helped."

"Excellent. Real manly stuff. Now tell me what I want to know."

Danny swallowed and nodded. "OK, well her name is Cori-Anne van Cleave."

"Cori-Anne van Cleave," repeated Don Jorge, rolling the name around his mouth. "Sounds more like a stripper than a yoga instructor."

"No, she just comes from Iowa," replied Danny as if that explained Cori-Anne's name. "She's actually a very good yoga instructor."

"Clearly, yes. She must be if she's taking your members."

"That's not it, Don Jorge. She has something that is very different to what we can offer. She has naked yoga classes."

"Did you say 'naked' yoga classes?" The don's pitch rose almost an octave.

"Yes, can you imagine anything more disgusting?"

The don certainly could imagine many things more disgusting, but at that moment he couldn't imagine anything more intriguing. Yoga did not play a part in any aspect of his life other than his investment in Danny's studio. But right then and there, the thought of a naked woman in one of those ass-up poses—he didn't know the name of the position he was visualizing—did something to him that he hadn't experienced for quite a while.

The truth was that nothing had turned Don Jorge on for months. When his mistress (and he only had one) complained about his lack of performance, he'd threatened to nail her tongue to her bedpost if she as much as opened her mouth. He'd tried Viagra and a penis pump, but the results were negligible. It wasn't that he was incapable of having sex, it was that he was simply uninterested in the act of copulation. He'd even had one of Los Angeles's top sexual therapists flown to his hilltop home in Sinaloa to see what was wrong. The man had examined him and run various tests and concluded that the only thing wrong with Don Jorge was that his libido had gone AWOL. He'd advised the don to take a subscription to Pornhub and scroll through the various categories to see if anything tickled his fancy. But after twenty minutes Don Jorge lost interest and gave his subscription password to one of his lieutenants.

Right now, though, at the very mention of naked yoga, he felt a stirring in his nether regions. It was as if someone had attached jump-starter cables to his penis. He licked his lips, which had suddenly gone dry, and raised his eyebrows. "So, tell me more about this naked yoga...this woman, Cori-Anne van Cleavage—"

"Van Cleave," interrupted Danny.

Don Jorge ignored him. "She is totally naked during the class?"

"Yes, Don Jorge. She is. But not just her. Everyone in the class. It is a horrific sight I am told."

"Hmm," said the don, wondering just what would be horrific about extremely flexible naked young women in erotic poses. Perhaps it was because Danny was gay that naked women were not appealing to him. *Just don't look at the women*, Don Jorge thought, *just as I will not look at the men.* "And tell me, Danny, why can't you offer naked yoga here at your studio?"

"Legal issues. Too big, and much too public. We

couldn't keep the classes private. Her studio is small and enclosed. It's no problem for her."

"But looking at these numbers, it's a problem for you."

"A temporary setback, Don Jorge. I am working on a way to shut her down."

"Really?" replied the don, trying to keep his voice calm. That was the last thing he needed Danny to do. He squeezed his legs together, trying to stifle his excitement. No way he'd let Danny close it down before he'd visited the studio and met this fascinating woman, Cori-Anne van Cleave. His imagination was going into overdrive, and if this bastard Danny screwed it up, he'd kill him. He held up his hand. "Before you shut down her studio, maybe you should think of a creative way to regrow your own business."

"I have been thinking, I assure you, Don Jorge. My head is aching from all the thinking."

"Let me put it to you this way, Danny." The don's voice had gone into bad-cop mode. "Your head will ache even more when I nail it to the front door of your studio as a warning to anyone else who doesn't do their job properly."

Danny gulped. He'd heard stories of the don's favorite method of execution. "I will do my best, Don Jorge."

"Ah, you're a good boy, Danny," replied the don, patting Danny's face in what could have passed for a slap. "You do that, and everything will be just fine. Now, I have other business in Miami. I'll come back in two days to find out what your plan is." He stood up, put on his Panama hat, snapped his fingers at his bodyguard Yuri (who was lounging in a chair outside Danny's office reading a magazine), and walked out to his SUV that was double parked in front of the club.

"Where to, boss?" asked Yuri.

"I need you to look up the number for Cori-Anne van Cleave Yoga. It's not far from here." Don Jorge knew this would be a tough order for his bodyguard, who had an IQ lower than a school-zone speed limit, but his own prowess with an iPhone was severely hindered by the thickness of his fingers.

By the time Yuri had found the number, Cori-Anne was just finishing her last class of the evening. She laughed and chatted with the men who were pulling on their sweats. The evening class was a much younger group of gay men and women who took naked yoga seriously. The geriatrics in the morning class were certainly more joyful if less spiritual. It had taken her over a month to see beyond the pendulous breasts and testicles that seemed to dominate her visual field in the morning. Now she saw only glee and happiness, and she had to admit that she'd never had students who enjoyed their classes quite as much. In the beginning she'd wondered how and why they wanted to twist themselves into different positions, exposing bodies that in her opinion should only be exposed to medical practitioners specializing in arthritis and goiters. Marvin had explained it to her in a way that made perfect sense.

"You know, sweetheart, one of the things about getting old is that you never look in the mirror and see yourself as you are. The person looking back is always the person you remember from years before. In these classes we see each other's wrinkles and saggy asses, and that's how we know the truth of who we really are. No one judges you. No one looks that much better. It's the most liberating thing you can imagine."

As the last student waved goodbye, Cori-Anne's phone rang. "Cori-Anne van Cleave Yoga," she said, not recognizing the number.

"Hello," said a voice with a heavy Hispanic accent. "This is the naked yoga studio of Cori-Anne van Cleave?"

"Yes, this is Cori-Anne. To whom am I speaking, please?"

"My name—uh, my name is uh…Viktor Cruz." Don Jorge decided he didn't need to use his real name. "I think I would like to join one of your classes."

"Well, of course, Viktor. That would be wonderful. I would have to meet with you first, though, to see what level you're on before you join one of the classes."

"What level I am on? Oh, I understand. Well, I am not a yoga aficionado, but I am very flexible and extremely strong."

"Good to hear, and that will help," replied Cori-Anne. "But I still have to see you before you join a class. When can you come in? I don't suppose now would be good?"

"Yes, now would be perfect. We are in the area. I can be there very soon."

"Excellent, I'll be waiting."

Ten minutes later the doorbell to the studio rang, and Cori-Anne, dressed in a pale green and blue robe she'd put on after the last class, unbolted the door. The man outside was dressed in a white linen suit that matched his thick white hair and mustache. He looked to be in his early sixties, and his short stature oozed a kind of strength that both fascinated and frightened Cori-Anne.

"You must be Viktor," she said with the most disarming smile she could muster.

"I must be...?" For a second Don Jorge forgot that he'd used another name.

"Yes, that's the name you told me on the phone."

"Indeed, Viktor, that's who I am. Viktor is my name." He smiled back at Cori-Anne, who couldn't hide her confusion. "So, now should I undress so you can examine me?"

"Oh, no, that's not necessary. Maybe you could just take off your jacket so I can see how flexible you are." She didn't like the way Don Jorge was eyeing her, but she'd got used to the way her elderly students first looked at her: the women as if she was their favorite granddaughter and the men as if she was someone else's. Erections happened occasionally, but they were few and far between. She had a horrible feeling Viktor would be a little different. There was something about him that just felt wrong.

"You must understand," she said, "that there is a very strict policy about lewd thoughts and consequent behavior. This is a spiritual form of yoga, and it's all about you feeling free and uninhibited. It's not about the person in front of you. You have to look inwards, not around you. This class is meant to take you to a state of inner vision and peace."

Don Jorge nodded his head and half closed his eyes as if he were already in some deep, contemplative state. He was most definitely having visions, but not the kind Cori-Anne was referring to.

"This is all perfectly clear," he said. "When do I start?"

His get-up-and-go which had got-up-and-gone was back where it belonged, and he was determined to keep it there. He held his jacket in front of him to hide his erection. Cori-Anne didn't appear to notice.

"Well, OK then. If you're sure naked yoga is something you will feel comfortable doing, you can join our eleven o'clock class tomorrow morning."

But comfortable was not what Don Jorge had in mind. He wanted to feel uncomfortable. He wanted to feel the way he'd felt at twelve years old when he'd found his uncle's copy of *Booty Queen* at the back of the gun safe.

"Of course, I am sure. Now, what do I owe you?"

"The classes last an hour and cost $100 and then $500 a month after that if you decide to continue."

Madre de Deus, thought Don Jorge. You can't get a South Beach hooker for less than two thousand dollars an hour. That sorry bastard of an LA therapist had charged him twenty thousand for the session that had done absolutely nothing. He rubbed his hands and gave Yuri a large and rare smile as he walked back to the SUV.

"Are you going to kill her, boss?"

"No, Yuri. Believe it or not, I am going to do one of her classes."

"That's good, boss. It will help you to relax more. You have been a little tense lately."

Under normal circumstances he would have admonished Yuri for his presumption, but not today. Today he was the very essence of bonhomie.

He had Yuri drive him back to his Miami house, lit a cigar, and poured himself a large glass of Barrique de Ponciano Porfidio tequila. The bottle had cost a small fortune, but at that moment he was happier than he'd been in months. If the mere thought of naked yoga could restore his libido, then what could an actual class of naked young women do? He shivered in anticipation.

Meanwhile, back at Ram-Dann's Hard Core Yoga and Pilates, Danny Ramirez sat in the chair in his office staring at a picture of a cow that his three-year-old nephew had painted. The thought of having his head nailed to the front door filled him with horror, so much so that he could think of nothing else.

By eight o'clock Danny finally gave up. There was absolutely nothing he could think of to do to entice those members who'd flocked to Cori-Anne's studio to return. The only potentially doable idea he'd had was to open a ceviche and martini bar, but even a generous bribe to a certain city official couldn't guarantee him a liquor license for at least two months. That was probably a month and a half longer than the don would give him.

He took a small sip of his celery juice, wondering what size nail the don would use on his head, and suddenly it hit him. He was thinking about it all wrong. The solution to his problems lay, as he'd intimated to the don, not in making his studio more attractive to his ex-customers but in making Cori-Anne's less so. The way to do that was to perpetrate an act so odious, Cori-Anne would be forced to close her studio permanently.

Yes, he smiled to himself, in a day or two the only stretch Cori-Anne would be doing was a long one in prison. He had detected a slight hesitation and perhaps a note of reluctance in Don Jorge's demeanor when he brought up the idea of ruining Cori-Anne's studio. But he had no idea why, and after all, he'd always found that it was better to ask forgiveness than permission. But why would he need to? When Don Jorge found out that all the students were back, he would be thrilled.

Danny went to his safe and withdrew two small sachets of pure heroin. Even though he received a "friends and family" discount on the stuff from the cartel, it was still expensive. But no mind; this was going to be worth every penny. He carefully inserted the bags into a condom and changed into black jeans and a hooded sweat top.

At midnight he easily picked the lock of the back door at Cori-Anne's studio and walked into the small storeroom. There was a half-empty case of The Mountain Valley Spring Water on the floor and two towels together with a blue and green silk robe hanging on an old hat stand. He thought of putting the condom in the pocket of the robe, but there wasn't one. He opened the door to the studio and crept in. His flashlight swept around the empty room until it rested on the table that held the bronze Buddha. A little obvious, perhaps, but there was no time for subtleties. He tiptoed over to the table and carefully placed the condom with the two sachets behind the statue. It was invisible from the front but easily detectable from the side. The police wouldn't miss it when they raided the studio.

The next morning at nine o'clock, he called his ex-lover at the DEA and gave him the information. It cost Danny $2500 to get an assurance that at 11:20 the DEA would burst into the studio, find the heroin, and expose Cori-

Anne and the old nudists for the degenerates they were. If that didn't put the final nail in the coffin of Cori-Anne van Cleave Naked Yoga for good, then his name wasn't Ram-Dann Anubis.

Of course, it wasn't. So, it didn't.

At ten to eleven, Don Jorge "el Clavo" Morales attended his first—and last—naked yoga class. He'd gotten there early, paid his fee, and after removing all but his boxers on Cori-Anne's suggestion placed his yoga mat at what he assumed was the back of the class. It was his intention to gorge himself on naked flesh. Cori-Anne, still in her robe, stood at the front of the room.

"Am I good back here?" Don Jorge asked, wondering when she'd disrobe and the other hot women would arrive. He didn't have long to wait for his answer.

The door opened and a group of chatty people entered and immediately took off their clothes. The don removed his boxers, being careful to hide the beginning of an erection with his towel. His tumescence vanished when he realized that most of the class were older and saggier than him. His anger and disappointment rose when the woman in front of him went into what Cori-Anne called extended puppy pose and her splayed buttocks, larger even than his wife's, totally obscured his view of Cori-Anne, the only person worth looking at. His anger was assuaged when Cori-Anne began to walk around the class correcting the students and adjusting where necessary. She moved behind him as he got into the second downward dog.

"Push your butt up a little higher, Viktor," she said. "Yes, that's it."

Suddenly he felt a sharp pain and intense discomfort in the region of his anus. His first thought was that he'd ruptured a hemorrhoid. He gave a high-pitched screech and jumped up just as three DEA agents burst through the door, demanding to know where the heroin was.

Chapter 4

New York and Miami, two days later

The Sorites Paradox and its application in the Decline of the Cultural Integrity of the State of Florida

Eliot Hart M.S. Neuroscience (failed) Princeton

Abstract

The Cultural Integrity or Cultural Quotient of a state relates specifically to the survival of traditional indigenous culture, new cultural dynamics, and the tipping point at which the quality of the culture shifts into a negative space. This paper does not focus on the politics of an ignoble and contemptible governor but rather the impact of the "Florida Man" phenomenon on the Cultural Quotient of the state. It uses the sorites paradox to try to determine the following: *At what instant did Florida Man cause non-Floridians to finally accept Florida was populated by halfwits?*

E liot pushed his chair back from the cluttered desk and brushed his long black bangs out of his eyes. He was extremely pleased with his progress on the paper, which was now exactly twelve lines longer than it had been the night before when he finally opened his computer after Belinda had called from London to say she'd be staying a little longer and to remind him that it was due in four days. He wasn't in the least bit worried. He'd thought through his arguments and visualized exactly how the finished work would present. He couldn't imagine it would take him more than a day to finish.

Eliot looked at his list of "Florida Man" headlines to make sure he'd ranked them in order of what he'd called "Progressive Stupidity." He wondered whether *Florida Man threatens to kill man with Kindness: Uses Machete named Kindness* was in fact better than *Florida man denies condom filled with heroin in rectum is his*. The former was more obvious, but the latter had an intrigue that gnawed at him like a hungry rat. Despite Belinda's admonition about the embarrassment it would cause her if he used it in his paper, there was something about it that begged further investigation. He pulled up *The Sun Sentinel* page on which the story had run two days before and reread it.

The possessor of the rectum in question, whose name had been withheld, was attending a yoga class when DEA agents acting on an anonymous tip burst into the studio. After questioning the instructor, who was also unnamed, the agents performed a full-body search of the unknown man who'd been "squirming suspiciously" and discovered the heroin in a condom dangling from his rectum. The man, protesting his innocence, had been arrested and was now the subject of an ongoing investigation by the Florida department of justice headed by special prosecutor Thomas Mortimer Jones.

It was the last part of the paragraph that held Eliot's attention. *Thomas Mortimer Jones.* There couldn't possibly be two people with that name. And if he was right, then it had to be the Thomas Mortimer Jones he'd been best friends with in high school. Eliot Googled the name, hit "images," and saw the grinning face of his friend in front of the seal of the state of Florida. He didn't look that much different to the last time he'd seen him at their New Trier High School graduation twenty years before. He knew Thomas had been accepted to Stanford Law School, and Eliot's congratulatory email was probably the last time they'd even communicated. Maybe this was the perfect time to change that.

Eliot stood up, adjusted his sweatpants, and walked over to the window. He looked out over the Hudson River at the ferries making their way towards Ellis Island and the Statue of Liberty and took a decision. If Belinda had been there at the time, she would have said it was the quickest decision he'd ever made. And the worst.

At six o'clock that evening, an Uber dropped Eliot off at the Eden Roc hotel in Miami Beach. He'd considered a smaller hotel, but his mind had gone to something someone had once told him: smaller hotels, bigger problems. He'd thought about that statement and for the life of him couldn't work out why that would be true. Just because you can't think of it doesn't mean it isn't true was the conclusion he'd arrived at, and so the Eden Roc it was.

Eliot checked in and was shown up to his ocean-facing room by an extremely friendly young man called Boris, who was determined to point out every feature the room and hotel offered.

"You got a great room wid a good view of de ocean."

"I think it's more a good room with a great view of the ocean," Eliot corrected him.

"Well, it's not permitted for me to argue wid de guests, so let me explain how de TV works. You got your remote here...."

"Boris," said Eliot, reaching into his back pocket for his wallet, "I have a pretty good idea of how the TV works. Now let me ask you a question." He pulled five twenties out his wallet.

"You got my full attention, Mr. Hart," replied Boris with his eyes fixed on the money.

"When are your days off?"

"I just got on duty today. But may I enquire as to why you are asking dis question?"

"Well, I often find that I when I give the bellman or concierge a tip for services rendered and services yet to be rendered, they go off duty for the next few days. Seeing as the recommended tip is $5 per bag and I had only one bag, the amount of money in my hand is for services I may require at a future date."

"So long as those services are on de level, Mr. Hart, I am only too happy to oblige. Now, let me tell you about de restaurants."

Eliot listened politely and asked Boris to book him a table for seven-thirty at the Malibu Farm restaurant.

"You got it, Mr. Hart, and if you need anything else, call

down and ask for me, Boris. And may I say your generosity is—"

Eliot shut the door in his face. He unpacked his small carry-on and connected his phone and iPad to the Wi-Fi. Then he lay on the bed to think through his plans for the next day. He'd begin with a short, conscience-easing visit to the gym followed by the kind of breakfast he was unable to eat in Belinda's presence without some nasty reference to his weight. After that he'd get hold of Thomas Mortimer Jones, invite him to lunch, visit the yoga studio...and that's when he realized how weak his plan was.

The chance of being able to speak with Thomas let alone get him for lunch were, he calculated, less than 10 percent, and interviewing the yoga instructor (provided he could find out who he or she was) possibly 7 percent. He did a quick equation based on Ease of Conscience plus Pleasure of Breakfast minus Probability of Interview Success over Cost of Trip and came to the conclusion that this whole thing was a bad idea. Even factoring in Enjoyment of Evening Cocktail and Good Dinner didn't really change things. He stared up at the ceiling for a minute or so and decided that though it was after six-thirty, he'd try to call Thomas at his office and at the very least leave him a message. If nothing else, it would raise the Probability of Interview to over 18 percent.

It wasn't hard to find the number for the Miami-Dade County Department of Justice, but as expected it went straight to a recording. "You have reached the Miami-Dade County District Attorney's office. If you know your party's extension you can dial it now...." Eliot didn't and was about to hang up when the recording continued. "For a directory list, dial zero." He did. "Now enter the first three letters of the last name of the party you wish to reach. For Elizabeth Jones push 256, For Constantine Jones push 348, for Thomas Jones push 273." He hit the number and waited. Three seconds later someone picked up.

"Hello," said the someone, who sounded both annoyed and tired.

"Hello...." replied Eliot. "Um, is this by any chance Thomas Mortimer Jones?"

"Who wants to know?" The voice went from tired and angry to anxious and angry.

"It's, it's Eliot Hart."

There was a pause. "Eliot? Eliot Hart from New Trier?"

"Yes, yes...is this, uh, Thomas?"

"Good fuckin' grief, man. Yes, it's me. But to what do I owe this unprecedented pleasure?"

"Jesus, Tommy, it's good to hear your voice."

"Eliot Goddam Hart, Jesus. Where the hell are you...how the hell are you?"

"I'm here in Miami and I'm great. How are you?"

"To be honest, I'm exhausted. Fucked up and barely functional. You caught me just as I was about to go home, have a large scotch, eat whatever crap I can find in my refrigerator that isn't about to crawl out on its own, and then go to sleep."

"Sounds horrible," said Eliot sympathetically. "I tell you what: Postpone your sleep for an hour and come over to my hotel. You can have a scotch and a decent meal with me."

"Nah. I'd love to, but I'm fried."

"C'mon Tommy. One drink. We haven't seen each other for twenty years."

Thomas took a deep breath and Eliot knew that the Probability of Interview had just gone up to over 90 percent. "OK, one drink, quick bite. Where are you at?"

Twenty-five minutes later Eliot nearly toppled out his chair when a hand the size of a baseball mitt slapped him on the back.

"Eliot Hart, I thought you'd forgotten about me," said Thomas Mortimer Jones, squeezing his six-foot-five, 250-pound frame into a chair designed for someone half his size. "What the hell are you doing here?"

Eliot had thought about what he'd say to Thomas while he stared at the ocean waiting for his old friend to arrive. His initial idea was to come clean and simply tell Thomas that he was quite desperate to find out exactly why the police hadn't considered that the heroin in question could possibly belong to someone else, but after further consideration he'd settled on a different tack: A slow, steady catch-and-soften-up followed by a cat-like pounce once he felt Thomas was at his most vulnerable. However, seeing his friend once again made him realize just how much he missed him and liked him. He made the decision not to lie. Or if he had to, just a little.

"Well, I want to hear all about your life, and then I'll tell you about this paper I'm writing. It focuses on the whole 'Florida Man' phenomenon in pop culture."

"Blagh," went Thomas, making a sound like a punctured

football. "The Florida Man thing is an unhappy reflection on the disparity between the haves and have-nots, mental health, the fentanyl problem, and a whole bunch of other miserable issues. It also has overtones of bigotry. Like Polish jokes or Irish drinking stories. In any case it's sort of last year's meme."

Fortunately for Eliot—because the truth was in all the time he'd spent thinking about his paper, he'd never once considered the obvious points that Thomas had raised—the sudden appearance of a waitress interrupted his response. She handed Thomas a menu, took his scotch order, and offered Eliot a refill on his martini. It was sufficient time for Eliot to ease up on his mental accelerator and put his brain on cruise.

"Well," Eliot said, trying his best to look noble, "the points you raise are precisely what I'm concerned about. You see, I'm writing a paper about the effects of racial or ethnic jokes on the psyche of a community to get a job at a local college."

"Sounds interesting," Thomas said, looking at the menu, "but why the hell are you looking for a job? I thought you'd made a billion dollars from that company I read you'd sold a few months ago."

"I did," Eliot said—he'd looked at the menu while he was waiting and already decided on a pizza—"but I left most of it on the table when I walked away from the company. Still got a ton but couldn't handle the corporate culture. Anyway, it's a long story and I don't want to bore you when you're exhausted. This is about old friends catching up after twenty years. Now, tell me about yourself."

"My life," replied Thomas, putting down the menu, "is

work, more work, sleep, work, more work. There's been fuck-all time for anything else. Where's our waitress with the damn drinks?"

Eliot could tell Thomas was strung out and tired, and he began to feel bad about his initial deception and the fact that Thomas had followed his career while he hadn't even thought about his friend since he'd gotten into Stanford. They ordered their food, and Thomas knocked his drink back in one go and immediately asked for another. They got into personal lives and all the things they'd done after school, and Eliot found out that Thomas had left a prestigious Miami Law firm to get into something he felt better served the public good.

"Unfortunately, when I left the firm," said Thomas, swirling the scotch round his mouth as if he were rinsing with Listerine, "my wife left me."

"I'm sorry," Eliot said, "that must have been tough."

"In a way it was and in a way it wasn't. You think things will get better in a damaged relationship. That your partner will come around to your way of thinking or you theirs. But that isn't always the case. Certainly wasn't in ours. We didn't have kids, and she was a shallow person who was clearly with me for the money, which I hadn't really made yet. In truth I don't have time for a personal life with this job. But you, how come what's-her-name—your high-powered girlfriend—didn't dump your ass when you walked away from that money?"

"Belinda probably has more money than I do. Her bonus last year was about the same size as the GDP of a small island nation. No, we're good together...well...probably... sometimes."

"Probably, sometimes?" Thomas asked, swallowing half his hamburger in one bite. "That's my whole point about damaged relationships. Probably isn't definitely, and sometimes isn't all the time. Are you happy?"

"I'm not sure I'm happy, but the relationship works, and I think she cares for me in her own way."

"Sounds like bullshit to me, pal. Either she's going to dump you, or you will walk away from her, like you did from the money. I remember you, Eliot. When you're not entirely focused, you worry. And when you worry, you overthink everything. Anyway," Thomas said, realizing he'd hit a nerve, "it's good to see you, and I'm glad you decided to look me up." He held up his depleted scotch glass and clinked it with Eliot's martini.

"Same here, Tommy." Eliot began to wonder if he'd ever be able to bring up the case of the heroin in the mystery butt without totally screwing up the evening. Just as he came to the conclusion that he couldn't and it wasn't worth doing because he was actually having a great time with his old friend, Thomas surprised him.

"You know, I'm working on a case which the papers ignorantly and erroneously labelled 'Florida Man.' If you could use it, it would be perfect for the paper you're working on. Unfortunately, you can't."

"I totally understand," lied Eliot, trying to suppress both his enthusiasm and disappointment. "You don't want to talk about work in any case."

"Not really, though this case is a real doozy. You'd love it."

"Don't tell me something you're not supposed to...."

"It's pretty fuckin' interesting, though. I suppose I

could tell you as long as you don't say anything to anyone. And you're going to have to swear to it on your life."

Eliot laughed, remembering that Thomas had a hard time keeping a secret. "Who am I going to tell? And I will swear—I do swear." He shrugged his shoulders, pinched his lips as though they were still at school, and crossed himself, which as he was a non-believer made no sense at all.

"Well, OK. I'm surprised you didn't see it if you're looking for Florida Man headlines. It was in *The Sun Sentinel* two, three days ago."

"Not the one with the guy with heroin in his rectum?"

"Ah, you did see it. Hard to miss, I suppose."

"It was the first article that came up when I Googled 'Florida Man' a few days ago."

Thomas nodded and signaled the waitress for another scotch. He was on his fourth and sounding a lot less stressed than he'd been earlier. Eliot was on his third martini and doing his best to sip slowly, though losing the battle.

Thomas looked around for a second to see if anyone was eavesdropping. The only person in the vicinity was a very elegant woman at the next table who'd come in about the same time he had. She was drinking a glass of wine and engrossed in a crossword puzzle. Satisfied she wasn't listening, he leaned forward.

"They fucked up in calling the guy a 'Florida Man.' He's actually from Mexico."

"Wow," said Eliot. "OK, now I see your point about bigotry." He didn't really, but his acknowledgement seemed to placate Thomas, who nodded once again before continuing. Thomas leaned forward till Eliot could smell the whisky on his breath.

"Not only is he not from Florida, but he turns out to be one of the top guys in a Sinaloan drug cartel. Jorge Morales, known to both his friends and enemies as "el Clavo", The Nail, and I bet you don't know why."

"No idea."

"Because when he kills someone, he nails them to a wall. Horrible fuckin' death I'm told."

"Jesus," said Eliot. "I wonder what kind of wall?"

"What?"

"Well, technically a dry wall wouldn't hold the weight of an average size man. Have to be a wooden wall."

"For fuck's sake, Eliot. I don't know what type of wall. It's irrelevant."

"Sorry, when you said it, I just got this picture in my head. As you remembered, I have an overthinking problem. Please, carry on."

Thomas took a deep breath and exhaled slowly. "OK, like I said, he's an infamous drug lord. Someone we've been after for years."

"Why was he in Miami?"

"Better question than the type of wall. It seems apart from killing, he's also in charge of the cartel's money laundering operation, a lot of which takes place right here in Miami. But why he was here pales in comparison to what he was doing when the DEA guys apprehended him." Thomas sat back and sucked up what remained of his scotch. He had what Eliot thought was a slightly smug look on his face. Then his face broke out in a massive grin. "He was taking a goddamned naked yoga class."

"I'm sorry, did you say a naked yoga class?"

"That's precisely what I said."

"That wasn't in the paper."

"No, sir, it wasn't. And it wasn't because I kept it out. The same way as I kept his name out and the name of the young woman who runs the studio. She'd be in horrible danger if anyone knew who she was. And you'd better believe that if the news media got hold of the fact that we'd caught el Clavo Morales in her yoga class, it would get back to the cartel. Then a nail through her head would be the least of her worries. Those bastards would slice her to ribbons."

Eliot blanched. He'd watched enough episodes of *Narcos* to know precisely what Thomas meant.

"Who is she?" he asked, not really expecting Thomas to tell him.

"I can't tell you, and to be honest, her name's probably going to change if we feel she needs to go into witness protection, which she is reluctant to do because she feels the people she teaches would be screwed without her. My word, not hers. And now I've probably told you a little too much."

"Don't worry. I said I'm not going to mention this to anyone. But I do have a question—actually maybe two or three."

"Shoot."

"If this el Clavo guy said the cocaine wasn't his, why didn't you try to find out whose it was? And second, why the hell would he be in a naked yoga class with a cocaine-filled condom up his ass?"

"Don't know and it doesn't matter. Of course he's going to say it's not his. Claims he felt someone—he believes

48

the instructor—stick it up his ass while he was in the downward dog position. Bullshit, bullshit, and more bullshit. And trust me, I know bullshit when I hear it. What's your third question?"

"How did the DEA know he'd be in a naked yoga class?"

"Not going to say anymore. I've already told you much more than I should have. Not that I don't trust you, but this is super sensitive, and if anyone who shouldn't find out, finds out, people are going to die."

"But surely members of his cartel will know where he was. Doesn't that make this young woman very vulnerable?"

Thomas shook his head and sighed. "Yes, it does, and I tried to explain that to her, but she's not interested in protection. We took Morales' bodyguard into custody as well, and hopefully he was the only other person who knew where his boss was at the time. Anyway, we're taking him to DC tomorrow to officially arraign him on federal charges. After that it will be all over the news. Hopefully we can keep the naked-yoga instructor out of it until then. Now your turn—tell me about your life and why you left half a billion dollars on the table like an asshole."

They talked for about twenty minutes more, mostly reminiscing, and agreed to hook up again in a few days when Thomas got back from DC and if Eliot was still there. As they stumbled out the restaurant together, the elegant woman who'd been sitting at the next table doing a crossword puzzle removed a small hearing amplifier from her left ear. She clicked the pen, which was also a directional microphone, picked up her cell phone, and hit a number.

"I have some news," she said to the person who answered her call.

Chapter 5

Miami, the next day

Eliot woke up with a slight headache. He'd drunk what seemed like a gallon of water before falling asleep and had taken two Advil, but the last martini had made a hangover inevitable. He hoped Thomas was feeling better than he was for his trip to DC that morning.

After three minutes of deliberation with his conscience, Eliot came to his first conclusion of the day: a workout was off the table, but a Belinda-horrifying breakfast was very much on. He struggled out of bed, opened the curtain, and looked out on a perfect Florida day. There wasn't a cloud in the sky, and a gentle breeze made the palms appear to be waving at the sun. Even the ocean looked less green than it had the day before. Nausea grudgingly gave way to happiness as he thought of how great it had been to see his old pal even though it meant an adjustment to his paper was inevitable. He showered, took two more Advil, and rode the elevator down to the lobby focused on what he'd order at the Malibu Farm.

As he exited the elevator, Boris the bellman rushed up.

"Mr. Hart, I have every hope dat you're enjoying your stay. How was de Malibu Farm last night? Food's great, isn't it?"

"Good morning, Boris. Yes, thank you. It was excellent, and I'm headed there now for breakfast."

"Most important meal of de day."

"I've heard that. Although of course the data doesn't necessarily support it."

Boris shrugged as if he didn't have an opinion on the subject. "Anything you need, Mr. Hart, you let Boris know."

Eliot smiled and walked off. Then he stopped and turned around and asked something he'd only minutes before decided not to ask.

"I tell you what, Boris, there is something I need you to find out for me. I believe there is a naked yoga studio here in Miami. I'd like to know where it is and a phone number if you can get it."

Boris hesitated for a moment. "As I said last night, anything dat's legal, but I don't know so much about naked yoga. Is dat like code for a, uh, you-know-what?"

"If you're implying a brothel, then no, it isn't. Naked yoga is perfectly legal, and I go to a class in New York. I'm considering taking a class here before I fly back."

If Boris picked up on the lie, he pretended not to, though he did rub his thumb over his fingers in a that's-going-to-cost-you gesture.

"I gave you a hundred last night, but OK." Eliot took three twenties out his wallet and slipped them to Boris. "If you can get me the info, you'll find me in the restaurant."

Malibu Farm was relatively empty except for a few tables occupied by parents of small kids who were either running around shrieking or spilling most of their food on the floor. The hostess, seeing Eliot's expression, told him he'd be better off sitting at the counter, which was as close to quiet as he'd get. He ordered a fresh fruit platter and the huevos rancheros, considered a Bloody Mary, settled on an Americano, and looked at his phone. Belinda had texted him from London at four his time saying that she wouldn't be back for another three days and when she did return, she wanted to have a serious conversation about their relationship.

Eliot took a deep breath and snorted it out through his mouth. It wasn't entirely unexpected. As far as he was concerned, every conversation they had was serious. He thought of what Thomas had said last night about their relationship sounding like bullshit and came to the rapid realization that he was right. It was bullshit, and that should have been obvious and would have been to anyone but Eliot. Realization turned rapidly to resolve. He wasn't happy, and he didn't want to teach at some trade school masquerading as a college. He took another look at the text and decided that like Belinda, it was devoid of emotion. For some reason the idea of standing up to Belinda made him happy. Happy enough to reconsider the Bloody Mary.

Eliot wrote back to say he was in Florida doing some research and wasn't sure when he'd be back and that he'd thought about it some more and didn't want to apply for the teaching post or work for an old bat like Cynthia. He ended it with a smiley face emoji that he knew would piss her off. It was a dangerous strategy, but one he felt worth the gamble.

Three minutes later Belinda returned his text. *Eliot, no one likes a 38-year-old child. I seriously believe we should rethink our relationship. In fact, unlike you, I don't think. I know.* So that was it. There was a certain sadness to the finality, he supposed, but he didn't feel in the least bit scared. Liberated? Slightly. Elated? Maybe not quite, but close. He began to think what he'd do. Perhaps he'd stay in Miami for a while and really research the paper. Turn it into something worthy. Then he smiled to himself. Things were moving quickly, but for once they were actually moving instead of getting stuck in his head.

That's when Eliot came to his second—or possibly third—conclusion of the day. He would write the paper for his own enjoyment even though the *Florida Man heroin/rectum* headline was out. The *Machete Called Kindness* line would serve to demonstrate the tipping point in his version of the sorites paradox. Options lead to insanity, he reminded himself, and he'd just removed two major options. Belinda and the drug lord's ass. Coming to a decision put him at ease.

His serenity lasted no more than a few seconds.

He stared at the various vodkas on the shelves behind the bar and wondered again about a Bloody Mary. This unfortunate maneuver dislodged the cog in his brain that had engaged to keep his resolve in place, and once again his head began to swim in possibilities.

If *The Sun Sentinel* reported that the heroin-in-ass guy was from Florida, then did it really matter if Eliot knew the truth? No one reading the paper would need to know that he was a Mexican drug lord. It was a pity to toss it out so cavalierly because it was the one headline that really intrigued him out of the hundreds he'd looked at. On the other hand, it would be a betrayal—be it ever so slight—of his friendship with Thomas, and wasn't that important? Although if he tried to find out a little more about the scene of the crime, would he really be betraying Thomas's confidence?

By the time the fruit bowl and coffee arrived, the conflict was bouncing around his brain like a ping pong ball. He popped a raspberry into his mouth and realized the dilemma on which he teetered so precariously was shifting towards give up and go home. But the fickle finger of fate wasn't as easily swayed as Eliot was, for at that moment Boris came up to his table with a huge grin on his face.

"Well, Mr. Hart, it seems you're in luck. De studio...." Boris looked around to see if anyone was listening. Other than a toddler eating something off the floor like a dog, no one was. "De naked yoga studio is only a ten-minute cab ride from de hotel. I called but de recording says classes only start at eleven. You may want to get there early, though." He handed Eliot the address on a piece of note paper, gave a smart salute, and walked off. Eliot crumpled the paper and put it in the saucer of his coffee cup. He'd made up his mind not to pursue the rectally-located heroin story, and he wasn't going to change it.

His resolve remained strong through the huevos rancheros, but by the time the last of the side order of bacon entered his mouth, it had vanished like a mist before the sun.

It was ten-thirty when Eliot arrived at the address Boris had written down for him. The sign on the frosted-glass door read "Yoga by Cori-Anne. Group classes at 11:00, 2:00, and 5:30." There was no reference to "naked," and though he couldn't see into the studio through the frosting, he could tell that it was dark. There was a small coffee shop across the street where Eliot thought he'd wait for Cori-Anne—whoever she may be—to open the studio.

A mind with a thousand thoughts tumbling around like clothes in a dryer is not necessarily adept at observation, and Eliot failed to notice the black SUV parked in front of the studio where two men also waited for Cori-Anne. Surprisingly enough, though unknown to Eliot at the time, their aim—to discover exactly how Don Jorge happened to find himself with heroin in his rectum—was the same as his. The methodology they planned to employ to extract the information, however, differed somewhat.

At 10:50, a very attractive raven-haired woman in a pink sweatsuit walked up to the door of the yoga studio and proceeded to unlock it. She was followed shortly thereafter by a group of older people laughing and joking as they made their way into the studio. Eliot threw his empty coffee container into the garbage and crossed the street just as the two men in the SUV got out and pushed open the studio door. Things happened very quickly after that. The two men, who were both short and squat with thick black hair and wearing Hawaiian shirts, made a sudden exit with the dark-haired woman, now wearing a blue and green bathrobe, struggling between them. Eliot, who was so preoccupied with what he'd say to the woman when he spoke to her, walked right into the man on Cori-Anne's left, causing both he and the man to stumble. Cori-Anne screamed and, pulling her right arm free, slammed her fist into the face of the man on her left. Eliot, totally confused as to what had just happened, stood up quickly. A little too quickly. The chin of the man he'd just walked into was at that moment perfectly positioned under Eliot's head. An uppercut from a welterweight boxer would have been no more effective, and the man's head snapped back like a dry twig.

"And then," as the waiter in the coffee shop across the street, the one recently vacated by Eliot, told his friend that evening, "you won't believe what happened. Six naked old people rushed out the studio and piled on the two thugs. It was a sight I hope to forget, though I probably never will. Dicks were flopping, balls were swinging, breasts undulating. I have seen the future of our bodies, and it isn't pretty. In fact, I think it may have put me off sex forever."

Inside the studio, seven minutes after the attempted abduction, things were marginally less chaotic than they'd been on the sidewalk. Eliot, slightly dazed and with a lump on the top of his head the size of a pigeon egg, was sitting against the wall while Cori-Anne, still wearing her blue and green robe, tried to get him to drink some water. The two thugs were lying on the floor tied up with an assortment of belts and sneaker laces, and the rest of the class were in the process of getting dressed.

"He saved you, Cori-Anne," said Marvin Gotlieb, who'd walked over to where Eliot sat. "You saved her, young man," he shouted at Eliot, just in case the thump to his head had affected his hearing. Eliot looked up and attempted to smile, which Marvin mistook for the grimace of someone about to throw up. "Grab a bucket, he's going to vomit. He must have concussion!"

Eliot shook his head. "No, I'm OK, thanks."

"Shh," said Cori-Anne gently. "Don't talk. Just drink this water." She held the bottle to his lips, and he took a sip.

Then Eliot looked at her and decided that he'd never seen anyone quite as beautiful. Her oval eyes, black-as-pitch hair, button nose...

"Thank you, I honestly feel better."

"No, thank, you," she said softly. Even her voice sounded angelic. "Marvin's right. You did save me. If you hadn't have slammed into that guy, I don't know what would have happened. Were you just passing by or were you coming in?"

For a moment Eliot couldn't decide how to answer. If he was just passing by, would she simply thank him and end the interaction? If he said he was coming in to do a class, would that make her suspect he was a pervert? After all, he would have been the youngest student by forty years. He opened and closed his mouth a few times, which Cori-Anne fortunately saw as a request for more water.

And then the police arrived.

Most of the group were now completely dressed except for one of the men who'd taken charge of restraining the prisoners. The two cops—one a young woman and the other a tall, solid man—both had their hands on their gun belts close enough to their Glock 22's in case they needed to draw their weapons. Both took a step back when the still-naked Robert Ludlow stepped up.

"Officers," he said, extending his hand, "I'm Bobby Ludlow. I was a homicide detective in Toledo, Ohio before I retired."

"Sir," said the young woman, whose badge identified her as Officer Cortez, ignored his outstretched hand, "you need to put on some pants."

"Oh," replied Ludlow, looking down in surprise. "I was so busy making sure these bozos were secure." He turned towards the two thugs who lay in the middle of the studio looking as sullen as it was possible to look. Officer Cortez wasn't sure which was worse, Ludlow's front or back.

"Sir," she repeated, "put on your pants!"

"Here you go, Bobby," said Gladys, his wife, handing him his sweatpants, which he put on commando style.

"Now," said the male officer, whose badge read "Jefferson." "Tell us what happened and what y'all are doing here."

"We do yoga...naked yoga," said Tina Constantinedes. "Very calming, and yet at the same time quite stimulating. Seeing your friends in the raw—"

"Jesus Christ," Jefferson gulped. He had a sudden traumatic flashback to when he was ten years old and saw his grandfather, who suffered from dementia, rushing through the house without any clothes yelling that he was a fire extinguisher. "You tackled these guys while you were naked?"

"Yes," replied Theo Minsky. "What do you think...we had time to put on our underwear?"

There was a chorus of voices as the class simultaneously tried to convey their feelings, observations, and roles in the apprehension of the two "suspects" as the female officer, who was doing her best to restore some semblance of order, insisted on calling them.

"Suspects, my ass," said Bobby Ludlow, who silenced his fellow students with a wave of his hand.

"We've already seen your ass," said the male officer, "so that doesn't help your credibility, and if you were a homicide detective, you'd know they're suspects until the law determines they're not. Now once again, what happened?"

Ludlow didn't like Jefferson's tone and informed him and Cortez in no uncertain terms that as far as he was concerned, the police were soft on crime and back in his day, they would have beaten the shit out of the two thugs before hauling them off in a paddy wagon. Many of the others agreed and joined in the haranguing. Marvin Gotlieb, to demonstrate his total disregard of modern law enforcement, tried to kick one of the prisoners but fell over when his laceless sneaker flew off.

Cori-Anne, who hadn't said a word up until then, decided she'd better step in before things got too far out of hand. "Three days ago, there was an incident in this studio involving drugs. DEA agents arrested a man, a very dangerous man I was told, and I was warned that something like this could happen. I was also informed by the district attorney not to say anything to anyone about the actual details. The fact is these two men barged into the studio just as we were about to start the class and grabbed me and began to drag me out the door. If it weren't for this man"—she pointed to Eliot—"they would have succeeded."

"Exactly," Leo Goldberg interrupted. "He stopped them, and we smothered them."

There was a moan from one of the prisoners, who was still trying to recover from the absolute horror of the cellulite-encrusted buttocks that had nearly suffocated him in the scuffle.

While Jefferson went over to cut the sneaker laces that had been used to tie the suspects' hands behind their backs and replace them with cuffs, Cortez walked outside to call the precinct. When she came back, she gave her partner a strange look and whispered something to him.

"OK," she said, "we're going to get these guys over to the precinct, and the DEA will take it from there. You lot should go home and take care of yourselves. And keep your clothes on in public."

"In private, too," Jefferson whispered under his breath.

Cortez turned to Cori-Anne. "You'll be getting a call from someone higher up a little later. You should go somewhere safe until then."

"What about me?" asked Eliot.

"No one mentioned you," replied Cortez. "You should probably forget this ever happened." Then she and Jefferson hauled the two suspects to their feet and marched out to their squad car.

After the cops had left, the class crowded round Cori-Anne and Eliot, who wasn't sure whether he should hang around or just slip out.

"Cori-Anne, dear," said Shelly Gotlieb, "you shouldn't be by yourself right now. You'll come home with us until the police think you're safe. Those two bastards weren't going to take you on a date, you know."

"Shelly's right," said Bobby Ludlow. "I remember punks like those. They've got friends, and unless those cops suddenly find some balls, they'll probably be released tonight with a pat on the back. In my day it would have been a bullet in the back of the head and their bodies dumped in an alley. That would keep them off the streets."

Two things about the group were clear to Eliot. First, they were as bloodthirsty as a pack of rabid dogs, and second, they loved Cori-Anne. He was about to tell her that he agreed with everyone when she suddenly turned to him.

"What do you think...and I haven't even asked your name."

"It's Eliot. Eliot Hart. And I think what everyone's telling you is right. You need to be somewhere safe."

"You see," said Marvin, "the boy's got a head on his shoulders. With a big lump on it, mind you. You may want to see a doctor, Eliot."

"I'm fine, thank you," replied Eliot. "But Cori-Anne, if Mr. Ludlow is correct and whoever is after you decides to try again, you should be somewhere really safe. Maybe even in another city."

Cori-Anne scratched her ear and pursed her lips as she did whenever she was thinking. "No, I've got classes this afternoon."

"Listen," said Shelly, "we aren't going anywhere, and I'm sure all your students would rather miss a week or two than have anything happen to you. You should listen to this young man."

"Talking of which," said Tom Ludlow, "who the hell are you? For all we know, you could be one of them."

"Technically," replied Eliot, "you're right. I suppose I

could be. Though I'd have to have concocted some elaborate scheme to make it look like I wasn't part of whatever organization those two belonged to in order to shove the suspicion onto them and off me."

Ludlow looked at him dumbfounded.

"But," continued Eliot, "I'm really not."

"So, who are you?" asked Sylvia Goldberg.

"As I said, I'm Eliot Hart. I suppose you could Google me if you're worried." He looked over at Cori-Anne, who surprisingly had a sweet smile on her face.

"Good idea," said Ludlow, beginning to type on his iPhone. "OK, here we go...Eliot Hart. Hmm, well, it looks like him." He held his phone out to the group, and they nodded in recognition. "I see," he continued, "that you walked away from six-hundred million dollars when your company was bought."

"What a schmuck," said someone.

The others agreed.

"It's a long story," replied Eliot. "But that's me. So now you know I'm not part of some gang."

"OK, everyone," said Cori-Anne, stepping up to Eliot. "Why don't you all go to lunch? Leave me to think about what I'm going to do. I'll be perfectly fine. When I decide, I'll send a group text to let you know. Eliot, if you're not in a hurry, could you wait?"

"Yes, of course, I can. Goodbye," he said to the departing septuagenarians.

"Schmuck," said Marvin Gotlieb.

Chapter 6

Miami, that afternoon

"I really want to thank you for what you did," Cori-Anne said to Eliot. "Can I at least take you to lunch?"

"I'd love that, but honestly, there's no need to thank me," Eliot replied. "I'd like to say I did everything you all think I did on purpose, but I'm not sure I did."

"Well, whether you stopped those men on purpose or not, it doesn't matter." Cori-Anne patted his arm. "The point is, you could have just walked by and left me. But you didn't and that's what counts."

Eliot nodded his head and gave Cori-Anne an awkward smile. There was no point in confirming his ineptitude before it became obvious. In any case, he justified to himself, what had happened wasn't so much a distortion of the truth as it was a twisting of the facts.

"You know, Cori-Anne, you seem awfully calm. I mean, what happened was pretty traumatic. You may be in shock."

Cori-Ann looked at Elliot and bit her lip. For a moment he thought she was about to tell him to mind his own business. Then she crinkled her nose and laughed.

"I probably am in shock, but for some reason—and don't ask me what it is because I don't know—I don't feel scared. I know what could have happened, but it didn't— mainly because of you—and that makes me feel hopeful that everything is going to be alright."

"OK, if you're sure you're feeling up to it, let's have lunch. I do think we should get out of here as quickly as possible and go to somewhere more crowded...more public. It'll be safer until you decide where you'll be secure. If you like we can go to the Malibu Farm restaurant at the Eden Roc Hotel. I'm staying there."

"Perfect. Let me just change out of this." She let her robe slip to the floor.

For Cori-Anne, exposing her body to people in her studio was completely natural. For Eliot, on the other hand, it was unanticipated and almost incapacitating. He tried to look away, but his neck refused to budge, and he found himself staring at one of the most exquisite bodies imaginable. If Cori-Anne noticed or felt him scanning her like a barcode reader, she didn't show it as she pulled on her underwear, leggings, and pink sweat top.

"There," she said with the sweetest smile Eliot had ever seen. "Do you want to call an Uber while I lock up?"

Unlike in Manhattan, Ubers in Miami seem to be there almost before you hit "send," and a white Toyota Camry was waiting for them as they stepped from the dark studio into the bright sunlight.

Fortunately for Eliot, Cori-Anne made small talk on the ride, which gave him time to consider how much he'd reveal to her. As he had become accustomed to over the last eighteen hours, he vacillated somewhere between the whole truth, the truth, and total bullshit, and finally settled on the truth. He felt he could spin it sufficiently to make her feel comfortable without betraying Thomas— or at least not throwing him under a bus.

"I have to ask you a question," he said once they had a table and Boris, who'd hovered like a deranged bee, had left. "Was it your yoga studio where the guy was caught with heroin?"

Cori-Anne, who was about to take a bite of her Salmon Niçoise, put down her fork. The smile faded, replaced by a look of either fear or suspicion. Eliot couldn't work out which.

"Why are you asking me? How do you know?" she asked.

"Well, you said something about an incident when the cops arrived, and I had dinner last night with Tommy Jones, who's an old friend of mine from high school. He told me a few things about the case, and he mentioned an incident at a yoga studio, but he wouldn't tell me any more. After what just happened, I figured it must be your place."

"Well, I'm not sure what to think," she replied. "That's quite a coincidence that you suddenly showed up as I opened and just as those two bastards were trying to kidnap me."

"I know it sounds a little fishy, Cori-Anne. The timing seems like a coincidence, but statistically it's not because it's predicated on when you opened. But let me try to explain so you don't think I have any ulterior motive."

"Well, your explanation better be good, Eliot. Because

if it isn't, I'm going to get up and walk out. So, tell me, and I'm warning you right now: if you're lying, I'll know."

Eliot shook his head and adopted a look that he hoped came across as both sincere and grave. "Three days ago," he pushed away his chicken tortilla salad (an unusual move for someone who loved food as much as Eliot), "I saw a headline in *The Sentinel* about a Florida Man who claimed the heroin in his rectum wasn't his."

"It was his, but he didn't put it there," replied Cori-Anne. "But carry on."

Eliot wanted to ask her to elaborate but decided he wasn't even close to allaying her suspicions to pursue that line. He told her about his paper, gave what he thought was a simple explanation of the sorites paradox, and said he'd seen Tommy's name in the paper as being the DA in charge of the investigation.

"I don't have the foggiest idea what you mean by the sorites paradox, and I don't really care, either. What I'd like to know is why would you fly all the way here to find out about the story? Why couldn't you just call him?"

"That's a good question, and it's a weird answer."

"I'm beginning to think all of your answers are a little weird."

Eliot looked at her carefully, trying to decide if she was being sarcastic. Then he noticed a dimple beginning to form on the corner of her lips and realized she was more amused than suspicious.

"I have what my girlfriend Belinda calls an overthinking problem."

"So, you have a girlfriend?" The dimple vanished.

"Well, no...I mean I did...but—"

"It's none of my business," she said dismissively. "And that 'problem,' as your girlfriend or ex-girlfriend calls it, doesn't explain why you didn't simply call your friend."

"I didn't think he'd just open up to someone he hasn't seen since high school graduation. The truth is I would have let the whole thing go because I could have chosen another Florida Man headline, but for some inexplicable reason, I couldn't stop thinking about why the police didn't investigate the guy's claim that the heroin wasn't his. When Tommy told me who he was, I guess it made sense. Anyway, that's why I decided I'd fly out, hopefully see him, and get an explanation. I was lucky he was free for dinner."

"And he told you about me?"

"No, he told me my Florida Man premise wouldn't work because the guy involved was from Mexico, not Florida. He mentioned he was a big deal in a drug cartel, and he'd been doing naked yoga at the time of the arrest. But that was it. He wouldn't tell me any more or answer my question about how the heroin got into the guy's butt. I promise you he never mentioned your name or where your studio was. In fact, he was very protective of your identity."

"OK, so how did you wind up at my studio?"

So far everything had been the truth. Not the whole truth as we've established, but certainly in the vicinity. It was at this point that Eliot decided he'd have to move from the borders of veracity to a slightly risky fabrication.

"I started to look up yoga studios—not big ones because I realized it could never have happened at a large studio—and yours was on the list. The rest was just serendipitous."

"Hmph," went Cori-Anne, who liked the sound of "serendipitous" but wasn't entirely sure what it meant. She'd been watching Eliot carefully as he spoke. He had soft eyes and a kind face and had sounded genuine until perhaps the last part about finding her studio when his nostrils flared. She decided to let that go for the moment.

"OK," she said, "your story is just ridiculous enough to be true, and you did save me, even if it was accidental. If I sounded suspicious, then you've got to understand I'm actually quite worried and I really don't know what to do. Hopefully when the police or DEA or your friend Thomas calls me later, they'll tell me."

Eliot had an almost uncontrollable urge to take her hand, which hovered close to her water glass. Almost, but not quite. His hand moved in the general direction of hers, but then he stopped and pulled back. It felt a little presumptuous. He was sorry for her. Desperately so. She looked so vulnerable and lost, and he made up his mind that he'd help her in any way he could. He wasn't clear as to what this rather unanticipated decision entailed, and he hoped it didn't include further violence, but his determination was resolute.

If she noticed his aborted hand gesture, she didn't acknowledge it, though she did lean forward. "Up until two days ago, I thought my whole life had turned around, and now, kerplunk, it's hit the floor. I have to send a text to my next two classes to cancel them." The glint of a tear forming in her right eye caught the light reflecting off the sea. She wiped it away with her napkin and sniffed. "They're not like the group you saw this morning who'd stick with me no matter what. These are younger and a lot less loyal. I really don't know what to do."

"Well," said Eliot quietly, "I'll help you."

"Why?" she asked. "Why would you do that—put yourself in more danger? I mean, you don't even know me."

"That is true," he replied, trying to think what his motivation should be or even what it was. "I'm not sure why, but if I had to conjecture, I'd say it was because my life is a bit of a muddle, too. Up until this morning I was about to do something I don't want to do for someone I don't actually care about. But doing something to help you would be something I want to do…and you seem like someone I could care about. Or do care about. Or at least hope to care about."

Cori-Anne shook her head as if trying to comprehend exactly what had just been said. "You know, Eliot, I'm having a hard time understanding you. What exactly are you trying to say?"

"I know, I know. It's my overthinking issue." He took a deep breath and exhaled slowly. "What I'm trying to say is that I'd prefer to help you do whatever you want to do rather than do what I was going to do before. Or was going to do before I decided not to do it."

Cori-Anne looked confused, and Elliot did his best to clarify and failed miserably. "You see, my now ex-girlfriend Belinda wanted me to write a paper I didn't want to write to work at a place I have no interest in working. I was working hard to make someone happy who believes I can never make her happy."

"OK," she muttered, even more confused. "Let me try to get this straight: You'd rather help me than write that paper that Belinda wanted you to write because you don't really care about Belinda anymore?"

"Precisely, but I don't want you to think that I've just taken a cavalier decision to dump Belinda, because she's the one who dumped me. Or says she's going to do it. I suspect she's found someone else. And I can't say I blame her."

"Why ever not?" asked Cori-Anne.

"I don't think I'm that easy to live with. Anyway, it's a complicated story, and I'd rather know about you." He paused for a second, then raised his eyebrow as if he suddenly had a brilliant idea. "Hey, why don't we have a margarita? You don't have any more classes, and I don't have anything at all."

"Why the heck not?" she replied. "It'll probably make both of us feel a lot better." Eliot signaled a waiter, and they ordered their margaritas. Then much to Eliot's surprise and delight, she reached across the table and squeezed his hand.

"I can't imagine why you'd be difficult. You seem like a very sweet and generous man."

"Thank you," Eliot said. "I try to be, but I suppose it doesn't always come off that way. Belinda said I was indecisive and indolent."

"Indolent?"

"Yes, lazy. She's a very active person and I'm not."

"Maybe you just need the right motivation." She squeezed Eliot's hand again, and he felt a sudden glow as if he'd just fallen into a vat of warm chicken soup.

He gave a snorty laugh. "You're probably right, and maybe this is my opportunity. But I still want to know more about you. How did you end up in Miami? Unless this is where you're from, although no one seems to be from here."

At that moment their drinks arrived.

"Cheers," said Eliot, clinking glasses.

"Good to meet you, Eliot," Cori-Anne replied. She took a large gulp of her drink and pursed her lips as if considering his question carefully. The only other person she'd shared her life story with was Coachella, and that was after two martinis and a joint. There was something about Eliot—an innocent naivety, she thought—that made her feel safe or perhaps complacent, and so she began to talk.

She told him how she'd come to Miami to get away from her mom, who had become a religious fanatic after her dad died, how she'd met and divorced her husband after the mule fiasco, and how she'd opened her yoga school after doing a course in an ashram in California for six months. Eliot laughed as she explained how she'd moved from regular yoga to naked yoga on the advice of her old-timer students. He asked her why, and she explained how the drug-cartel-controlled studio run by Ram-Dann Anubis was poaching her students.

"Everything was going great. I was getting more and more students. Many, I suppose, from the Ram-Dann place. And then I got a call early that morning from my friend Coachella de Ville—"

"That can't be her real name."

"No, that's her stripper name. She's the one who warned me about the heroin and DEA raid. Coachella's brother is a DEA agent, and he knows the two of us are friends. Apparently one of his agents had got an anonymous tip that

I was selling heroin in my studio, and he told Coachella to let me know in case it was true."

"Jesus. Who'd do something like that?"

"Well, as it turns out, Ram-Dann Anubis himself. According to Coachella's brother, the agent who got the 'anonymous' tip told him that Ram-Dann—whose real name is Danny Ramirez—planted a condom filled with heroin so that the DEA would shut my studio down because I was taking his business."

"But why would the DEA raid if they knew it was a set up?"

"Well, obviously they didn't know it at the time. The agent told Coachella's brother afterwards. Something to do with Danny offering him a bribe that didn't materialize."

"They didn't mention a condom in *The Sentinel*...but more importantly, how did you find it, and why did you decided to shove it up that guy's ass? The cartel boss...why his particular ass?"

"It was pure luck that I found it. As I was walking around the room, I saw it stuffed between the Buddha and the incense diffuser. I grabbed it. I was going to toss it into the street, but at that moment the DEA guys burst through the door and, well, the cartel boss's ass was the closest ass to me. I can't explain why I shoved it in there. It's not something I'd normally do. To be honest, I do my best not to look at my students from behind. It's not something you get used to."

"I can't imagine it would be."

Cori-Anne paused and took a long sip of her drink. "I didn't trust the guy from the word go. It seemed like he had an ulterior motive in coming to the class. I didn't know he was a drug boss until your friend Thomas told me. From what I now know, Danny Ramirez had no idea that Don Jorge had come to the class. So, I imagine Danny's in real trouble. Let's have another margarita."

They called the waiter over and ordered another round. Halfway through their second drink, Cori-Anne's phone began to vibrate.

"Take it," said Eliot when he saw her about to shut it off. "It could be the DEA guys."

It turned out to be Thomas Mortimer Jones, and he wasn't happy. "I'm glad you're OK," he told Cori-Anne, "but if you see Eliot, tell him I'm going to kick his ass."

"You can tell him yourself, Mr. Jones," replied Cori-Anne. "But really, instead of threatening him, you may want to thank him. If it wasn't for him, the cartel would have kidnapped me. He saved me and now he's going to help me. So why don't you be nice to him." She handed Eliot the phone.

Eliot hadn't heard Thomas's threat of an ass-kicking. The expletive that followed his timid "hello" more than made up for any physical threat that Thomas may have had in mind.

"What the fuck, Eliot? I thought I could trust you, you son-of-a-bitch."

"Hold on there, Tommy—"

"Don't you fuckin' *Tommy* me. Why the hell did you go to her studio, and how the hell did you even find it?"

It could have been the second margarita, or perhaps it was a hint of the new Eliot-to-be. The one that, in the past few hours, had made subtle changes to his thought process resulting in monumental changes to his life. In any case, the man on the receiving end of Thomas Mortimer Jones's ire did not back down.

"Of course you can trust me. You said don't tell anyone, and I wouldn't, and I didn't. All I did was look for a naked yoga studio. It wasn't that hard. I was just curious. And it was damn fortunate that I did find it. So much for your guys protecting Cori-Anne."

There was a deadly silence on the other end, and Eliot braced himself for what he assumed would be a full-frontal assault of threats and expletives. But Thomas had calmed down.

"Well, you're right, I should have been a little more forceful in getting Miss van Cleave to be careful. And perhaps we should have arranged some sort of protective custody. So, whatever you did was a good thing I suppose. But look, there's a real problem...can you put me on speaker?"

"Hold on," replied Eliot. He put the phone on the table. "Thomas has something we both need to hear. Let's move to that end of the bar. There's no one there." He picked up the phone again and told Thomas they were moving to a quieter spot.

When they got to the bar, they ordered another margarita from the bartender and Cori-Anne put the phone on speaker.

"Jesus Christ," said Thomas when they indicated it was OK to talk. "Are you really ordering drinks? Does that seem responsible with a bunch of crazed killers after you? Never mind, doesn't fucking matter. Just get the hell away from Miami."

"It sounds like Cori-Anne's in imminent danger," said

Eliot. "Or should I say, even more imminent danger than she was in this morning."

"That's exactly what I'm saying except I'll be a little more articulate. You are both in serious shit. We had to let Jorge Morales go on a technicality, and I have no doubt he's coming after you, Cori-Anne. And he'll be relentless. After your stunt this morning, you're not safe either, Eliot."

"How did that happen?" asked Eliot.

"There were so many things wrong with the raid, the judge just threw it out. Morales flew straight back to Mexico, but he won't let this go. Of that you can be sure. Now, I can have you picked up and taken to a safe house, but my gut feel is you'd be a lot better off out of Miami. These cartels have spies all over, including inside the DEA and police."

"I suppose I can go to my mother in Iowa," said Cori-Anne in a voice that conveyed both fear and reluctance.

"That could work. How about you, Eliot?" Thomas asked. "A small town in Iowa is one thing, but New York is too big to be safe."

"Well," replied Eliot, whose mind had been going a million miles an hour. "I have a better idea."

"What's that?" asked Thomas.

"What do you think about going on a safari to Africa? I've always dreamed about it, but I've never had anyone to go with."

"That sounds ridiculous," said Cori-Anne.

"That sounds brilliant," said Thomas.

Chapter 7

Sinaloa, Mexico, the next morning

"Round" Ronny Rundo had never been on a plane before, let alone a private jet. He'd been slightly nervous on takeoff, but the four Xanax he'd swallowed with a shot of Jim Beam had put him into a state of euphoria similar to that of elephants who've eaten fermented berries from the marula trees in southern Africa. Ronny was on his eighth packet of peanuts when the pilot announced over the intercom that they were about to land.

He fiddled with his seat belt until his boss, the Reverend Clayton Calvin Cripps, finally reached over to show him how it buckled. It wasn't easy. Ronny was certainly in the low to moderate mental disability range on the IQ scale, but he also stood six foot six from the soles of his heavy black size 15 boots to the tip of his shaved head and weighed well over three hundred pounds. So, getting a seat belt round his waist, even with a double extender, was more a feat of engineering than intelligence.

"Now you listen, boy," said the Reverend Cripps, who styled himself as "The Flaming Horror of Gomorrah" on the Church of the Uber White Nazi website, although in prison his nickname had more to do with Gomorrah's twin city. "Your job is simply to be at my side during our meeting with these wetbacks. You ain't required to say anything other than if I ask you something. Is that clearly understood?"

"Yes, Reverend. I think so," replied Ronny, who could have fitted the diminutive preacher into his back pocket. Not that he would even contemplate such an egregious act, of course. He was terrified of the skinny middle-aged man whom he'd first met at Ellis Unit, the prison in Huntsville, Texas. He'd attended the reverend's Sunday mass—or massacre as it was called after the congregation killed four black inmates who'd wanted to attend. After his release, Ronny had sought out Reverend Clayton Calvin Cripps at his church compound near Canyon Lake, just outside Wimberley in the Texas Hill Country.

The reverend, who was as close to a man of God as a chimpanzee is to a popcorn machine, had been ordained online through a white supremacist organization in Michigan and welcomed Ronny to the church. It was here that young men and women of all shapes and sizes (though not of all colors or religions) were taught to hate, fight, kill, and distribute heroin and cocaine for the Jesús en lo Alto cartel in Sinaloa, Mexico.

"That's good, son. The beaners may be our partners, but they don't like us white folks one bit. So we have to be on our toes, and your job is to protect me in case things turn nasty."

"I ain't gonna let nuthin' happen to you, Reverend."

"Good boy, Ronny. Now these greaseballs, they're gonna pay us a shitload of money to take care of a problem, the details of which I do not know as yet. How'd you like your first plane ride, by the way?"

"I like the peanuts a lot, Reverend, but I gotta go to the bathroom real bad. The one in the front was locked the whole flight."

"That's not a bathroom, boy. I told you, that's the cockpit."

"I thought that was a fancy word for urinal on a plane."

"Jesus H. Christ boy, I despair of you sometimes. Well, now you gotta wait until we land."

Ronny wasn't sure he could and squirmed around until the plane touched down. He was out and running towards a clump of trees almost before the plane had rolled to a stop on the runway that had been cut into the dense jungle.

A black Cadillac SUV was waiting at the end of the runway to meet them. Neither the driver nor the young woman who sat in the front seat said a word while they waited patiently for Ronny to finish peeing. Reverend Cripps smiled politely at the welcoming committee.

"I do apologize for my boy over there pissing like a mule. God be praised he didn't manage to open the door to the pilot's cabin, or he would have drowned the poor bastard."

"It is no problem, Reverend," said the young woman. "Don Jorge is very happy for you to settle in and will see you at lunch in about an hour and thirty minutes. Ah, it seems your boy, as you call him, has finally finished his ablutions. Good, let us be on our way. It is no more than a twenty-minute drive."

They drove in a silence broken only by Ronny telling Cripps how much better he felt and some spattered gunfire from somewhere in the jungle, which fazed neither the young woman or driver. The dirt road wound its way through the trees and emerged into enormous fields of poppies that stretched to the horizon. There were hundreds of people working in the fields and men on horseback, who reminded Cripps of the overseers when he'd been on agricultural detail at the prison.

He wasn't in the least bit nervous about meeting with Don Jorge and his compatriots. They'd been working together for almost five years, and while the distribution of the drugs was their main business, the Church of the Uber White Nazi had carried out numerous successful killings and kidnappings for the cartel. The Moraleses paid well and had treated Cripps with respect, although he suspected they hated him as much as he hated them. His only concern was with Ronny, who despite Cripps' admonition to keep silent was likely to blurt out something inappropriate for no apparent reason. He knew should have reminded Ronny not to use the terms "wetbacks" or "beaners" in the presence of their hosts and hoped he'd get a chance to do so before lunch.

The hilltop hacienda belonging to Don Jorge "el Clavo" Morales and his twin uncles Mateo and Santiago—neither of whom styled themselves *don* nor had a sobriquet—was a huge modern structure composed of three separate units, one for each family. Both uncles were now well into their eighties, and both their sons had been killed in different drug wars. They were shrewd businessmen who'd invested the billions made by the Jesús en lo Alto cartel in offshore banks after Jorge had laundered the money. Their greatest worry was that their nephew, whom they considered a moral degenerate like his deceased father, would ruin the business once he finally took over.

Ronny and the Reverend Cripps were shown to a small suite consisting of two separate bedrooms, two bathrooms, and a common sitting room to freshen up. There was a bottle of mezcal and a bowl of fruit on the coffee table. Ronny wanted to have a glass of the mezcal, but Cripps, who didn't touch alcohol, told him to take it as a souvenir instead. Cripps knew alcohol made Ronny uncontrollable, and that was the last thing he needed. Ronny pouted for a moment until Cripps slapped him across the face, and then he proceeded to eat an entire pineapple without bothering to peel it. Neither had brought a change of clothes and so, wearing their same outfits now heavily sweat-stained and smelling awful, they were shown onto a bricked patio surrounding a large pool. There they were greeted by Don Jorge, who was lounging on the U-shaped orange couch smoking a cigar. Yuri and another man, who looked like an accountant in a white button-down shirt and khakis, stood to the side.

"Welcome to my home," said Don Jorge, wrinkling his nose at the foul stench emanating from the two sweaty gringos. "Here, come sit, Reverend Cripps, and your man...boy...whatever you call him can go sit with Yuri by the pool. This here is my accountant, Rodolfo, who will discuss the details of the job and payment. After that I must leave you, but lunch will be served and then you can fly back." In truth Don Jorge had planned to eat lunch with his white supremacist business partner, but the horrendous body odor was making him feel sick.

"Ronny, son, why don't you go and laze at the pool with Don Jorge's fella over there. I'll call you if I need you."

"But Reverend Cripps, what happens if these—"

Cripps cut him off before any derogatory term could find its way from Ronny's pea-sized brain to his mouth. "Shut your damn piehole, boy. Now git over there and wait for me to call you." As Ronny waddled off, Cripps sat down on the section of the couch opposite Don Jorge.

"May I say, Don Jorge, it's a great pleasure to be back here at your magnificent estate. May I also enquire as to the health of your uncles, whom I have not laid eyes on for a while."

"Well, Reverend Cripps, let us hope it stays that way. They are my family and I love them, but they are out of touch with the world as it is today. They would not approve of what I am going to ask of you."

"And pray, sir, what is it you desire of me?"

"I need you to kill a woman named Cori-Anne van Cleavage—"

"It's van Cleave," corrected Rodolfo, earning a sneer from Don Jorge.

"Van Cleave, then. *Madre de Deus*, Rodolfo, why do you always feel the need to correct me?" He made a mental note to have Rodolfo's feet dipped in hot cheese to remind him who was boss. "As I was saying, my dear Cripps, I need you to kill this woman who lives in Miami, from which I have just last night returned after a troublesome arrest on some stupid falsified charge. Fortunately, I have a very good lawyer who showed those bastards just how dumb American drug agents are. The point is, I can't go back for a while."

"I'm mighty sorry to hear of your misfortune, Don Jorge, and if you provide the details, it will be my pleasure to kill this whore of Satan."

"Well, she is not exactly a whore as far as I know, but she may well be under the influence of Satan judging by what she did to me."

"And may I enquire as to what that was, Don Jorge?"

The don's face darkened, and he thumped the coffee table. "No, you may not. No one may know. In fact, as much as I hate the thought of not being able to torture her myself for her disgusting act, I need you to make sure she never reveals it to anyone."

"Oh, Lord. One of those women," said the reverend, not really knowing what he meant by that.

"Yes, indeed," replied Don Jorge. "One of those women." He wasn't sure what Cripps meant by that either. "So, capture her, kill her as quickly as you can to make sure she says nothing to anyone. And while you're at it, she is with a man named Eliot Hart, who prevented two of my men from abducting this van Cleave woman and cutting out her tongue and attaching it to her head with a large nail. You can kill him, too."

"Excellent," said Cripps, who'd jotted the names down in his notebook. "I'm thinking that perhaps we'll take them both back to our church and use them in our religious ceremony."

"I want them killed, not baptized," said Don Jorge,

wondering why it was that people didn't understand his instructions. He thought of Danny Ramirez, who was now waiting in the cellar of the hacienda contemplating a well-deserved encounter with a nail gun.

"Hee, hee," laughed the reverend with a high-pitched cackle. "Oh, they'll be baptized alright—with the venom of some pissed-off rattlesnakes. We don't use holy water in the Church of the Uber White Nazi. No sir, we do not."

"No," yelled the don, "absolutely no! You do not take her anywhere. Just kill the bitch and make sure she says nothing. Is that clear?"

Cripps leaned forward in his chair and sneered at the don. "I'm not used to being addressed in such an unmannerly tone, sir. I think I will take my leave."

"You will not do anything of the kind," replied Don Jorge. "Remember where you are and who I am." Then he smiled and reached over to pat the reverend's arm, a move he immediately regretted as his hand came back all clammy. "My apologies, dear *Reverendo* Cripps. It's just that this woman could say something that would damage my reputation, so I'm a little, as you say, grumpy."

"Very well, I accept your apologies," replied Cripps, now more determined than ever to find out exactly what this Cori-Anne van Cleave had done.

The don looked at the small man with the neatly combed greasy hair. He'd never understood why his uncles had got into business with such a despicable creature, whose large incisors made him think of a field rat. Though he had to admit that Cripps was efficient and carried out his assignments with a cruelty that appealed to the don's sense of justice.

"Tell me something, Reverend," he said, trying to inject a conciliatory tone into his voice. "This is something I have never understood about the name of your church. Why do you have to include the word 'white'? It seems redundant."

"Because, sir, neither the Lord nor I would permit a black man into our church."

"That much I understand. But do you seriously think a black person would want to join a church full of Nazis?"

"Perhaps not. But we consulted a marketing expert who said people value an organization whose name communicates exactly what it is. Like Fender Guitars. They could easily just call the company Fender, but they do not want some person coming into the store wanting to buy a fender for his '67 Mustang. Or General Motors. No one goes in and asks to see the general. See what I mean?"

"I do," said the don, who deeply regretted asking the question. "Well, it's been a great pleasure talking to you. *Caramba*, look at the time. I must be off, but your lunch will be served, and then I wish you a good return flight. Rodolfo will give you all the details." He yelled for Yuri to follow him and walked off without bothering to shake hands.

"Your boss is short on manners," Cripps said to Rodolfo as they sat down to eat. Ronny had joined them after wishing Yuri goodbye. He was having a hard time understanding why the reverend hated Mexicans so much. The two bodyguards had got on like a house on fire as people of diminished brain capacity are wont to do.

"Don Jorge can be a hard man to be sure," replied

Rodolfo, watching in horror as the two Americans drank their soup directly from the bowls and thinking the reverend had some nerve commenting on Don Jorge's manners. "And yet he is fair. Now, I too have a meeting soon, and we must not delay your flight back to Texas. So, to business. We will pay you $45,000 for the woman and $25,000 for the man. You must eliminate both within the next four days. Our people in Miami are watching them and will inform you as to their precise location."

"To be honest, Rodolfo," said the reverend, stuffing roast chicken into a corn tortilla and smothering it in salsa, "that seems a little low for a hit of this nature. Hardly worth our time and effort. Why don't you just do it yourselves.?"

"Too risky for us just now," replied Rodolfo. "The DEA are watching us very carefully."

"That may be, but if the woman has done what Don Jorge says she has, then $45,000 is far too little and four days not long enough. Those sorts of women are dangerous, and it's gonna require special planning to take her out." He'd decided to see how far he could push Rodolfo to reveal what had happened that made the don madder than a two-headed calf.

"Believe me," replied Rodolfo, "Cori-Anne is hardly what I'd call dangerous. She is simply a naked yoga instructor, and I hardly think sticking a condom of heroin into Don Jorge's buttocks would constitute dangerous behavior or require special planning for people like yourselves. The problem is—and this where your discretion is necessary—if any other cartel bosses heard about what happened to Don Jorge, he would become...

how'd you say? A laughing stock."

"Indeed," said Cripps. "He'd become the butt of their jokes." He began to laugh so hard at his own witty response that Ronny, who hardly ever laughed because he very rarely got the joke, made a sound like a foghorn.

Then the Reverend Clayton Cripps sat back and smiled, and Rodolfo knew he'd made a grave error. "Look," he said, trying not to sound nervous, "why don't we do this: I'll make it an even $100,000 for both."

"Make it $150,000 and you can be sure I will be as close-lipped as a terrorist at a waterboarding."

Rodolfo, who'd been willing to go up to $200,000, smiled weakly and shook hands with the reverend.

"I think we have concluded an excellent arrangement," said Cripps, trying his best to sound calm. "So now let's not waste this bountiful feast. Pass me those beans and we'll be on our way."

"I thought you said we couldn't call these wetbacks 'beans,'" said Ronny, who was shoveling the carne asada into his mouth with his hands.

Rodolfo snorted loudly. Then he stood up, scowled at the Americans, and silently vowed he'd make them pay at some point.

Cripps was too full of bonhomie to correct Ronny. "Go easy on those tortillas, boy. We got us a lengthy plane ride ahead, and shitting on the pilot is a federal offense."

Chapter 8

Miami, the previous afternoon and later that same evening

Eliot had wanted to go on a safari for as long as he could remember. At the beginning of his career, he couldn't because he didn't have the resources, and then when he did, Belinda had pooh-poohed the idea. She had absolutely no interest in seeing animals in any shape or form in any setting other than on her plate. When she took time for holidays, they'd been in the south of France or northern Italy. Eliot tolerated these destinations but ultimately found them boring because all they did was eat—which he enjoyed—or go to galleries—which he didn't.

Cori-Anne's initial reaction had been similar to Belinda's, though she was less dismissive of the idea. This would be her first trip out the country (not counting Mexico), and she wasn't sure Africa had much appeal. She was comfortable with farm animals, which she'd grown up around, but the idea of being close to an elephant or lion terrified her. An even more important concern was the cost of the trip. She had barely enough money in the bank to make next month's rent.

It was Thomas who convinced her that the Jesús en lo Alto Cartel, which he said roughly translated as "Jesus on High," had tentacles in most of Europe and even parts of Asia, and that somewhere remote in eastern or southern Africa would be far safer. Eliot had a slightly more difficult time in getting her to agree that he'd pay for the trip.

"But you don't have any money either," she said. "You told us that you gave it all back."

"Not all of it." Eliot laughed. "I kept $200 million, and what's the point of having all that money if you can't spend it on something you really want to do with someone you really want to do it with?"

"But we don't even know each other, Eliot. That's a long way to go and a lot of money to spend on someone you may not even like. Or may not like you. Oh, no. Now I've made you feel bad, haven't I?"

Eliot knew she was right, and he'd hardly thought this through the way he normally thought through everything. It was an odd feeling.

"No," he replied gently, trying to sound reassuring. "You haven't made me feel bad. And in any case, it is kind of presumptuous of me to even ask you."

"No, it's not that. But this is really my problem, and you've got caught up in it."

"It was my choice. And I'm not in the least sorry I made it. Look, unfortunately we are—like it or not—in the same boat, and going on safari somewhere really remote makes sense for you and for me."

Cori-Anne nodded and pursed her lips as if she were considering his proposal.

"We can have separate rooms," Eliot continued, sensing an imminent approval. "And from what I understand, most of the time we'll be with other people. So, there's nothing to worry about. We can just be friends traveling together." The last part sounded pathetic even to Eliot, but for some reason it resonated with Cori-Anne. Then again, it could just have been the third margarita. Whatever it was, she leaned over and kissed him. It was not a romantic kiss by any means. A casual observer might have labelled it as no more than a peck on the cheek. But for Eliot, on a starvation diet of affection, it was like the first taste of the hot fudge sundae he remembered so well from his first trip to Rumplemayer's on Central Park South when he was five.

"My suggestion," said Thomas, who'd been patiently waiting on the line for Cori-Anne to agree, "is that you leave as soon as you can. Tonight, if that's possible. You do have passports, don't you?"

Eliot had his in the room, and Cori-Anne said she thought hers was in a drawer next to her bed. "I hope it's still valid. I only used it to go to Mexico on honeymoon and that was six years ago."

"If that's when you got it, then it's still good for four more years."

"I'll get the hotel concierge to try to book our trip," Eliot said, taking his last swig of margarita.

"No, you won't," Thomas said. "You'll tell no one where you're going. I'll send a car to take you to Cori-Anne's apartment, and you can go online and book stuff from there on your iPad. If you have any issues, just let me know and I'll do what I can from my office. But I'm going to repeat this: tell no one where you're going."

Twenty minutes later, with a puzzled Boris carrying Eliot's bags, they got into an unmarked police car and were driven to Cori-Anne's apartment. The two plainclothes detectives said they'd be outside waiting until Eliot and Cori-Anne were ready to go to the airport.

While Cori-Anne packed, Eliot went online to BA and booked two business class tickets to Cape Town through London. He then looked up companies that arranged safaris and found one he liked called &Beyond. He called their New York office and talked to a woman named Annie, who said she'd consult with her colleague Jodie at &Beyond's head office in Johannesburg and put together several itineraries.

"When do you want to go, Mr. Hart?"

"Well, we're going to fly to London tonight. So, I guess starting the day after tomorrow."

"Good grief," Annie said. "I've never arranged a trip so quickly. Most people book a year in advance. I'm not even sure what camps are available, and it's the middle of the night in Johannesburg."

"I'll pay whatever it costs, but this is a bit of an emergency. What happens if we got to, let's say, Cape Town, which I hear is amazing, and spent a day or two there? Would that give you time?"

Annie promised she'd do her best and said she'd book them into the Mount Nelson Hotel in Cape Town and arrange for someone to meet them at the airport with all the details. The detectives outside the building must have been on a coffee break because at that moment, two people entered the building looking for Cori-Anne.

"OK," said Cori-Anne, slipping her passport into a large tan Kate Spade bag. "I have no idea what to wear on safari, so I've just packed some of my workout gear and jeans."

Eliot wondered what workout gear she wore during her naked yoga sessions and was just about to ask when someone knocked on the door of the apartment.

"Oh, my God," said Cori-Anne, clutching his arm.

"It has to be the cops," Eliot replied, feeling as if his heart had pole-vaulted into his mouth. "I'll open the door. Maybe you should go to the bedroom."

"Hello, hello," said a voice from outside the door. "Cori-Anne, are you there?"

"That sounds like the Gotliebs," Cori-Anne said. "Open the door."

"No," Eliot said, putting his arm out to stop her. "It may just be someone who sounds like them."

Cori-Anne pushed his arm away and turned the handle. "Believe me, no one sounds like them but them."

"Thank God," said Shelley Gotlieb as she and Marvin burst into the apartment. "We thought something had happened."

"And I see you're still hanging out with the schmuck," Marvin said, taking a look around the small living room as if he were expecting trouble.

"Marvin! Shelley!" Cori-Anne exclaimed, giving the diminutive seventy-year-olds a mutual hug. "What are you doing here?"

"We waited for your text..." Shelley answered.

"...which never came." Marvin finished the sentence with a soupçon of admonition in his voice.

"I know," Cori-Anne replied, "and I'm so sorry. Things have been going so fast. I honestly didn't realize what time it was."

"Don't worry, darling," Shelley said, giving her cheek a pinch. "We were just concerned, that's all."

"Thank you so much. We're good."

"We're good? You're together now? With the schmuck?" asked Marvin.

Eliot, who'd decided he didn't really care for Marvin after being referred to as "schmuck" perhaps once too often to be a term of endearment, cleared his throat.

"Yes, as it happens, Cori-Anne and I are in this together, and the police have told us we need to get away from here for a while."

"I don't want you to worry," Cori-Anne said. "We'll be far away from danger. We're going on a safari."

Eliot made a sound like a cartoon horse. "Remember we're not supposed to say?"

Cori-Anne bit her lip. "You're right, sorry, sorry. Look, Marv and Shelley. The guys we're trying to avoid are very dangerous, and we have to get away to somewhere remote. It's best you don't know where."

"A safari, you say," said Marvin as if he'd missed the last part of the conversation entirely. "Well, those are expensive, I hear. You're gonna need money." He reached into his pocket, withdrew his wallet, and took out five twenties. "It's not much, but it'll help."

Eliot pushed Marvin's hand away gently. "You're very generous, Marvin, but we don't need money. I've got enough to cover us. Thank you, though."

"Where'd you get enough? You got nothing. We all saw that."

"No, you read I gave back $600 million. They paid us a lot more than that. Don't worry."

Marvin shrugged. "OK, if you say so. But at least let us drive you to the airport." He gave the money to Shelley, who slipped it into Cori-Anne's handbag while she wasn't looking.

Cori-Anne kissed both Marvin and Shelley with as much affection as she could muster and patiently explained that the police had provided transport.

"You should get with the others," Eliot said as they shepherded the two old people out the door. "You'll be a lot safer in a group. And please don't mention that we're going on safari."

"You can count on us," said Marvin.

An hour later while Cori-Anne and Eliot were making their way to the BA lounge at Miami International Airport, Shelley and Marvin met the rest of their group at the Purple Ibis Diner.

"She's good?" asked Tina Constantinedes.

"I believe so," said Shelley. "Provided she doesn't get eaten by a lion."

"Shelley!" Marvin yelled a little too loudly. "For God's sake. What's wrong with you? You can't hear so good?"

"Pipe down, Marvin. I never told them she was going on safari. Hmph, you'd think I'd given away a secret."

"A safari," said Tom Ludlow. "That's a hell of thing to

do. I imagine they're going to South Africa."

"No, more likely Tanzania," said Leo Goldberg, who'd just watched a National Geographic show on the wildebeest migration.

The debate on where in Africa Eliot and Cori-Anne were going carried on through the Chicken Cordon Bleu and wasn't resolved after coffee—or even by the next dinner. They were disappointed about the cancelled classes but glad that Cori-Anne was safe for the moment. No one in the group observed the woman who'd followed Marvin and Shelley from Cori-Anne's apartment to the Purple Ibis. Unlike the dinner she'd eavesdropped on between Thomas and Eliot when she'd had to use her directional microphone pen, she could have heard the septuagenarians yacking from across the room.

As soon as they shuffled out of the restaurant, the woman paid her bill and called her boss. He in turn called a TSA agent on the cartel payroll, who confirmed that a Mr. Eliot Hart and a Ms. Cori-Anne van Cleave had just boarded a British Airways flight for Heathrow connecting to Cape Town two days later. Phone calls to a number of safari companies yielded results ten minutes later.

"Some friends of mine, Eliot Hart and Cori-Anne van Cleave, just booked a safari this afternoon," said the same woman who had overhead the conversations in the restaurant. "It's their anniversary, and I'd like to surprise them with a bottle of champagne in their hotel room, but I don't know where they're going to be staying."

"How very sweet of you," replied Annie from &Beyond. "Well, I don't normally give out our clients' information, but seeing as you're a friend...I booked them into the

Mount Nelson Hotel in Cape Town while we work on their itinerary."

"Thank you," said the woman. "You're most helpful." She hung up and called Rodolfo.

Very strange, thought Annie once she'd hung up with the woman. *I wonder why a couple celebrating their anniversary have booked separate rooms.* She shrugged and decided it wasn't really her business.

At nine-thirty the old flip cell phone belonging to the Reverend Clayton Calvin Cripps rang.

"Dangfuckinnabbit!" yelled Cripps, who'd been watching *Hairy Potter and the Philosopher's Bone* on the porn channel in his room at the cheap motel he and "Round" Ronny Rundo were staying at in Miami in preparation for their kill the next day. He hastily stuffed his tumescent penis back into his underpants and answered.

"Who's calling at this time of night?"

"It's me, Rodolfo."

"What in the hell do you want? We ain't done the job yet."

"I am aware of that, Reverend Cripps. But there's been a change of plan. How would you like to go on a fully paid trip to South Africa?"

"South Africa? Ain't there a lot of black people over there?"

"I believe so," replied Rodolfo with a smirk. "I believe so."

"I don't like the idea of operating on foreign soil."

"We do understand, but we have arranged for you to be assisted by an organization very similar to yours which we use in our animal trafficking operation."

"I don't know nothing about animal trafficking, and in any case if this organization is of a similar belief as us, why do you need the Church of the Uber White Nazi to carry out these killings?"

"Because, my dear reverend, no one is as skilled as you and that big *idiota* of yours."

"Well, I take your point. Of course, it will cost you extra. Let's say $250,000 plus expenses."

"Absolutely no problem," said Rodolfo, who would have agreed to any sum because he had no intention of paying the disgusting little man. Unlike his boss, who tolerated bigots if they were essential for the task at hand, Rodolfo did not.

He believed even a criminal had to have some standards. That's why he'd contacted Piet "Die Poffadder" van Tonder of *Die Afrikander Weerstandsbeweging,* or as it was known in English, The Afrikaans Resistance Movement, a white supremacist group that the cartel used to traffic endangered pangolins and lion bones to Vietnam and China. Their job would be to help Cripps and Rundo kill the Americans and in turn dispose of Cripps and Rundo.

"I imagine you don't have passports," said Rodolfo.

"You imagine correctly," replied Cripps.

"Not to worry, my dear *reverendo.* We have a man in Miami who will take care of that."

Chapter 9

The next day

Both Eliot and Cori-Anne were exhausted when they checked into The Rosewood Hotel on High Holborn in London's West End at around 10:45 the next morning. They were also cold as neither, in their haste, had packed warm clothes—Eliot because he'd only planned to go to Miami and Cori-Anne because she really didn't have any. They'd also not planned to spend the night in London, but the plane to Cape Town for that night was fully booked. Cori-Anne was thrilled, and Eliot was concerned, not because he feared running into the cartel but because he was terrified of bumping into Belinda, who as far as he knew was still there.

Unlike Cori-Anne, Eliot had been to London a few times before with Belinda, whose normal hotel was The Lanesborough on Hyde Park Corner, where her company had a special rate. Eliot had chosen The Rosewood because the concierge at the BA club at Miami Airport had recommended it, and it seemed far enough from The Lanesborough to avoid any embarrassing encounters with his now-confirmed ex-girlfriend.

"This looks expensive," Cori-Anne said when they got out the cab in the courtyard of the majestic old building.

"Um," said Eliot. "It's quite expensive, but look, Cori-Anne, promise me you aren't going to worry about that again. I told you last night I haven't had anything to spend my money on since I got it, and other than the fact that we're actually running for our lives, I can't think of anything else I'd like to spend it on right now."

Eliot had done his best to stop Cori-Anne bringing up the cost of the trip and other aspects of her lifestyle which she believed put her in a deficit position with Eliot, but he could tell she felt extremely uncomfortable.

"I can't believe you bought us business class tickets," she'd said, taking a sip of the champagne they'd been served just after takeoff. "I've never sat in the front of the plane, and honestly, it's not necessary. I'd have been perfectly fine in coach." She looked at the faces in the back just behind the curtain and thought they were looking at her with both resentment and longing.

"Well," replied Eliot, "as I said, we're in this together and that's how we're traveling. I promise I'm not trying to act like some spoiled rich dude because I'm not. Well, I suppose I am rich, but I'm not spoiled. I didn't grow up with money and I've only really had it for a short period of time. There's no reason for you to feel bad. If I couldn't afford to do this, I promise you I wouldn't. And remember: we agreed we're friends going to have an amazing experience."

Cori-Anne could tell he was embarrassed, and she felt awful. It was just odd for her. She'd never taken anything from anyone including her ex-husband, and now she suddenly felt like she needed help. And yet there was something about Eliot—she couldn't put her finger on it just yet—that was completely disarming, an almost naïve innocence that made her think he needed her as much as she needed him. She squeezed his arm and blew him a kiss.

"I think I'm going to try to sleep. Now, how do you put the seat back?" He showed her, and she laid back and closed her eyes, allowing the margaritas and champagne to work their magic.

She woke up a few hours later when someone on their way to the toilet bumped into her seat. She looked over at Eliot, who was snoring gently. This time she leaned over and kissed him on the cheek. He opened his eyes and smiled at her. Then the lights came on and the captain announced they'd be landing in ninety minutes.

As promised, Eliot had booked her a separate room at The Rosewood. They rode the elevator together in awkward silence and agreed to try to sleep for a bit and then meet up at 2 p.m. for a late lunch at the Holborn Dining Room in the hotel.

Eliot was already sitting at the table when Cori-Anne walked in. He saw her talking to the maître d' and waived. She saw him and waived back. Eliot wasn't sure whether he was still tired, but in his mind she looked more beautiful than she had the day before. Her hair was combed back, and she wore jeans and a black Lululemon hoodie. She'd also put on makeup, which covered nothing bad but instead accentuated everything good. And there was, Eliot thought, a lot of good.

"I'm starving," she said as she plonked down opposite him. "Did you sleep?"

"I did," he replied. "I set my alarm for 1:30 and passed out. How about you?"

"I slept about an hour, but I did some yoga—there's a mat in my room—and I feel OK. Do you think they have fish and chips? It seems like the thing to eat here."

"They do," Eliot responded with a big grin. "I looked at the menu while I was waiting. And they have a curried mutton pie, which I am definitely having."

They gave the waiter their order. Eliot wanted to order wine, but Cori-Anne talked him out of it, saying they shouldn't drink at every meal and that she was going to have him doing yoga. She sounded a little like Belinda when she said it, but somehow it worried him less.

"Now," he said, "we have this afternoon and most of tomorrow before we need to leave for the airport. We absolutely need to get some clothes, but maybe we should just get something to walk around in here and then safari gear when we get to Cape Town. Do you have any idea what you'd like to see?"

"Yes, I really want to see Buckingham Palace." She wrinkled her face. "Does that sound too touristy?"

"No," Eliot replied more enthusiastically than he felt about seeing it yet again or bumping into Belinda. Not that she'd deign to stand amongst the riff-raff gawking at the king's residence, but The Lanesborough Hotel was just a short walk from the palace itself. "That's what we'll do this afternoon. And we can probably walk there and back if we get a warm jacket."

They finished their meal, asked the concierge where they could get jackets, and took a taxi to the Uniqlo in Regent Street, where they both bought parkas and down vests, though not in matching colors. Cori-Anne had insisted on paying for her own outfit, and Eliot decided not to fight it. Then, feeling a lot warmer than they had getting out the taxi in the morning, they walked up Piccadilly and cut through Green Park till they came out at Constitution Hill.

They'd walked closely together, occasionally bumping into each other (deliberately so on Eliot's part and perhaps a little less deliberately on Cori-Anne's), but the minute Buckingham Palace popped into view, Cori-Anne grabbed Eliot's arm and pulled him towards her.

"Ooh," she almost squeaked, clapping her hands like a little girl. "This is so exciting! I've wanted to see Buckingham Palace forever. I wonder if we'll see the king?"

"I doubt it, but you never know. Look, his standard is flying above the palace, which means he's in. But I imagine he's either taking a little afternoon nap or having a cup of tea and a scone. Which reminds me...would you like to go for a typical English tea? Cucumber sandwiches, scones, little cakes...there are some great old hotels around here that serve it to foreigners like us."

Cori-Anne poked him in the stomach. "Eliot, we just ate an hour ago. Let's walk around for a while at least. We can have an early dinner if you're desperate, but not just yet."

Eliot took the gut prod good-naturedly. It was something

Belinda would have done and said to him, but she wouldn't have said it with any hint of affection. Cori-Anne hadn't let go of his arm, and he put his hand up over hers and they began to walk down The Mall. They turned into Stable Yard and passed Clarence House, where Cori-Anne swore she saw Kate looking out one of the windows. They turned onto Cleveland Row and then Pall Mall and walked for what felt like hours through St. James's and then Mayfair towards Covent Garden, with Eliot filling Cori-Anne in as much as he could and making up what he didn't know.

"You seem to know an awful lot," she said.

"I do," he replied. "And that's part of my overthinking problem. I can't stop looking up everything I can about anything that pops into my head."

"That's pretty obvious. Have you always been like that?"

"Yes, ever since I was a kid. I've spent my life collecting knowledge and filing it away in my brain. The problem is as soon as I learn something new, I connect it to something I already know. It's like a never-ending loop, if that makes any sense."

It didn't to Cori-Anne, but she nodded as if it did. She'd never met anyone quite like Eliot. Her ex-husband had incredible sex appeal and he made her laugh. And then one day he stopped being funny and became abusive. Whether it was the cocaine or the people he hung out with, she didn't know and she didn't care. All she wanted was to get away from him and the incident with the mules. The jail term had provided the opportunity to finally leave him.

"I honestly could tell you something about virtually

anything. I'm not saying that to make myself sound smart or anything, but when it gets too much, when I start to bore you, please tell me to shut up. I promise I won't be offended." Eliot was totally unaware that for a moment Cori-Anne had been in another place.

She gripped his arm even tighter. Then she laughed as if she'd just got the gist of what he'd been trying to say. "You're not boring, but if you ever drone on too much, I promise to let you know."

"Thank you," he said, putting his hand over hers and squeezing it. "I have a feeling that we can be honest with each other. Which is entirely different to the feeling I had with—"

"Shh," she said, cutting him off. "You don't need to explain anything. Just let it be. Now…." She pulled out her phone and looked at the time. "It's nearly six-thirty, and I'm sure you're feeling as tired as I am, so if you want to grab something to eat…maybe on the way to the hotel."

They found a small Lebanese restaurant which had great food and awful wine, but by then they were both so desperate to get some real sleep that the wine didn't really matter.

"It's weird we're together like this but we know so little about each other," Cori-Anne said.

"I know, and I can't wait till we're not falling asleep at the table to actually find out more about you," Eliot replied. "At least Cape Town's only an hour ahead of London. By the time we get there the day after tomorrow, we'll have caught up on jet lag. We have most of the day in London tomorrow, so why don't we at least plan what we—or rather you— want to see. Hopefully it won't be raining."

"You said the flight's nearly twelve hours?"

"That's what it says."

"Well, then I want to walk as much as possible if you're up for it."

"Me? Always up for it," Eliot lied, his nostrils flaring. "This is definitely a walking city." He took a last sip of his wine and raised his empty glass. "*And so to bed.* You know who said that?"

"Other than you, I'm sure a lot of people say it around this time."

"No, it was Samuel Pepys. That's how he ended his daily diary entry."

"I have no idea who Samuel Pepys is."

"Was. He was a naval administrator and member of Parliament here in London at the end of the seventeenth century." He saw her eyes glaze over. "Anyway, that gives me a great idea for our walk tomorrow. We can look for blue plaques."

"You'll have to tell me what those are, too. And don't make me feel stupid."

Eliot's heart thumped and then he saw her smile. "Well, that would be the last thing I ever think about you. And when you start to teach me yoga, you'll see how clumsy and uncoordinated I am. I've just read all these things, and for whatever reason I don't forget them. Anyway, there are blue plaques all around London on all types of buildings that tell you what famous person lived there, slept there, ate there, and got up to all sort of stuff there."

"Including sex?"

"I'm sure, but I doubt if they'll say that on the plaques."

"Sounds good, but to quote you and whatever his name was, *And so to bed.*"

Cori-Anne held his hand all the way back to the hotel, and when they got to the point where they were forced to separate, she kissed him on the lips and immediately pulled away.

"I'm beginning to like you, Eliot Hart," she said. "See you at breakfast." And with that she turned quickly and made her way to her room.

Eliot stood for a while staring after her. His mind was turning over like a Ford flathead V8 trying to work out exactly what she'd meant by that statement. Did "beginning to like you" imply that she didn't fully like him yet? Or did it mean that she hadn't liked him before? Or was it meant to be a pre-emptive segue into a potential "love you"? By the time he eventually fell asleep, he was no closer to an answer.

In Miami, at about the same time that Eliot finally managed to close his eyes, the Reverend Clayton Calvin Cripps was doing his best to help "Round" Ronny Rundo fasten his seat belt for their flight to Cape Town, also through London. They were not in business class, and Round Ronny was having a horrendous time trying to squeeze into the seat, which was a good deal smaller and more cramped than the one on the private jet they'd been on two days before.

Ronny may have been uncomfortable, but the poor woman in the seat between him and the reverend felt as if she was about to have a panic attack. She began to breathe heavily and whimper until the reverend said, "Shut yer yap before I shove something in it you won't like." The woman twisted her head as best she could and looked at the little rat-faced man who bared his teeth at her. She felt the blood run from her head and then everything went dark. The cleaning crew found her an hour after the plane landed in London. She'd been stuffed under the seat as if she were a piece of hand luggage. She was still alive but incoherent, muttering only that she'd seen the devil, who looked like a turnip with greasy hair.

Chapter 10

London, the next day

There are nearly one-thousand blue plaques scattered around the different boroughs of London. Cori-Anne, who'd already done an hour of yoga before joining Eliot at breakfast, was keen to see as many as possible.

"Well, technically," said Eliot as he smothered the last of his kipper with the remnants of his poached eggs and popped it into his mouth, "I don't have a map, so I can't calculate the actual walking distance, but I estimate it would take us over three days if we didn't stop for food and pee breaks to see all of them. However, I have put together a route which should take us a few hours. Then we can have lunch, pop back to the hotel for a shower, and head off to Heathrow in plenty of time to catch the plane."

"You're very focused on food, aren't you, Eliot?" Cori-Anne said. She'd ordered half a grapefruit and a slice of wheat toast, which she ate with just the thinnest film of butter.

Eliot didn't take this badly because in essence it was

the truth. He was focused on food. He absolutely loved eating but believed his ingestion of nutriments was fully under control. He didn't snack between meals, and he avoided sugar and fried foods as best he could. Belinda had encouraged him to try various diets, but he'd become so despondent that she'd finally given up. Eliot was by no means fat, but he could do to lose a few pounds. He knew this, but up until now the pleasure to pain ratio between food and no food was, as far as he was concerned, unacceptable. He looked over at Cori-Anne and decided that he'd probably do anything she wanted him to do.

"Um, yes, I do enjoy eating, but I know I should cut down and exercise more, and that's why I'm looking forward to our walk."

"Good," she said, patting his hand as he reached for another slice of toast. "And I am going to help you do that on this trip. Hopefully when this craziness is over, you'll want to continue."

"I have a feeling I'll want to continue," Eliot said, thinking—or rather wishing—that what Cori-Anne had meant referred to being together rather than eating well and exercising by himself.

By one o'clock Eliot thought he'd probably never walk again. They'd schlepped through Bloomsbury and Fitzrovia, Soho, Mayfair, and St James's, along with places he'd never heard of. They'd seen where Mahatma Gandhi lived as a law student, where Karl Marx had stayed from 1851-1856, the house where Frederic Chopin had left from to give his last public performance, and countless others. Cori-Anne loved every step of the way and each story that Eliot magically pulled from whatever section of his brain held his filing cabinet. They ended up at The Grenadier on Wilton Row in Belgravia, where Cori-Anne once again had fish and chips and Eliot reluctantly ordered the roasted cauliflower and lentil curry, which he actually enjoyed.

They walked back to the hotel holding hands. Eliot had initiated the move, and Cori-Anne had endorsed his initiative with a squeeze.

"Don't you find this whole situation quite mind-blowing?" she asked when they were on the Heathrow Express from Paddington Station on their way to Terminal 5 at Heathrow Airport.

"If you mean that you've gone from running a yoga studio to running from the Jesús en lo Alto cartel, then yes, I suppose that is quite a change."

"I should call my mom; I'm sure she'll be wondering where I am. I'm not sure what to tell her, though. I suppose I can say that I finally found 'Jesus,' but hopefully he doesn't find me."

Eliot waited for her to laugh at her joke, but she didn't.

"How about you?" she asked. "I'm sure your brain must be working over-time with everything that's happening."

"Strangely enough, I find this whole sequence of events almost linear. You have to think of it as a co-ordination grid where the vertical axis is unhappiness, and the horizontal axis is happiness."

"I have no idea what you mean."

"You don't? No? Well, let me go back a few weeks. I'm

in my apartment doing nothing with someone who I thought cared for me—slight movement on the horizonal axis. Though if I'd analyzed her actions rather than my own, I would have come to the conclusion that she really didn't care and there would be no progression no matter what I did. Then I get forced to consider a job that I didn't want at a place that I didn't know by a person I didn't like. Huge movement on the unhappiness axis. But then—" he emphasized *then* by tapping on his nose "—I decide to write something that really interests me on a subject that brings me into contact with someone I already like, going to a place I've always wanted to go, to do something I've always wanted to do. Massive movement on the happiness axis. Now we imagine the origin, where the lines cross and we see that—"

"You really are an over-thinker," Cori-Anne said, shaking her head in amazement. "To me the only thing that makes sense in all of that is that you said you really like me. And you may as well know, I really like you too."

Eliot looked at the beautiful woman in front of him and raised his eyebrows, almost as if he didn't believe what she'd said.

"What?" she asked. "Are you surprised?"

"No, I...uh...I just can't believe...or more accurately I'd never have believed someone as amazing as you would ever say that to me." Before she could respond, the train pulled into the station at Heathrow Terminal 5. They grabbed their wheelies from the luggage rack at the door and took the escalators up to the check-in. Much to their delight, they'd been upgraded to first class and were directed to the Concord Lounge.

"This is very cool," Cori-Anne said after they'd both, on the bartender's recommendation, ordered a glass of Domain Jean Chartron Saint-Aubin. To Eliot's regret—though still not annoyance—Cori-Anne declined the menus. "We have an eleven-hour flight. Let's eat on the plane."

"Of course," replied Eliot with a sheepish grin. "That's exactly what I was about to propose."

Terminal 5 at Heathrow is a large terminal with thousands of people walking around aimlessly looking at shops with designer-brand clothing or luxury watches they can ill-afford. The wiser ones can be found eating the fare at the numerous restaurants that they know will be better than anything served on the plane. Others—like the Reverend Clayton Calvin Cripps—are slumped in lounge chairs staring at the information screens spinning through the myriad flights departing to everywhere but their destination.

Cripps was tired and desperate to go to the bathroom after the eight-hour-and-twenty-minute flight from Miami and what seemed like hours and hours hanging around the terminal waiting for the Cape Town connection to board. He'd developed an aversion to using public toilets after his stint in prison, and his bladder felt like it would burst at any minute. "Round" Ronny Rundo, on the other hand, had no such issue. He'd consumed both his dinner and that of the poor woman he turned into hand luggage on the plane, and he wasn't about to wait for any reason to relieve himself.

After they landed and went through security, he'd seen Pret a Manger, where he bought five sandwiches and washed them down with two bottles of orange juice. The terminal was packed with anxious travelers, and Ronny had had to toss an Albanian family that was taking up six seats onto the floor so he and Cripps could sit in comfort. Ronny had wandered off to find the toilets shortly after consuming his food. On his return he hissed at the Albanians, who were cowering on the floor against a pillar.

"What took you so long?" asked Cripps, desperately regretting asking the minute Ronnie opened his mouth to reply.

Ronnie filled the reverend in on his success in the bathroom and how he'd almost drowned a man in the toilet for complaining about the noise. That's when he dropped the real bombshell.

"You know the two peoples we're supposed to kill when we get to Africa?"

"Yes, I do," said Cripps, trying his best not to show the exasperation he felt with the giant moron. "We have photographs, which I do hope you've managed to store in that pea-sized brain of yours."

"Oh, yeah, it's in here." Ronny tapped his head with a finger the size of a salami. "I know because I just saw 'em walking into some fancy club."

"Holy shitnagle," squeaked Cripps, jumping up. "Maybe we can kill them bastards right here so we don't have to get on another plane and travel to that Godless continent. Show me where they went, boy."

Most people got out the way of the bald giant and his companion when they saw them—or felt them—approaching. The young woman who sat at the desk outside the Concord Lounge, however, was made of sterner stuff.

"Are you travelling first class, sir?" she asked Cripps.

"First class? You must be real thick, young lady. Your goddam airline is as far from first class as a biscuit is from a bucket of horse piss. Now allow me and my friend here to enter. First class, what a joke."

"I'm sorry, sir," said the young woman, totally unfazed by the rude little man. "Unless you can produce a first-class ticket, I am going to have to ask the two of you to leave."

Very few people ever stood up to the reverend. Almost none when he was accompanied by Ronny. And yet here was someone whom Ronny could have used as a toothpick telling Cripps to go about his business. Cripps blinked twice and then much to Ronny's surprise—because he'd expected the reverend to ask him to squeeze her head till her brain popped out like a cherry pit—turned around and walked off. He'd have to go to Africa; there was no choice. He prayed he wouldn't encounter too many black people.

Chapter 11

Cape Town, the next day

Eliot and Cori-Anne emerged from passport control perhaps not quite as fresh as daisies but certainly a good deal fresher than the Reverend Cripps and "Round" Ronny Rundo, who'd once again had to endure cramped coach conditions.

Neither party had checked luggage, and so the first time they laid eyes on each other was when they were met by their respective welcoming guides after going through passport and customs control. Of course, neither Cori-Anne nor Eliot knew about Cripps and Rundo, and their only acknowledgement of the pair was a slightly derogatory remark by Eliot as to the oddness of the two and a giggle from Cori-Anne in return. Cripps and Rundo, on the other hand, stared at their prey with a great deal of interest until a big blond man in a khaki shirt and shorts introduced himself.

"My name," said the man in an accent that was as foreign to Cripps as Cripps' was to him, "is Ben Terre'Blanche, and I have been sent by our Kommandant to take you to our headquarters. Now, where is your suitcases?"

"We ain't got none," responded Cripps. "That damn Mexican didn't give us no chance to get any clothes before he sent us on this cockamamie mission."

Terre'Blanche had no idea what "cockamamie" meant but assumed it meant important as he been tasked by Kommandant van Tonder to treat these two as VIPs.

"That is no problem. I am sure we can find some clothes for you. This big boy here may be a problem, though. Jesus, he's a big bastard."

Ronny grinned at Terre'Blanche. He was struggling to understand the Afrikaner's accent and just assumed he was being asked if he wanted food and to use the toilet.

"Yes, please," he said.

"Yes, please what?" asked a puzzled Terre'Blanche.

"Don't mind him," Cripps said before Ronnie could respond. "He's as dumb as a baloney sandwich. He just needs to void his bowels and fill his gullet."

"You mean take a shit and eat?" asked Terre'Blanche, slowly realizing he was in the presence of complete imbeciles.

While Ronny went to foul the Cape Town International terminal toilets, Terre'Blanche bought him a stick of biltong—the South African version of jerky— that was as long as Ronny's forearm.

"By the way," said Cripps, "I assume you know that those two there talking to that black fella are the people we are here to kill?"

"Oh, indeed yes. We are very aware of them and my colleague, that man over there with the big beard and the hat with the zebra-skin band, he is watching them and will follow them to their hotel. Once we know where they're staying, we can work out the next steps."

"Good," said Cripps. "The sooner we're out of this hell hole, the better." Terre'Blanche could not have been in more agreement. The thought of being around the little imp and his gorilla-sized companion made him nauseous.

Terre'Blanche ushered them out to the parking lot towards a white Toyota Landcruiser. Five minutes later—with Terre'Blanche and Cripps discussing how much they hated black people, Jews, and homosexuals and Ronny happily sucking on his biltong—they pulled out of the airport and were soon barreling along the N1 towards Stellenbosch, the town where the AWB (the neo-Nazi Afrikaner Resistance Movement) had its headquarters.

The man who met Cori-Anne and Eliot at the airport introduced himself as Jannie September. He was a freelance guide contracted by &Beyond to take them around the Cape Town area while their safari itinerary was being finalized.

"You're very lucky," he said. "It's still off-season, so things aren't too crowded. Now, where is your bags?"

"All we have are these carry-ons," replied Cori-Anne. "We need to buy clothes for our safari. We unfortunately had to leave in a hurry."

"Jussus," said Jannie. "I never had Americans here with such small bags. You people never travel light. Well, no worries. I will pick you up from the Mount Nelson Hotel this afternoon and take you clothes shopping. You have two great rooms reserved with views of the mountain." He was a little unsure why they weren't sharing a room but decided he'd wait to ask or try to ascertain for himself.

"Perfect," said Eliot as they followed Jannie out to a minivan. "When do you think our itinerary will be ready?"

"The lady, Jodie from &Beyond, she will call you later, but I think you'll be in Cape Town for a day or two. So perhaps I can give you some options for things to do. There is so much to see here—you won't believe it."

On the way to the hotel, Jannie gave them a brief history of Cape Town and its people. He explained that he was a Cape Colored, a separate ethnic group descended from black, white, and Asian slaves brought in from the Dutch East Indies and that his last name, September, referred to the month his ancestors had arrived in Cape Town. He told them that he spoke three languages: English, Afrikaans, and Xhosa, the main black language in the Western Cape of which Cape Town was the largest city. To his family and friends, he spoke Kaapse Afrikaans, which incorporated both English and Afrikaans.

Eliot, as Cori-Anne expected, knew a great deal of the history of South Africa and the apartheid system. "You know," Eliot said, "if you referred to someone as 'colored' in the states, you'd be in serious trouble."

"I understand," replied Jannie, "but that's the problem with many of your countrymen. You look at everyone else's culture through your own eyes. My ouma—that's 'grandmother' to you guys—always said, use a new pair of glasses every time you look at something different. Of course, she was as blind as a bat and refused to wear glasses."

"She sounds like a wise woman," said Cori-Anne. "I'd like to meet her."

"Not possible," said Jannie. "About a year ago she was

hit by a bus. Anyways, because this is a short stay, why don't we focus on the beauty of the Cape rather than its sad past and save that for when you come back. Start off happy, as my oupa—that's 'grandfather'—used to say. There's always plenty of time to be sad."

"Is he still alive?"

"No, ag shame, he died of a broken heart after my ouma was killed by the bus. Now look, you can see the mountain that made this place famous, Table Mountain, with the tablecloth of clouds covering it. Unfortunately, that means you won't be able to take the cable car up to the top."

"That's too bad," Eliot said. "But, talking of tablecloths, where should we go for lunch?"

"Let's get you checked into the hotel, then I'll take you to the V&A Waterfront. You can eat there. Lots of places in the mall with great food. You'll love it." He rattled off a number of places that Eliot said sounded terrific.

Clearly, Cori-Anne thought, Eliot and Jannie had a common interest in food. The rest of the trip from the airport focused even more on food with Jannie insisting that they try Cape Malay cooking if they had time and that his Auntie Aneezah made the best curry imaginable.

"Aneezah, that's an interesting name." said Cori-Anne.

"Oh, ja," replied Jannie. "It's a Muslim name. Means 'she-goat.' Which is very appropriate because she likes to butt in on every occasion."

"Good grief," said Eliot, suddenly pointing out the window as they passed by what looked like a Roman temple on the slopes of Table Mountain. "Are those goats?"

"Where, where?" Cori-Anne yelled. "Oh God, yes. Our first African animals!"

"Sorry to disappoint," Jannie said. "Those are Himalayan tahrs, whose ancestors escaped from a zoo in 1930. They're ruining the bloody ecosystem on the mountain. But the good news is you'll soon see plenty of wild animals. Maybe tomorrow I arrange for you a hiking tour near Cape Point and you'll see herds of zebras and eland. And now here we are, The Mount Nelson Hotel...the 'Pink Lady.'"

The minivan turned through an arch, past a security point, and onto a winding, palm-lined driveway up to a splendid portico where a uniformed bellman greeted them enthusiastically, raised his eyebrows at their sparse luggage, and ushered them up to the reception desk, where the greeting was if nothing even more effusive than that of the bellman.

"Oh, dear," said the receptionist, looking at her screen. "I was hoping to have both rooms ready for you to check in. But one room is still occupied, and they've still got an hour till check-out time. I'm so sorry. However, if one of you would like to shower and change beforehand, you're very welcome to do so at the spa."

"That's fine," Eliot said. He turned to Cori-Anne. "You take the room and I'll go to the spa."

"Give us a minute," Cori-Anne said to the receptionist with what she hoped was a disarming smile. "Look," she said, taking Eliot's hand and walking towards the end of the reception area. "I don't think we need two rooms."

Eliot felt a little thump in his chest, and then his mouth broadened into what Cori-Anne thought was a very goofy smile. He'd been wanting to hear her say that, hoping to hear her say that, and had he been able to understand his own jumbled unconscious mind, desperate to hear her say that. He'd thought about it ever since the afternoon in Miami when he'd suggested that they have separate rooms. The problem was he hadn't come up with a suitable rejoinder for when she did say it. He'd been through "are you sure?" and "this is a big step" and "Cori-Anne, I don't want you to feel pressured," although he'd decided the last one was a little patronizing. He looked at her and suddenly knew the answer. So he put his arms around her, pulled her in tightly, and kissed her full on the lips.

"I'm going to assume that's a yes," she laughed, pulling back.

Jannie, who'd been waiting for them to register from a chair near the reception desk, saw what was happening. He stood up and walked over. "You know, why don't I come back in about two hours? That should give you plenty of time." He didn't say what for, but Jannie's instincts were better honed than Eliot's, and he'd seen the way Cori-Anne had looked at Eliot on the trip from the airport.

"That should be perfect, Jannie," said Cori-Anne. "We'll meet you down here at one."

By the time the bellhop showed them to the huge cream-colored room with a balcony that overlooked Table Mountain, the machinations inside Eliot's head— should they have come to the attention of a competent neuroscientist—could have drawn an analogy to that of a whirling dervish on methamphetamine. What had Cori-Anne meant by "two hours should be perfect?" Would she want to shower and sleep? What would she think when she saw that he wasn't exactly in great shape compared to her? Why would anyone so utterly beautiful and lovely and every other word related to pulchritude and lubricity that he couldn't come up with want to be in a room with him?

"Fortune favors the brave" as Pliny the Elder is purported to have said, but *bonne chance* favors the unassuming, for just as Eliot stood frantically wondering what was about to happen, Cori-Anne stuck her head into the bathroom.

"There's a huge shower," she said.

"Um, well, if you'd like to go first...."

"I was thinking," she replied as she began to unbutton her blouse, "that perhaps we could share it."

They began their lovemaking in the shower and then retreated to the bed when Eliot slipped on the soap. When they were done, Eliot was firmly of the opinion that he'd need to take up yoga if he was to compete in any way with Cori-Anne's almost impossible and highly erotic flexibility.

At one o'clock, freshly re-showered and wearing their last remaining clean outfits, they walked down the stairs to the lobby, where Jannie waited to take them to the V&A Waterfront.

Chapter 12

Cape Town, same day

The accommodation at the headquarters of Die Afrikander Weerstandsbeweging, or AWB as it was known by people who couldn't be bothered to use what was a mouthful for most, was certainly not as luxurious as The Mount Nelson. Cripps and Ronny were shown to a whitewashed room at one end of a large gabled mansion on the outskirts of Stellenbosch on the slopes of Pappergaaiberg, or Parrot Mountain.

"There's a shower and a toilet down the hall here," said Ben Terre'Blanche, "and I will get you the clothes when you have finished showering." He was damned if he'd let these two foul-smelling Americans put on his clean clothes in their current condition. "Once you're dressed just come to the front there and I'll take you to the Kommandant, who is making a *braai* especially for you." He turned around and left them without explaining what *braai* meant.

The Reverend Cripps looked at the two bunk beds and scowled. The entire room reminded him of his prison cell.

He desperately needed to use the toilet and he was determined to do so before Ronny. He grabbed the towel that lay on his bed and said to Ronny, "You stay here and watch our stuff while I go and evacuate my innards."

"Don't be too long please, Reverend. That meat stuff is making my tummy sore, and I need to poop."

"Dagummit. I ain't interested in your crapola. I gotta mash one out that I been savin' since Miami. So, you just wait your gosh-darned turn. Now watch our stuff."

The problem for Ronny was that they didn't have any stuff other than the clothes they were wearing, and so after sitting on his bed watching the empty room for ten minutes, he fell asleep. He shot out of bed ten minutes later when a sound that reminded him of the howl of a prisoner the reverend had castrated a few months before ripped him out of his snooze. He rushed down the corridor where he bumped into Terre'Blanche, who'd also heard the scream. The bone-chilling screech finally died down and ended with a loud "Heil Hitler."

Terre'Blanche hammered on the door. "What's going on in there? Are you being attacked by a terrorist?"

"No, dammit, I'm not being attacked. I just passed a turd the size of a bowling ball. Now I'd thank you all to give me some peace while I complete my business."

Half an hour later, wearing a fresh pair of long lime-green polyester pants and matching shirt and feeling a lot better than he had earlier, Cripps emerged onto the back patio of the house, where a man with a large beard wearing a similar outfit was putting various cuts of meat on what looked like an upside-down ploughshare over a hot charcoal fire. A minute or so later they were joined by

Terre'Blanche and Ronny, wearing khaki shorts that were too tight and a black t-shirt with a strange swastika-like symbol that strained every artificial fiber used in its manufacture to keep his girth contained. Ronny looked at the meat and clapped his hands delightedly.

"Welcome," said the man with the big beard. "I am Kommandant Piet *Die Poffadder* van Tonder." He had a long coil of sausage in one hand and a spatula in the other, which he held out as if he wanted to shake hands. The reverend hesitated for a moment and then shook the spatula, wondering what other strange customs these people had.

"Good day to you, sir," Cripps said. "I am the Reverend Clayton Calvin Cripps of the Church of the Uber White Nazi, and this here is my enforcer, Ronny Rundo. We are grateful that you have availed us of your hospitality and help in this matter."

"Ag, no problem, Reverend," replied van Tonder, tossing the sausage onto the ploughshare. "Don 'l Clavo' or whatever his fucking name is personally called me to do him this favor, and of course I'm happy to help. Now before we get down to business, let me ask you this: Have you ever had a South African *braai*?"

"We ain't had a South African anything yet," replied Cripps.

"I had me a bull tongue," Ronny said, rubbing his stomach, which still hurt.

"What?" asked van Tonder, looking confused.

"He means *biltong*, Kommandant," said Terre'Blanche. He tapped his head. "*Ek dink hy is n'bietjie befok in sy kop*," he said in Afrikaans, which translated roughly as *I think he's a little fucked in the head.*

"No worries. Well, a *braai* is what you yanks call a barbecue."

"I would ask you, sir," said Cripps, "not to refer to us as 'yanks.' To us yanks are northerners, and we view them with only slightly more regard than we do Blacks and Jews and homosexuals. Which is to say just above that of a snake's belly in a wagon rut."

Neither van Tonder nor Terre'Blanche knew what the hell the little man was talking about, but van Tonder decided to let it go.

"Ja, ja, ja. Apologies, man. Anyways, this here is a *braai*, and I'm cooking this *lekker boerewors* on a *skottel.* You will eat like a beast."

The small talk progressed with neither party really understanding what the other was saying until van Tonder was finally finished cooking and invited them to the table, which held various other foodstuffs.

"Reverend," said van Tonder, "maybe you could lead us in saying grace."

"I'd be delighted," said Cripps. The Church of the Uber White Nazi wasn't a church in the way that van Tonder or Terre'Blanche thought of a church, and the Reverend Clayton Cripps most definitely wasn't a reverend in the way that the two South African white supremacists thought a reverend ought to be. Cripps considered himself to be a worshipper of Hitler, and *Mein Kampf* was his bible. Or at least that is what he told his followers. If someone had put Cripps into a mental washing machine and rinsed off all the fabrication he'd built up around himself, they would have found a deranged psychopath who believed he was put on earth to inflict as much pain as possible on those he had learned to hate from an early age growing up in Calico Rock, Arkansas.

Cripps' father had been an actual preacher in a local church until he was fired for stealing church funds and blaming it on the janitor, who happened to be black. The janitor was a popular man, and no one was prepared to take the word of a preacher—who most considered a wastrel, a drunk, and an unholy bastard— over his. When the older Cripps came home after being soundly admonished and ignominiously fired by the church elders, he beat his wife and children most awfully, all the while bemoaning that at the root of all their woes were black people who fouled God's earth, Satan-worshipping Jews who controlled everything and everyone, and homosexuals who brought the Lord's ire down on the rest of God's children. Shortly after making that terrible pronouncement, he told his wife to join him in their bedroom where he blew her head off with his shotgun before turning it on himself. This left Clayton Cripps and his brother Bobby alone in the world.

The two Cripps boys were moved from one foster home to another, where they caused sufficient mayhem and mischief to get a lengthy sentence in a reformatory for incorrigible boys. Here Bobby Cripps died when he "accidentally" fell out the warden's fourth story window. On his release, Clayton was now even more convinced that the Jews, blacks, and homosexuals were behind his misfortune (even though no self-respecting Jew, black, or gay person would have had anything at all to do with him) and went on a rampage of hate crimes, eventually ending up in the Ellis Unit prison in Huntsville, Texas. It was in prison that despite his diminutive size, his deep-rooted ferocity and hatred shot him up in the ranks of the Aryan Brotherhood at an almost unheard-of rate. After serving his time and with the backing of some of the wealthiest sponsors of the Aryan Brotherhood, he set up the Church of the Uber White Nazi. And this was why the Reverend Clayton Calvin Cripps was slightly tongue-tied when it came to saying grace.

"Mein Fuhrer," he began, "who now sits at the right hand of Jesus, we ask you to make this food digestible by those of us with sensitive stomachs and rain thunder on those we mutually believe are responsible for this antwacky world. Amen."

"Very interesting version of grace," said van Tonder, wondering whether he should offer up a more traditional prayer in case Cripps' one had offended Jesus. "You know we, uh, also think very highly of Hitler, though not quite as a godlike figure."

"Well, some people let the Lord into their heart. I have let in der Fuehrer. Here he rests, sir." Cripps thumped his chest. "And he does not rest easy because there is work to be done in his name and enemies to smite. He emerges from me when I need him to."

Van Tonder gulped. He'd heard Cripps scream "heil Hitler" in the bathroom and wondered if Cripps felt the fuehrer had come out during the evacuation of his bowels.

"Anyway," he said, pushing the vision of Hitler's head emerging from Cripps's anus out of his mind, "it seems we both believe in the same principles, so let me first explain what this is because this will be good for your stomach." He cut Cripps a large piece of the still-sizzling sausage and put it on his plate. "This is what we call *boerewors* or 'famer's sausage' in English. Full of very interesting pieces of meat, including bull penis. We have a saying, *Dit maak die boere sterk,* which means it makes the boers strong."

Cripps felt himself heave. He had no desire to eat a penis. He looked over at Ronny, who was piling his plate with everything in sight.

"I can see your friend there needs no invitation to eat," said van Tonder, pointing his knife at Round Ronny.

"He ain't got many manners, Kommandant," said Cripps, seeing the look of disgust on van Tonder's face. "But then again manners is not what he's here for. He can pop a person's head like it was a pimple on a mule's ass. It's a joy to see, and I hope we will be able to demonstrate it for you when we get hold of those two mud-suckin' maggots."

"I look forward to that, Reverend. Now, here is my proposal. These two maggots, as you call them, they are going into the bush in a day or two."

"Into the bush, you say?" interrupted Ronny, laughing gleefully.

"Ja, into the bush."

"I thought they were going on safari?"

"They is. They're going into the bush—what is confusing you? I'm not sure what the joke is."

"You said they's going into the bush. Not on safari."

"Yes, exactly, they're going on safari into the bush. What's the problem? What do you call the bush?"

"We call it poontang," replied Ronny, swallowing a whole lamb chop.

"Very well," replied a now-frustrated van Tonder. "They are going on safari into the poontang if you prefer. But we don't know precisely where as yet. Our contact at the hotel will let us know tonight. With any luck it will be close to where we have some poaching operations, which will give us a huge advantage. Now eat up, gentlemen, and then Bennie over here can drive you around the area. It's very pretty, apart from the people."

Terre'Blanche gave him a horrified look. The Kommandant shook his head and said in Afrikaans, *"Neem een vir die span, man,"* which translates roughly as "take one for the team, you fucking cowardly bastard."

Terre'Blanche scowled. Hanging out with a psychopath and a deranged idiot went far and beyond anything to do with being a team player. He felt for his 9mm, which was tucked into the waistband of his shorts. If he had to shoot them, he would, and to hell with the consequences.

Chapter 13

Cape Town, that afternoon

Eliot and Cori-Anne were having an entirely different experience. They were sitting outdoors at a restaurant called Harbor House overlooking the dock at the V&A Waterfront. They'd ordered a huge seafood platter with giant prawns, langoustines, crayfish, mussels, and calamari, which they washed down with a bottle of Spier 21 Gables Chenin Blanc, a varietal neither of them had tried before.

"Maybe we should have another bottle," said Eliot, who was at a point where he was prepared to throw all caution to the wind. Their lovemaking had left him feeling happier than he could remember, and every moment with Cori-Anne, every story, and every funny little look left him more elated.

"No," she laughed, punching his shoulder playfully, "we have shopping to do, don't forget, and I think we want to be sober enough to talk to the agent about our itinerary when they call."

At that moment Jannie, whom they'd asked to join them for lunch but he had to visit one of his sick relatives, came up to their table.

"If youse two is finished with lunch then we can go shopping now for clothes. I spoke to the lady from &Beyond, and she is sending your itinerary to the hotel for you this evening. You can call her then with questions, but I believe you will fly out of here in two days. That means we can talk about activities for tomorrow."

"That sounds perfect," Eliot said, signaling the waiter to bring the check. "So now on to clothes."

Jannie took them to the Cape Union Mart, an outdoor and hiking store at the waterfront, where they picked outfits that they believed would not make them look like American tourists about to go on safari. Jannie shook his head, knowing that's exactly what they would look like. Their next stop was into the mall itself, which housed several more casual clothing boutiques.

"Don't buy more than you can put in a small duffel," Jannie advised them. "You'll be on small planes with limited luggage space, and in any case your clothes will be laundered every day at the camps."

To Eliot's relief Cori-Anne had given up on wanting to pay for herself. "You'll make it up to me with yoga lessons," he told her. "And in my opinion, your yoga class prices are ridiculously high."

"What do you mean?" she asked, looking slightly hurt.

"But worth every penny, because from what I've heard you're the best damn yoga instructor on the planet."

"Well," she said, getting what he was doing, "that means you're going to have to work extra hard beginning tomorrow morning."

On the way back to the hotel, Jannie asked them if they'd like to hike in the Cape of Good Hope Nature

Reserve. If they were interested, he offered to see if his friend Mary, who led hikes all over Cape Town including up Table Mountain, was free.

"The common trails are very short and easy, but Mary knows places that most people don't. She'll give you a good workout. The reserve is a very beautiful place, and you'll see the most southwest point of the African continent."

"That's not the tip of Africa," Eliot pointed out.

"No, the tip is Cape Agulhas, but that's a three-hour drive. My feeling is maybe you do the hike in the morning, and on the way back we can stop at some of the vineyards, where you can have lunch."

Both agreed it sounded perfect and said they'd meet Jannie outside the hotel at eight-thirty the next morning. When they stopped at the reception desk for the key, they were handed a leather pouch containing their proposed itinerary.

"This looks like a wonderful itinerary," said the concierge, a youngish man with a shaved head whose nametag read "Paul Ferreira."

"You looked at it?" asked Eliot in surprise.

"Oh yes, I always do. In my experience many of the safari companies will try to send you to places that give them the biggest commission rather than the best places. Obviously, I've been to many of these private game reserves, and so I make sure our guests are going to the right locations. Why don't you take a look and then I can provide whatever help you need?"

"Hmm," said Eliot, opening the leather pouch with the &Beyond logo on it. "I can't imagine that a company like &Beyond would send us to a bad place. They seem to have a great reputation."

"Oh, indeed," replied Ferreira. "Now, may I suggest that you take tea on the verandah where it's nice and cool. Look over the itinerary and then let me know how you feel about it."

"Seem a little weird, that he'd open something addressed to a guest," said Cori-Anne as they walked out the reception area through the large lounge where plates of cucumber and smoked salmon sandwiches, scones and cakes, and various savory-looking snacks competed for Eliot's attention and won.

"Eliot, we just ate…for goodness' sake." She grabbed his arm and dragged him through the doors to the verandah, where they both ordered tea and Cori-Anne spread the itinerary out on the table.

There was a note from Jodie informing them that she'd been incredibly lucky and managed to get accommodation at one of the most sought-after private game reserves in the whole of South Africa, Hunter's Folly. She recommended they next fly to Botswana to a camp in the Okavango Delta, which would provide a totally different experience. The trip would begin the day after tomorrow, as Jannie had mentioned earlier. She would give them a call at six-thirty that evening to discuss.

"Oh, my God," said Cori-Anne, "just listen to this. *On the banks of the Limpopo, adjacent to the vast Northern Tuli Game Reserve across the river in Botswana, lies the 31,000-hectare Hunter's Folly private game reserve. Here amongst the savannah grasslands and riverine forest, you'll find huge herds of elephant and prides of lion, both black and white rhinos, wild dogs, cheetah, leopard, and thousands of antelope, both the plentiful and the rare. The reserve is protected by one of the most effective anti-poaching units in Africa under the supervision of its first commander and current co-owner of the reserve, Bontle Warona-Modise. Bontle's husband and co-owner, Gosego Modise, is one of the most respected game scouts in all of Africa and prides himself as a martini mixologist in the camp's Storm in a Martini Glass bar, said to rival the famous martini bar at Duke's Hotel in London..."* Cori-Anne waxed on as eloquently as someone whose head is suddenly filled with the wonder of the bush can wax on.

"And just two days ago you were terrified of going somewhere where you'd be face to face with lions and elephants."

"Really?" she said, not bothering to look up. "I don't remember saying that."

Eliot stared at her and shook his head in delight as she continued to read the itinerary aloud. His mind was more focused on how they'd make love that evening. He realized that "love" as he understood it may have been a little premature. He was enchanted by her, perhaps even beguiled. She was as different from Belinda as a jelly donut is from a jellied eel, and once again he marveled at how someone so utterly beautiful could have feelings for someone like him. And yet, unless he was reading the situation incorrectly, she appeared to be exhibiting affection. In this respect Eliot believed he was correct. But affection, he reminded himself, was not love.

His reverie was interrupted by a sudden vibration from his phone. He looked down to find that it was Thomas Mortimer Jones.

"It's Jones," he said to Cori-Anne, who looked up from

the itinerary when she heard his phone buzz. "I guess I'd better take it. Hello?"

"Eliot?" said Thomas Mortimer Jones as calmly as he could.

"Yes, Tommy. I'm sitting here with Cori-Anne. We're just looking at our itinerary."

"Good," said Jones. "Can you put her on speaker...are you in a private area?"

"Not exactly. Should we go to our room and call you back? I'll just have to get the check."

"Here," said Cori-Anne, taking an old-fashioned wire out her purse. "Plug this in and then you take one ear bud and I'll take the other."

"OK," Eliot said, "I haven't seen a set of these for a while." Once the earbuds were in place, he moved closer to Cori-Anne to share the speaker, and for just a second her cheek brushed his. "We're listening."

"Now, I don't want you to panic," Jones said.

"Normally when people say that," said Cori-Anne, "it's time to start panicking."

"I take your point," he said. "However, there's no need to do anything differently just yet. We just learned that the cartel has hired some hitmen to go after you."

"Holy shit," said Elliot a little too loudly. "We need to get out of here."

"No," Jones said firmly. "That is precisely what you shouldn't do until I find out more. We don't know who the hitmen are or if they have the slightest idea that you've left the country. I'm using every resource available to find out, so sit tight. Are you on your actual safari yet?"

"No," replied Eliot, hoping his breath didn't smell in the

intimate environment created by the wire. "We're leaving the day after tomorrow really early, and it does seem from the itinerary that we'll be in the middle of nowhere. Should we be looking out for something...someone?"

"Just keep your eyes open and stay out of places that don't feel safe. As soon as we can find out who the hitmen are, I'll make sure that the FBI over here or Interpol over there knows about it. Stay in touch and I'll call when I know anything."

Cori-Anne pulled out her earbud and looked at Eliot. "Are you worried?"

"I don't know, are you? I mean it's not like I've been in a situation like this before." He realized he'd emphasized "I" and immediately regretted it.

"Well, neither have I—if you're implying that this is normal for someone like me." She, too, emphasized "I," but there was anger in her tone.

"I'm so sorry," he said, reaching for her hand which she immediately pulled away. "That's not what I meant. Look, we're in this together, and I realize neither of us knows exactly what to do. I mean, it feels like we're doing the right thing getting as far away from civilization as we can get. Honestly, I'd never...."

She was quiet for a moment, and then she put her hand on his wrist and tried to smile. "No, I'm sorry I overreacted. For a second, I just realized how different our lives have been up until now, and we still don't really know each other yet."

"No, we don't," Eliot said, wanting to lean across and kiss her. "But we know enough to at least like each other. Well, I like you a lot."

Cori-Anne laughed. "You do, do you? And I like you a lot, too, Eliot Hart. I have a thought: Maybe we should eat here at the hotel tonight, just to be on the safe side. And I'm not sure about tomorrow, either. Perhaps we should stay on the hotel property."

"I agree about dinner, but let's see how we feel tomorrow morning. We can always cancel the hike."

"Good." She stood up and put her hands on her hips. "Now, we have plenty of time before dinner, so let's go to the gym for your first yoga lesson."

His phone rang again. This time it was Jodie to ask if the itinerary was acceptable, and if it was, could she charge the trip to the credit card that Eliot had given her colleague over the phone in Miami. Eliot agreed, and Jodie told them she'd finalize everything and give Jannie all the details for getting them to the airport.

As they were about to leave, Paul Ferreira, the concierge, came up to the table. "May I assume that the itinerary is appealing?" His voice had a simpering quality to it that reminded Eliot of Uriah Heep.

"Yes," replied Cori-Anne. "It's perfect—very exciting."

"Oh, excellent," Ferreira said, putting his hands together in a decidedly Heep-like fashion. "Now, can I arrange something for tomorrow? I can put together a wonderful tour for you."

Before Cori-Anne could reply, Eliot jumped in. "No, thank you. We're just going to stay here tomorrow and relax at the pool."

"What a pity to miss out on things. But if that's your preference, then of course. If you change your mind, let me know and I can arrange things in a jiffy." He turned and walked back inside.

"I don't trust that guy one bit," said Eliot. "There's something a little off about him."

In that, his instincts were correct. The minute Ferreira got back to his desk, he took out his phone and dialed a number. It rang twice and then was answered by Ben Terre'Blanche, who'd just returned from driving Cripps and Rundo around Stellenbosch.

"Bad news and good news. They're staying in tomorrow, but they are definitely going to Hunter's Folly, so you can set up everything to happen there."

Terre'Blanche took a deep breath. He was hoping that Ferreira could have arranged for the targets to take a tour with him as their guide. Then he could have delivered them to some place near Cape Town where Cripps and Rundo would be waiting to kill them. Still, Hunter's Folly was in the vicinity of the huge farm where the AWB bred lions for canned hunting and from which they shipped the bones to Asia for traditional Chinese medicine. The only issue he saw was that he'd have to spend more time with two of the worst people he'd ever come across in his life. Perhaps if he planned it right, he could arrange for Cripps and Rundo to have a hunting accident. As far as he was concerned, they were a disgrace to the purity of the Aryan race.

Chapter 14

Cape Town, the next morning and evening

Cori-Anne woke up about ten minutes before Eliot. The sunlight was weak and thin, and she could see a layer of high clouds in the sky. They'd opened the drapes the night before when they got back to the room after dinner to look at the dark shadow of the huge mountain that stood like a giant sentinel protecting its city, and now she was glad they'd left them open. Rising early gave her a few minutes to think about everything that was happening so fast.

She looked over at Eliot, who was snoring softly on the pillow next to her. He had a strong face, she decided, with a softness around the edges that hinted at what her book on Buddhism referred to as an "uncorrupted soul." There was nothing classic about it. No high cheekbones. No special feature. He was handsome, she thought, in an uncorrupted-soul*ish* way. As gently as she could, she moved a strand of his thick black hair away from his eyes. He must be dreaming of something funny, she thought, judging by the goofy smile on his face.

She knew he'd wanted to make love the night before, but she was reluctant and he'd sensed that and so they'd simply kissed and fallen asleep in each other's arms. She thought of all the men she'd known over the years and couldn't think of one who wouldn't have been petulant at her unwillingness to have sex. Eliot, the man lying so peacefully beside her, was unlike the ones who had come before. There had been no tension with him. No disappointment. Just an acceptance.

It wasn't as if she hadn't wanted to make love. She had, but what had happened so spontaneously that afternoon in the shower and on the bed came from a different place, a lonely and frightened place. Last night was different. Over dinner and just enough wine to lift their inhibitions, they'd talked of their families and their childhoods and what they liked and didn't about their lives so far. It was more like a first date, and Cori-Anne had principles about what did and didn't happen on a first date.

Eliot stirred and opened his eyes.

"What time is it?" he asked, looking up at her as if she were his most favorite thing in the world.

"Just after seven," she said, resisting a sudden urge to lean down and kiss him. Not yet, but soon.

"Do you want to do that hike?" he asked, pushing himself into an upright position.

"I think so," Cori-Anne replied. "Don't you? I think we'll be safe enough. I mean, we don't even know if whoever's after us has any idea we're in South Africa."

Eliot looked at his phone. "There's no text from Thomas, so I think you're probably right. I'll text Jannie and tell him we'd definitely like to do it. Now," he said, standing up and stretching, "why don't we go down and see what's for breakfast."

Paul Ferreira spotted them the moment they got out the elevator. He noticed that they were wearing clothes more suitable for a hike than a lazy morning at the pool. Damn, they'd lied to him, the miserable bastards.

"Hello," he shouted, "Miss van Cleave, Mr. Hart...."

"Don't stop," Eliot said. "Keep walking. Pretend we don't see him."

But a good concierge is nether fooled by diversionary tactics nor gives up quite so easily, and their entrance to the restaurant was blocked by Ferreira who, like a shadow, had somehow managed to slide past them.

"May I enquire if you're headed to the dining room for breakfast?"

"Yes," replied Cori-Anne, sounding as annoyed as Eliot had ever heard her. "We are, thank you."

"And it looks like you have some activities planned for the morning?" he said, weaving in front of them as they tried to head to their table.

"We don't know yet," Eliot said, almost elbowing Ferreira out the way. "We'll let you know if we need your help."

Ferreira grudgingly acknowledged defeat and made his way back to his desk, where he called Terre'Blanche. "Those filthy swine lied to me. They're going hiking but I don't know where."

"Damn," replied Terre'Blanche. "How long do we have before they leave?"

"I don't know. They've just gone to breakfast."

"OK, no worries. We'll leave now, park in front of the

hotel, and follow them when they exit the grounds. I'm pretty sure they'll do what everybody does and go to Cape Point. Maybe these horrible buggers I'm with can push them off a cliff... and then I can do the same to them."

Jannie drove Eliot and Cori-Anne along Chapman's Peak Drive heading to the spot where they'd meet their hiking guide, Mary. The scenic drive as far as both were concerned was stunning.

"This has to be one of the most beautiful places I've ever seen," said Cori-Anne, who couldn't decide which view was better: the slopes of the Twelve Apostles Mountain Range on her left or the surf of the Atlantic crashing against the rocks to her right.

"Ja," agreed Jannie. "My old man was a fisherman, and he told me that everyone in the world should see this place before they die. Unfortunately, he was killed when his boat capsized along the other coast, so he never got to see it himself. But there you have it. More good advice from my family."

"I hate to say this," Eliot said, "but it seems that your family members die shortly after making pronouncements in a manner related to the very thing they're making a pronouncement about. So, my advice to you, Jannie, is warn the remaining members of your family not to make pronouncements."

Jannie nodded sagely. He thought Eliot sounded like a teacher he'd had in high school who'd attempted to teach the class classical philosophy. They turned into the Cape

Point section of the Table Mountain National Park and met Mary at what Jannie said was called the Olifantsbos (Elephant Bush) parking lot.

"Don't worry," he said, "there haven't been elephants here for a very long time."

"Then no doubt we'll be charged by one," whispered Eliot to Cori-Anne.

Mary was sitting in her car but got out when she saw them. She greeted them by saying, "I hope you're up for some decent exercise." Her weathered complexion and baggy clothes made it impossible to tell her age. "I'm going to take you on a trail that most people aren't allowed to go on, but I can because of this," she said, showing them a rather official-looking ID card. "We'll leave my car here, and Jannie can meet us at the lighthouse when we're done in about two hours, depending on how fit you are." She gave Cori-Anne and Eliot the once over. "Well, I can see how fit you are, my dear, but I'm not sure about this bloke. We'll have to prod him a bit to get him going."

Cori-Anne laughed at the indignant expression on Eliot's face. "Don't worry, this is part of his new exercise regimen."

The walk was less strenuous than Eliot thought, and he managed to keep up with Cori-Anne and Mary for most of the way except when they climbed from the beach to the higher plateaus. By the time he caught up, his thighs were aching and he was breathing heavily.

"Are you OK?" Mary asked.

"Perfectly fine," Eliot answered, doing his best to sound it. "I've been a little sedentary of late but...." He was about to explain further and then realized that Mary wasn't interested. Cori-Anne smiled at him. It wasn't a sympathetic smile but rather an encouraging one, and it made Eliot more determined than ever to get himself in some sort of shape.

"This whole area," said Mary once she was sure Eliot wasn't going to pass out, "is one of the six floral kingdoms of the world. There are over a thousand different species of fynbos including these proteas, South Africa's national flower. Now, quiet, look over there."

Cori-Anne gave a delighted squeak when she saw that Mary was pointing at a herd of zebra and some large antelope, which Mary said were eland.

"Should we be careful?" asked Eliot, who'd read extensively about zebra but not about eland.

"The only animals you have to be careful of around here are the people, especially the ones who believe the rules for where you can walk or what you can do don't apply to them."

Mary's point was perfectly demonstrated when they finally arrived at the end of the trail near the Cape Point lighthouse. A number of baboons were wandering around the carpark looking for things to eat or steal. There were signs all over warning people not to feed baboons and to keep their car doors closed, but most visitors were ignoring the signs. Only Mary, who seemed to be a lone voice as there were no park rangers in sight, managed to get them to stop with firmly delivered threats of prosecution.

Jannie was waiting for them in the parking lot and asked if they'd like to hike up to the lighthouse while he drove Mary back to her car. Cori-Anne was all for it, but

Eliot declined. He didn't think his legs could handle the steps.

"I'd rather just stand and watch the baboons for a bit. You go ahead—I'll wait."

As he walked around looking at the both the people and baboons, he noticed a white Toyota Corolla with three people in it who appeared to be looking at him. The minute they realized he'd seen them they looked away and slunk down in their seats. Eliot hadn't had a good view of them, but there was something about the one guy, a large man whose shaved head touched the roof of the car, that seemed familiar and he decided he'd take a closer look.

Inside the white Toyota, Cripps, who was in the back seat, rubbed his hands together. "Perfect, Goddamned perfect. He's seen us so he's going to stroll by casually to get a better look. So, boys, here's how we do this. You two get out and follow that bitch up to the lighthouse, and Ronny, as soon as you can, do your thing."

"What thing?" asked Ronny

"I don't know what damn thing, boy. Just make sure she falls over the edge or down the stairs or maybe come up behind her when no one's lookin' and twist her neck like a lobster crackin' a walnut. I'll wait here in the car, and as soon as that nosy bastard gets closer—and he will, believe me, he'll come right up to the car—I'll grab him and slit his throat with this here razor." He pulled an old-fashioned razor that he'd found in the bathroom at the AWB compound out his pocket. "Now git going so we can git the hell out of this Godforsaken place."

Terre'Blanche, who'd never heard a worse plan in his

life, decided he was having nothing to do with it. He got out the car and followed Ronny to the base of the steps, and then as soon Ronny began to climb after Cori-Anne, he turned and walked as far away as he could from what he imagined would be total carnage. Unfortunately for Cripps, Terre'Blanche left his door open.

Cripps, as has already been established, was not a tall man, so when he lowered himself in the back seat to prevent Eliot from seeing him, he was also hidden from a large baboon strolling between the cars looking for food. The baboon noticed the open door, and, knowing that the idiot humans usually left food in their cars, climbed into the front seat vacated by Terre'Blanche and began to rifle through the center console. Cripps heard the noise from his hiding place in the back seat and carefully opened the straight razor. Good, he thought, the bastard had saved him the trouble of having to jump out the car. He rose slowly from his crouched position and then as quick as a mongoose shot his left arm round the front headrest to grab what he imagined was Eliot's hair and his right arm around the other side to slit Eliot's throat.

There are a number of things about baboons that Cripps was unaware of at the time. First, they are incredibly strong. Second, they don't like surprises. Third, they have extremely sharp teeth that can rip skin from a man's arm like husk from an ear of corn. These three things and one or two others (like the expulsion of feces when alarmed) thrown in for good measure Cripps discovered in the next few seconds. As soon as his left hand came into contact with the baboon's head, the baboon screamed and shot forward. Seeing the shiny object in Cripps's other hand, he grabbed it and sank his large canine teeth into the bony flesh. Cripps let out a horrific yell of pain that startled several passersby. Cripps, who was still not aware that his adversary was a member of the genus Papio and not the genus Homo, dropped the razor and opened his door with his left hand. He jumped out the car and took a step back. The baboon, who'd recovered slightly, picked up the razor and admired it. He saw Cripps outside the car staring at him in what can only be described as abject terror, and then in a macabre shuffle, he lunged at Cripps in what one tourist from the UK who'd observed the whole spectacle told her husband "looked like a scene out of that movie we saw with Johnny Depp. You know the one: Sweeney Todd, the Demon Barber of Fleet Street."

Cripps, pretty sure the baboon was not about to shave him, ran off howling obscenities until the baboon, now bored with the razor, dropped it and went off in search of a less-traumatized visitor to harass.

Things hadn't gone exactly as planned for Round Ronny Rundo either. Halfway up the steps leading to the lighthouse, he was accosted by a tour group from China, who mistook him for a famous wrestler and insisted on taking selfies with him. Ronny was a pretty obliging person when not killing people or eating and so was only too happy to pose. By the time he was done, Cori-Anne was safely back with Eliot and Jannie, who was just pulling into the parking lot.

By the time the Reverend Cripps and Round Ronny Rundo had regrouped with Terre'Blanche—who'd observed the fiasco with some satisfaction from a safe distance—

Jannie, Cori-Anne, and Eliot were enjoying a plate of fish and chips at Snoekies, an institution in the little town of Hout Bay. After lunch Jannie suggested they visit one or two wine farms in the Constantia Valley before going back to the hotel.

Their first stop was Groot Constantia, the oldest wine estate in the Cape dating back to 1712. They walked around the grounds, took a tour of the mansion house, and sampled a few of the wines, which Eliot declared absolutely delicious. He bought two cases of Groot Constantia Cabernet Sauvignon that he shipped to his old apartment, wondering if he'd ever get to see it again.

"If I may make a suggestion now," said Jannie, "let me take you back to the hotel. When you come back, we can spend a whole day touring the Stellenbosch wine area. You need at least a day for that, and the traffic at this time is really bad." Both Cori-Anne and Eliot agreed, so he dropped them off at the hotel and told them to call him if they decided they were up for some Cape Malay cooking that night. If not, he'd see them at seven-thirty the next morning to take them to the airport for their charter flight to Hunter's Folly.

Eliot remembered that he'd seen the big skinhead and the little man who'd had the run-in with the baboon at the airport, but he didn't put two and two together to realize that they could be the assassins that Thomas had warned him about the night before and so didn't give it another thought.

"Are you up for trying Cape Malay cuisine?" he asked Cori-Anne when she got out the shower. She was wrapped in a towel which she dropped when she got to the bed, and much to his surprise and delight, she jumped in next to him.

"I am," she replied, "but...." She reached for his belt buckle and began to unfasten it. "First I'm going to have to work up an appetite."

"I thought you wanted to—"

"Shh," she said, putting her finger on his lips. "This time I've been doing the thinking, and this is what I want."

They ate dinner at Aneezah's Place, the restaurant belonging to Jannie's aunt in the Bo-Kaap area of Cape Town.

"Cape Malay food," said Jannie as he drove them past the colorful houses that made up the neighborhood, "is a mixture of Malaysian, Indonesian, and even Indian. It's sweet and spicy at the same time. My auntie is a fantastic cook, and she's going to give you a good time—you'll see."

He dropped them off outside the restaurant and told them he'd be back in an hour-and-a-half. Once again, they invited Jannie to join them. He apologized and said he had a prior engagement but would have lunch or dinner with them on their return.

After ten minutes of listening to Aneezah's stories about the mischief Jannie had got up to as a kid, they understood his reluctance to be there. Of course, the ribbing was all good-natured and they could tell the family bonds were strong. Aneezah was open and funny, and though the little restaurant was full, she spent a lot of time with them asking questions and talking about her food and what made it special. She insisted they try little bits of everything, and though Cori-Anne was nervous about eating stuff that was too hot, she found the food to be delicious and spicy without being fiery. Being a Muslim restaurant, there was no alcohol, but they made it back to the hotel with more than enough time to go to the Planet Bar, where they sat out on the terrace drinking glasses of red wine and talking about the next day.

"You know, Eliot," Cori-Anne said as it became clear that it was time for bed, "I told you this afternoon that I'd been doing some thinking."

"Yes," Eliot said, his mind whirling into action on *Possibility of Good Thought* over *Possibility of Bad Thought* and potential of a *good* or *bad* outcome. But before he could calculate the odds, Cori-Anne laughed.

"You know, you're very transparent when it comes to emotion. I've known you for four days, and I already have a pretty good idea of what's going through that complicated mind of yours."

He opened his mouth to say something, but she stopped him mid-breath.

"Let me finish. When we had sex yesterday afternoon, it came out of a place that was very different to when we made love just before we went to dinner this evening. Yesterday I was excited, but I was also scared. I desperately needed to feel something other than numb. I wanted to ache and breathe heavily and understand that the world wasn't as crazy as it felt at that moment."

"And did you?" he asked, his concern evident.

"Yes, I did. And I felt so good afterwards. Happier and lighter, almost as if the tension was lifting. That's why I just needed you to hold me last night. Tonight, I wanted to start again. I wanted to feel like that dinner was our first date and we were just beginning to explore each other, to know each other. And that's how I felt when I got in the shower this afternoon."

"Wow," was all he could say. He realized to his horror that he'd totally overlooked this side of Cori-Anne, and he felt ashamed.

"'Wow'? Is that all you have to say?"

"No, it's not, but in truth I don't know what to say other than I'm so happy you feel that way. I don't want to screw things up by saying the wrong things or things that may—"

"Eliot, Eliot, Eliot," she said, touching his cheek. "I know you overthink everything, but sometimes you just need to go with the flow. Sometimes you have to accept things for what they are. Not for what they could or couldn't be. I'm just going along with how I feel right now, and I have a pretty good idea that I'll feel the same way tomorrow. That's all I can do...as far as I can go."

He leaned across the table, knocked over his fortunately empty wine glass, and kissed her. Perhaps—although he didn't realize it at the time—this was the moment, the genesis of Eliot's metamorphosis from overthinking to spontaneity. It was as if a curtain began to close in one part of his brain and open in another. The awakening and transformation of Eliot Hart had begun.

Chapter 15

Cripps hadn't slept more than three or four hours. His hand ached from the five stitches and tetanus shot given to him by the vet, who looked after van Tonder's cattle on his farm near Stellenbosch. He had been all for simply bandaging it— he'd had worse wounds in prison—but Terre'Blanche said that a baboon bite could become infected and that he needed a doctor. The only doctor available at the clinic was named Khan, who van Tonder mentioned might be an Indian or a Jew. Cripps flew into a rage, proclaiming he'd never have either one touching him, which is why he ended up with van Tonder's vet. Still, Cripps supposed the vet had done a decent job despite the fact that he'd used a stitching needle designed for sewing up wounds on cows and had insisted on taking his temperature with a rectal thermometer the size of a turkey baster, the only type he had at his surgery. He was pissed off and desperate to get back home. He blamed Eliot and Cori-Anne for his current woes and was now determined to really make them suffer. When he got to the dining room, van Tonder, Terre'Blanche, and Ronny were already eating.

Cripps wasn't hungry so he poured himself a cup of coffee and picked up what looked like a stale chunk of bread.

"We calls those 'rusks,'" said van Tonder. "It's what we eat in the poontang."

Cribbs bit into one and nearly shattered his remaining teeth.

"Ag, no man," laughed Terre'Blanche, "you must dunk it in your coffee first to soften it. Don't you people know anything?"

"I tell you what we do know," replied Cripps. "We know this is a fucking dangerous place with them damn baboons, doctors shoving thermometers up your ass, and food designed to shatter your choppers."

Van Tonder laughed loudly. "You're a funny little bloke, Reverend, but you're very uptight. Relax, man. Here, try some of this *boerewors*, our breakfast version. Nice and spicy."

But Cripps refused. All he wanted to do was get down to the business of death. He poured himself another cup of the worst coffee he'd ever tasted, including the slop they served in prison, and sat back with a scowl. "Just tell me the damn plan for today."

"Right, well, this might cheer you up. We're flying to our farm in Northern Limpopo, right near the town of Alldays. Very beautiful country. It borders on a private game reserve called Hunter's Folly, where your targets is staying. Now, on our farm we breed lions for your countrymen to come over here and shoot. Of course, we make it simple for them. We drug the lions and then dump them in a place where they are easy targets."

"How does that help me?" asked Cripps. "I ain't particularly interested in your pissdiddly operation. I need to know how Ronny and me will get close enough to kill these bastards."

"If you're finished being rude," replied van Tonder, totally understanding why Terre'Blanche had wanted nothing to do with this evil little imp, "then I will tell you. There are two options. Number one: You and Ronny here will play the part of hunters. We know for a fact that one of the tracks that the Hunter's Folly safari guides use runs very close to our border. We will have you in one of our blinds in a tall tree from where you can see into their property. The minute the open Land Rover containing your targets comes into view, you shoot them. A tragic hunting accident...happens all the time out here."

Cripps rolled his eyes. "That's a dumbass idea, I tell you."

"OK," van Tonder said with a distinct sneer. "Then option two is we hijack their vehicle, kill their guide and tracker, and make it look like poachers were involved. We bring the man and the woman back to the farm and feed them to the lions."

"That's a better idea. I want to see them suffer. And you think we can pull it off?"

"Ja, of course, man," van Tonder said with a dismissive wave of his hand. "You think we're a bunch of amateurs?"

"I'm sure you're not," replied Cripps, realizing he needed to placate the AWB Kommandant if he was to get what he needed from Cori-Anne. He hadn't told Ronny his plan for obvious reasons, but his idea was to record Cori-Anne on his phone confessing that she'd inserted the condom into Don Jorge's ass while he was doing naked yoga. He would then contact some of the other cartels and sell the taped confession to the highest bidder. It would destroy Don Jorge's business and then he, the Reverend Clayton Calvin Cripps, would draw up a new contract with a bigger, more successful cartel.

"Well, good, because we is not amateurs. We'll get them for you, and you can do whatever you like to them before we feed them to the lions." Van Tonder thought he sounded convincing enough, though he knew the little reverend was anything but naïve. The real plan was for him and Terre'Blanche to shoot Ronny and the Reverend before they could kill Cori-Anne and Eliot. They would then video Cori-Anne confessing and send it to Rodolfo for whatever he had in mind. It's what he'd spoken to Rodolfo about earlier that morning and for which Rodolfo would pay the AWB an extra $150k. He smiled at Cripps and Ronny. "Now, if you gentlemen is ready, I suggest we drive to the airport, and I will personally fly you to the farm. It's a small plane, so it's going to be a bit cramped."

The old Cessna 185 Skywagon was a single-engine plane that was very definitely not designed to hold two very large men, one average size man, and a small man with a nasty temper. At least not comfortably. It was a tight squeeze and because their combined bulk exceeded the weight limit, van Tonder had to fly very low and make frequent stops to refuel. By the time they landed on the small airstrip at Groot Witdoosbos, the AWB farm, even

Cripps was ready for a large brandy.

Things were very different for Cori-Anne and Eliot. They'd got up at six and gone to the gym, where Cori-Anne gave Eliot his second yoga lesson. She didn't push him too hard because she wanted him to enjoy it, and he did because he was motivated by flexibility and felt he would soon be able to do things he hadn't previously imagined. They had breakfast, and at seven-thirty Jannie picked them up for the drive to the nearby private airfield where a Cessna 421, a plane rather more comfortable than the one Cripps and Ronny had squeezed into, was waiting to take them to the Hunter's Folly private game reserve.

"It looks like you'll be gone for at least ten days," said Jannie as he helped them unload their duffle bags. "You will have a great time. Hunter's Folly is one of those game reserves that is booked up nearly a year in advance, and it's only been open for a few years. Then on to the Okavango Swamps. Man, that is my dream."

"Will you be our guide when we return?" Eliot asked.

"Ja, sure. If you can call up Jodie and tell her then that will be great."

Eliot still had five hundred-dollar bills in his wallet plus a wad of South African rand. He gave Jannie $200 and promised to call Jodie and tell her they'd like him on their return.

Much to their surprise there were two other American couples who were also flying to Hunter's Folly. They were Simon and Steven Storm and their wives Tracey and Lisa. The Storm brothers told Cori-Anne and Eliot that their father, Roger Storm, was one of the original owners of

Hunter's Folly with Gosego but had gifted his half to Gosego and Bontle on their wedding day.

"He must be a very generous person," said Cori-Anne as they settled into the plane.

"Generous to a fault," laughed Simon, "but certifiably nuts. If you only knew what he'd been up to over the past few years...."

"Sounds like an interesting guy," said Eliot. "Maybe you can tell us a few stories when we get to Hunter's Folly."

"He may be able to tell you himself," said Steven. "He and his wife visit Gosego and Bontle pretty often from their own game reserve in Namibia. We're actually going to see them next. We've never met her."

As the plane took off it became too noisy for proper conversation, and the passengers either dozed or stared out as the land unfolded like a coloring book beneath them. Cori-Anne put her head on Eliot's shoulder. He wasn't sure whether she was sleeping or thinking. He tilted his head till his cheek touched her hair. It was soft and smelled of lavender from the shampoo at the hotel. He tried to take the advice she'd given him the night before about accepting how things were at the moment and not projecting. It was so antithetical to his natural instinct, but for an instant he closed his eyes and allowed himself to simply feel. He wondered if falling in love really was like falling asleep— something that just happened, and you couldn't resist it, no matter how hard you tried.

He lifted his head as gently as he could so as not to disturb her and looked out the window. Below him he could see vast farms and scrubland. The soil looked almost red in color, hot and dry, and he wondered how anything survived. Then he, too, fell asleep and only woke when the pilot told them to make sure their seatbelts were fastened for their landing at Hunter's Folly.

Chapter 16

Hunter's Folly, that afternoon and evening

Everyone looked out their windows as the plane made a sweep over the airstrip. "We do that to make sure there aren't any animals on the runway," said the pilot.

There weren't, though Lisa said she thought she'd seem some elephants off to the right, and as they touched down a herd of startled impala grazing on the edge of the strip scattered into the bush. Two open-top dark green Land Rovers that had been fitted with two rows of elevated bench seats were waiting for the guests. Their guides, Andrew and Keabetswe, introduced themselves while the trackers and pilots unloaded the luggage onto the Land Rovers. Keabetswe asked Eliot and Cori-Anne to get into her vehicle, and they drove off first to avoid a dust trail for the other group.

"Is this your first safari?" Keabetswe asked.

"First time anywhere in Africa," replied Eliot, who couldn't hide his enthusiasm. He was, he decided, more excited to be there than anywhere else he'd been in his life. "I've been dreaming about this for...I can't even tell you how long."

Keabetswe laughed. "Then we are going to have to make this extra special. How about you, Cori-Anne?"

"To be honest I hadn't even thought about a safari until a few days ago when Eliot suggested it. But I guess I'm excited—also a little scared."

"You have nothing to worry about," replied their guide. "We haven't lost any guest to a lion for over a week." She noticed the horrified look on Cori-Anne's face. "I'm joking of course. No, you will be perfectly safe, I promise. Now I know my name will be hard for you to remember, so you can call me Kea."

"But Keabetswe is such a beautiful name," Cori-Anne replied.

"Thank you. It's a Tswana name that means *we have been given*."

"And you're from here?" Cori-Anne asked.

"Yes, not far from here. Before I became a guide, I was in the Black Mamba anti-poaching squad led by Bontle, who now together with her husband owns the reserve."

"We heard that," said Eliot, who had been busy looking around and seeing nothing but thick bush. "And the two guys on the other Landy are the sons of the previous owner, Roger Storm."

"Yes," Kea said with a big grin. "Roger Storm, indeed."

"You say that as if he was a problem," Eliot said.

"No, no, don't get me wrong. We all love Roger Storm, and he is Gosego's best friend. But where he is, there is trouble about to happen. Big, big trouble. I am sure tonight at dinner after you have had a few of Gosego's martinis, he will be regaling the group with stories about their father's exploits. But look, there are some giraffes."

They watched the giraffes, whose gangly lope made it look as if they were walking in slow motion. Then Kea started up the Land Rover and they drove slowly towards the camp. It was hot, and Kea explained that most of the animal world was taking a noon siesta and that they'd be doing the same thing pretty soon. About ten minutes later they came to a wooden sign that read "Hunter's Folly Camp" and turned onto another dirt track that led directly to the main lodge. Neither Eliot nor Cori-Anne knew what to expect as the photos on their itinerary were the size of postage stamps.

"It's not fenced at all," said Eliot, making a rather obvious observation.

"No, the animals are free to walk through here to the river and back, but again, you are perfectly safe. During the day you can walk by yourselves from the main structure to your tents, but at night one of the guards will fetch you and walk you back after dinner. Same thing in the early morning. But look, here is Bontle to welcome you and explain all the rules. I will see you at four o'clock to take you on your first game drive."

Bontle stood at the entrance to the lodge with a young woman holding a tray with wet towels and glasses of what turned out to be pineapple juice. Cori-Anne thought Bontle was absolutely stunning. She was tall, taller even than Cori-Anne, who was above average height, and her bearing was almost regal. Long braids hung down below her shoulders, and her face was open with not a hint of vulnerability. Both Bontle and the younger woman were dressed in what looked like the standard Hunter's Folly uniform: long khaki pants and a matching short-sleeve shirt with the logo on the top left pocket.

"Welcome to Hunter's Folly," she said with a warm smile and outstretched hand. "Please take one of the wet towels to wipe off the dust, grab a drink, and follow me inside so we can go over everything. Your bags will be taken to your tent...and Jodie called me to say you'd only require one."

"Yes, we sort of made a change in Cape Town, and uh...." Eliot said feeling almost embarrassed.

Cori-Anne rolled her eyes. "What he's trying to say is that we decided we'd rather be together."

Bontle laughed. "I understand and I'm very happy for you. And the good news is we were able to get another couple for the extra tent, so there's no charge. Now, come sit and I will take you through everything you need to know."

"It's incredible how well the lodge blends into the surroundings," Cori-Anne said as she and Eliot stood waiting for Bontle to go through the camp rules.

"Most of the camps in the good reserves use eco architecture," replied Bontle. "When Roger Storm built this place, he was very insistent that the reserve be resilient to climate change, which is why we don't use any exotic materials unless we absolutely don't have a choice. This place is designed not to fit into nature but rather to be a part of it. Those of us who grew up in rural communities without all the modern conveniences of the Western world understand how the things we are given in nature work for us. I was not part of planning the original design, but to me it just feels right."

It did to Eliot and Cori-Anne, too. The main structure

had a thatched roof held up by huge wooden pillars on a highly polished concrete base. The walls were made of tightly woven reeds, open at the top, with slow-moving ceiling fans doing their best to cool the guests. The dining room was to the right of the reception. It had six tables covered in bright yellow tablecloths and was built around an enormous sausage tree that emerged from the top of the thatch like a giant in a car sticking his head through the sunroof. It overlooked a watering hole, where a few bored warthogs were on their knees scarfing in the mud for something or other.

Bontle was used to the reactions of first-time visitors, and Cori-Anne and Eliot didn't disappoint. "This is incredible," said Eliot as he slumped onto one of the couches looking around the space that was as stark as it was elegant. "I feel like I'm back in the nineteenth century in some British aristocrat's African hunting lodge."

"That's the impression we try to give, but of course there is no hunting around here. In fact, it's called Hunter's Folly because it would be really stupid for any hunter to set foot on our property."

"Have any?" asked Cori-Anne.

"Well, technically I'm not allowed to say, but yes, at the beginning a few people from the hunting farms nearby came onto the land. Let's just say in their present condition they won't be making a return any time soon. All 'accidents' of course. Now let's go through these details...."

She had them read and sign waivers, took a swipe of Eliot's credit card, and then walked them to their tent that was at the far end of the camp close to the banks of the Limpopo River. Calling it a tent, though, was like calling a migraine a slight headache. It was tent-like in that the walls and ceiling were made of canvas, but that's where the resemblance ended. There was a wooden deck with a small plunge pool and chaises overlooking the lawn that disappeared into a thick patch of trees. The wood was dark and highly polished and ran under the canvas into the main bedroom where a large four-poster bed draped with a mosquito net dominated the room. There were two lounge chairs that looked so plump that Eliot thought if he sat down, he might never get up. Like the main lodge, the room was sparse when it came to knick-knacks, but everything from the rugs on the floor to the brass bedside lamps and wine cooler oozed quality. The bathroom behind a screen at the back of the bedroom contained a tub made from beaten copper and a large rain shower and was filled—apparently by the way they were wrapped—with eco-friendly toiletries.

"There's even an outdoor shower off the deck," said Bontle. "But we don't recommend using it at night. Now a few things about the animals." She walked them back out to the deck and pointed towards the thick riverine forest. "That's the Limpopo River. On the other side is the Northern Tuli Game Reserve in Botswana. While the river is a little too wide and deep for lions to cross, we do get some of their elephants, so you may see a few wandering around. You'll also see hippos in the early morning and evening. When you do see them, make sure you stay up on the deck because they won't walk up the stairs. We have three prides of lions in our own reserve, and they come into the camp on occasion, which is why we ask our visitors not to stray too far from their tents. It's basic common sense. If you have any issues or questions about anything, just call us on the phone in your room. Oh yes, one last thing: Always make sure your tent is closed and you don't leave any food out on the deck, or your room will be trashed by the baboons. Any questions?"

Cori-Anne and Eliot, who'd read more about animals and safaris than she had, felt numb. Marauding baboons and ravenous lions sounded slightly more dangerous than they'd envisioned, but at the same time, thrilling. At least to Eliot. Not so much Cori-Anne. Both shook their heads.

Bontle knew precisely what they were thinking, but she also knew that if first time visitors didn't feel a little apprehensive, they'd be more likely to do stupid things. She gave them a big smile.

"Now, you are here to have fun and leave all your worries back in the city. So, if you want to unpack now, do so. Or follow me back to the lodge and you can have some lunch and wine if you wish and meet our chef so you can discuss any food issues or desires. My husband, Gosego, should be back later this afternoon. I know he is keen to welcome you."

"That would be great," said Eliot, looking around in case a dangerous animal was lurking nearby.

"OK, and because you and the Storms are the only guests here today, we thought it might be nice if we all sat at dinner together tonight. However, if you wish to be alone, that is no problem."

"Gosh, no," said Cori-Anne. "We'd love to have dinner with everyone and hear some stories about their father's exploits."

Bontle rolled her eyes. "You will hear stories alright, but don't encourage my husband too much or you will run out of here screaming. Or maybe I will run out screaming because I've heard them so many times."

When they got back to the main lodge, they were greeted by Simon, Steven, Tracey, and Lisa, who were already eating, and shown to their own table. A few minutes later a tubby man in a starched white chef's uniform came up to the table and introduced himself.

"My name is Luis Santo da Silva," he said, wiping his hand on his apron before offering it to Eliot and Cori-Anne. "I am the chief chef, and I can make for you whatever you like to eat. However, my specialty is Portuguese food, especially from the ex-colony of Mozambique, where I was head chef at the famous Polana Hotel."

"Sounds terrific," Eliot said. "I've been to Lisbon a few times, and the food was great."

"Well, I've eaten at Brazilian restaurants in Miami," said Cori-Anne, "so I guess I like it too."

"Psshaw," went the chef, sounding like a disappointed horse. "Then you have not had Mozambican food. It's the same but different."

"Well, I'm open to it as long as it's not too spicy," Cori-Anne said, wondering exactly what "the same but different" implied.

"Don't worry, for you I make it a little less spicy. For him a little more. He looks like he needs a little fire in his balls." Before Eliot could react, the chef told them he'd make them a prawn and papaya salad for lunch with fresh bread and he'd choose the wine for them. "I am also a sommelier, so you don't need to think about the wine."

They strolled back to their tent after what turned out to be a delicious salad and what Eliot thought was an only fairly decent wine, though Cori-Anne knew he was still a little peeved at the chef's reference to his testicles.

"We've got an hour-and-a-half before we need to be back for tea and...what did Bontle call them?"

"Bikkies," said Cori-Anne. "But I have no idea what she means. How about a little yoga stretching and a plunge in the pool?"

"I don't have a swimsuit," Eliot said.

"Neither do I, but no one can see us, and I thought you rather fancied naked yoga?"

She was right about the latter but not the former. Halfway through child's pose, a troop of curious baboons came and sat on the deck to watch them. Eliot grabbed Cori-Anne and they jumped into the pool, where they thought they'd be safe. No amount of yelling or pleading on Eliot's part for the baboons to "get the hell out of here, please," worked, and the baboons sat calmly picking ticks off each other and glancing at the strange creatures in the pool.

"I honestly don't like the way that big bastard is looking at you," Eliot said, splashing water at the baboon. "He's positively leering."

Cori-Anne clicked her tongue. "You're very sensitive at the moment. First the chef, and now you're jealous of a monkey."

"Technically, you're absolutely correct," Eliot said.

"Seriously? You're jealous of a baboon?"

"No, you're correct that baboons are monkeys. Most people think they're apes. And I'm not jealous at all. If anything I'm flattered."

"Flattered?"

"Yes, to be with someone that even a baboon thinks is beautiful."

"I'm sure you meant that in a good way, Eliot. But it didn't really come across that way."

They watched the baboons for fifteen minutes until the troop gave up on them and shuffled off to find something more interesting to do to while away the afternoon.

"Bikkies" turned out to be biscuits as they discovered when they got to the main lodge just after three-thirty and were poured a large cup of tea and offered some homemade bikkies by a friendly waiter. The other party was already there laughing and chatting with a huge man in the Hunter's Folly uniform. When he saw Eliot and Cori-Anne, he came over and introduced himself.

"I'm Gosego," he said, "the other and less-worthy half of Bontle. You must be Cori-Anne and Eliot. Welcome to what we believe is paradise, and hopefully you will too. Now here's what I've arranged with Kea for this afternoon." He took out his iPhone and opened a map of the reserve. "You can see we border the Limpopo River all the way along here. There are quite a lot of elephants in the area and a big herd of buffalo, so I'm sure that will be a good drive for you to get a feel for the bush."

"Are there any lions in that area?"

"Maybe, but I don't think so. We heard a pride to the west a little while ago."

"That means they're close, surely?" Cori-Anne asked, looking around nervously.

"No, they're quite far," answered Gosego. "The roar of a lion can be heard five miles away. There's lots of zebra and wildebeest there, too. So, I am pretty sure you will get to see them on your morning drive. Now, here she is."

They looked around to see Kea approaching them. "Are you ready?" she asked. "Then let's go."

Both Land Rovers left the lodge at about the same time going in opposite directions. "It's a big reserve," Kea said, "and because we only have ten visitors maximum at any time, we don't crowd the animals when we see them. They'll do the riverine forest tomorrow morning when we go to look for lions. Now let me ask you how much you want to know about insects and trees and birds. Because some people have no interest in them, which is a pity because they are fascinating."

Before Eliot could open his mouth to respond, Cori-Anne jumped in. She pointed at Eliot. "Be careful of what you ask, or you'll never stop talking. He will want to know everything you do provided he doesn't know it all already."

Kea laughed. "Good, well then, I'll make sure I tell Eliot what he wants to know without boring you, Cori-Anne. My suggestion is that we get the big picture today and then we can work our way down the food chain."

And that's precisely what they did. Fifteen minutes into the drive, they came across the buffalo making their way down to the river. Kea reckoned there had to be at least five hundred in the herd. They watched for a while and then drove deeper into the forest that ran along the banks of the Limpopo. The tracker, who was sitting in a seat attached to the left-front fender, suddenly held up his hand, and Kea stopped the Land Rover.

"Shh," she said, "sit quietly and listen."

Neither Eliot nor Cori-Anne could hear a thing until

suddenly what had looked like a shadow began to move and a large elephant appeared.

"It's the matriarch...be very quiet and the rest of the herd will follow," whispered Kea. Sure enough, the large female was followed by two more elephants, and much to Eliot and Cori-Anne's delight, both were trailed by babies. More and more elephants came out of the bush heading for the river, and Eliot counted at least thirty with more babies and juveniles. One or two looked at the Land Rover, and one of the juveniles—a male, Kea said— flapped his ears and did a mock charge at their vehicle, causing the intrepid passengers to squeak in alarm.

"What happens if one really does charge?" asked Eliot. "Do you have a gun at least?"

"No, we don't believe in carrying rifles except when we track poachers or have to put down some animal that has been caught in a snare. We are trained to know when an elephant is about to do a real charge, and I would have got us out of here in that event."

They saw more elephants a little further on and some beautiful antelopes with what looked like white circles painted on their rears that Kea told them were waterbuck. She pointed out the yellow-barked fever trees and the stunning red and aqua carmine bee-eaters and a large water monitor lizard that Eliot reckoned must have been at least four feet long. On the way back to the camp they stopped for cocktails and snacks to watch the sun set over the bushveld, and both Eliot and Cori-Anne thought—though they didn't share it with each at the time—that they were the happiest they'd been, possibly in their entire lives.

That feeling didn't last long. Fifteen minutes after they got back to camp and were in their tent dressing for dinner, Eliot's phone rang. It was a FaceTime call from Thomas Mortimer Jones, and he looked and sounded anything but calm.

"Well," he said, trying not to look at Cori-Anne who was still in her underwear, "it's not great news."

"Then it's good news?" asked Eliot.

"No, it's not. I just said it isn't great news."

"Well, then it could be good news...I mean if something's not great, it can still be good."

"Jesus, Eliot, I'm trying to say it's fucking awful news."

"What is it?" replied Cori-Anne as she finished dressing.

"First, we believe the two hitmen sent by the cartel flew to South Africa at about the same time you did. They're members of a white supremacist organization that the cartel uses in the US for distribution and enforcement. I'm going to forward photos so you can be on the lookout. The other thing we found out is that Don Jorge Morales and five of his men flew out of Mexico last night. We have no idea where they're going, but I have a bad feeling they're flying to South Africa as well. Don't ask me why."

"Why would Don Jorge come here?" Eliot asked.

"Christ, Eliot. I said don't fucking ask me. All I know is that there's definitely something weird going on because the body of his financial guy, Rodolfo Sanchez, was found by Sinaloa police yesterday morning. They found his head soon afterwards nailed to the door of his mother's house. I've contacted Interpol, who tell me they'll inform the South African authorities, who'll keep their eyes open.

171

But until they commit a crime on South African soil, there isn't much they'll be able to do. My gut feel is that you'll be safe where you are, and I'll let you know as soon as I hear anything else."

Thomas hung up after reminding Eliot to look out for the mugshots of the two white supremacists, which arrived on his iPhone just as the guard came to escort them up to the main lodge for dinner.

"Oh, my God," Eliot said, holding the phone up to Cori-Anne. "We've seen them. You remember at the airport, and then I saw them at the lighthouse yesterday...they must be on to us!"

"What are we going to do, Eliot?" She sounded as scared as Eliot felt.

"I don't know. I mean, there's no way they can get to us here."

"Unless they're also guests. Bontle said they only take ten guests at a time. Together with the Storms, we're only six. We have to ask Bontle who the other guests are."

"Ok," Eliot said, giving her a reassuring hug. "Let's do that, and let's try to stay calm and not panic."

"I'm not panicking."

"I was actually saying that to myself."

Cori-Anne and Eliot were the first to arrive at the main lodge, and they found Gosego behind a section of the long bar under a neon sign that read "Storm in a Martini Glass."

"My friends," he said, "welcome to the best martini bar in Africa and possibly the world. Named for my best friend, Roger Storm, who enjoys a martini more than anyone I know. Now, what will you have—and please don't ask me to shake. Only stirring is permitted."

Cori-Anne and Eliot watched in fascination as Gosego concocted their martinis the way a Michelin chef makes a gateau St Honoré. Not that either had sampled the classic French torte, but if they had, the complexity and precision required to concoct that seemingly simple desert would have left them equally impressed.

"By the way, Gosego," Eliot said after complementing him on his mixological skills, "the other guests who are arriving soon—do you know them?"

"One couple I know. They're taking the tent you're not using. The others are first-time visitors. Why do you ask?"

"Because," Cori-Anne replied, before Eliot could remind her that they weren't going to panic, "there are two white supremacist killers after us. Plus, a Mexican drug lord."

Chapter 17

Somewhere over Africa and in Johannesburg, that same evening

Technically, the Gulfstream G650 could have made it from Mexico City to Johannesburg, South Africa without refueling, but the captain persuaded Don Jorge that it wasn't worth taking a chance. So they stopped in Dakar to refuel and allow the four men accompanying Don Jorge el Clavo Morales—all of whom were in a desperate state—to use the bathroom. Don Jorge did not want them using his private toilet on the plane.

Now as the plane, still at 41,000 feet, crossed from Botswana into South African airspace, Don Jorge looked out the window at the land below. It had a purple glow tinged with gold from the sun as it set somewhere in the west. Don Jorge thought it was almost as beautiful—though not quite—as the sunset in Sinaloa, and he wondered why he'd never taken the opportunity to visit the continent before. He'd heard Pablo Escobar telling his uncles about the hippos and zebras and giraffes he'd brought over from Africa to his estate east of Medellin.

Personally, he believed the Columbian was soft because he actually liked to look at them, not kill them.

Don Jorge had no time for any living creature, man or beast, that could not provide some form of entertainment or monetary return, which is why on the advice of his Chinese associate, he'd gotten into the animal trafficking business. When Rodolfo—whom Don Jorge had put in charge—returned from his negotiations with van Tonder, he'd told the don how much fun it was to shoot the "canned" lions and other animals on the farms owned by the AWB. Well, he'd certainly give it a try while he was there.

He was desperate to give anything a try. Ever since Cori-Anne had shoved the heroin up his ass, he'd lost interest in most things. Even torturing Rodolfo after he'd overheard him discussing with van Tonder how to get the video confession from Cori-Anne hadn't done much for his mood. *What the hell is wrong with the world today?* he wondered. First that idiot Danny Ramirez totally ignores his very clear instructions to leave the naked yoga studio alone and focus on his own business. Then that filthy bitch Cori-Anne performs an act so foul and unforgivable on his person for no earthly reason. This treachery, as horrific as it may have been, was followed by the incomprehensible act of his trusted money manager, Rodolfo, telling the very thing he was supposed to keep secret to those two gringo racists. And finally, Rodolfo himself performing the ultimate act of betrayal by demanding that the AWB extract the videoed confession from Cori-Anne to distribute it to other cartels to eternally shame him.

Well, Don Jorge had taken care of Danny Ramirez and he'd taken care of Rodolfo. All that was left was for him to take care of Cori-Anne after van Tonder had eliminated the gringo assassins. So much of it was unnecessary. Danny could still be doing his thing in Miami instead of nearly pulling the front door to his mother's house off its hinges when they nailed him to it. Rodolfo's execution had very nearly turned into a disaster. His head was so large that the don's enforcer couldn't find a long enough nail at the local hardware store. In the end he'd resorted to a kebab skewer, which rather defeated the purpose of Don Jorge's moniker "el Clavo." As for Cori-Anne, well, he had something special in mind for her.

After they landed in Johannesburg and cleared passport control and customs, Don Jorge and his men were driven to the Michelangelo Hotel in Sandton City, one of Johannesburg's northern suburbs, where they showered and changed. Then they headed to The Butcher Shop and Grill in the Nelson Mandela Mall adjacent to the hotel to meet Nguyen van Duc, the Vietnamese agent for one of the largest animal trafficking organizations in Asia. Quite frankly, if the lion bones and pangolin scales weren't so profitable, the don would never have gotten involved. It was a complicated arrangement. Technically the cartel owned the AWB farms that bred the lions and arranged for big-game hunters from America and Europe to shoot them and extract the bones to ship to Vietnam, Laos, and China. Van Tonder and his cohorts ran the farms and were paid 50 percent of the profits, which was far higher than any other group the cartel did business with and which Don Jorge would take care of when he met van Tonder face-to-face. The Vietnamese distributors were, if anything, even greedier and less trustworthy than the South Africans.

Right now, though, he needed Nguyen van Duc to smuggle something else out of South Africa to one of his establishments in Asia. Oh yes, Cori-Anne van Cleave would regret her actions for the rest of her miserable life. And miserable, as far as Don Jorge was concerned, wasn't a word that even came close to how awful her life would be.

Don Jorge sat at a table by himself and his four bodyguards at a table to his right and slightly in front of him. The don ordered a glass of red wine and looked around the restaurant. Most of the patrons were men chowing down on steaks, drinking wine, and speaking loudly. He had no idea how many indigenous languages were spoken in South Africa, but his ear was sensitive enough to pick up different sounds, and he was fascinated by the rhythm of the words. Many were conversing in English and mainly about business. They were all dressed in casual clothes—some drab khaki, some colorful native. The don felt out of place and conspicuous in his cream silk suit.

"Mr. Morales?"

The don looked up to see a small man with hair as white as his. The man stuck out his hand.

"I am Nguyen van Duc. But if you like you can call me just Duc."

"Ah," replied the don, shaking Duc's hand, "we finally meet. And of course, you may call me Jorge."

"Jorge, Jorge," repeated Duc. "That's a funny name. Sounds like you are calling a prostitute—whore hey!"

Under normal circumstances Don Jorge would have

punched the little Vietnamese man for his bad attempt at a joke, or at least called over one of his bodyguards to do it for him. But at this moment he needed the Vietnamese trafficker's cooperation, and so he decided to retaliate with a joke of his own.

"Very amusing. And your name sounds like you should stick your head under the table when I say it. Duc, Duc!"

"I don't understand sticking head under the table unless you are looking for blow job. Better if you say like quack, quack. Like a duck. Now that is funny."

"Yes, it is," said Don Jorge, hoping he could get this whole business over with as quickly as possible. "Let's order and then get down to business." He signaled a passing waiter, who was carrying a large tray of steaks and seafood. He pointed to a T-bone, and Duc ordered the Mozambican prawns.

While they were waiting for their food, they made small talk about people they'd killed and the incredible size of the animal trafficking business. Don Jorge was amazed to find out that the annual revenue of animal trafficking was only slightly smaller than drugs and human trafficking.

"Well," said Don Jorge, taking a bite of his steak and chewing it slowly, "it's human trafficking that I want to speak to you about. I need you to get a woman out of here."

Duc looked around and then leaned forward. "We must be careful; there are many ears around here. This place and the hotel you are staying at are where some of the biggest deals in these sorts of trades are discussed with people from many countries. I look over at that table and I see some Nigerians who are my competitors in smuggling abalone out of this country. Those Somalis at the back table are in the arms trade, and those Chinese are also in the bone and pangolin business."

"I am amazed that there is anything left to smuggle out of here," said the don. "Doesn't seem like a long-term proposition." He made a mental note to check with Rodolfo until he remembered that Rodolfo was dead. He'd have to replace him soon or he'd be saddled with the kind of paper work he had no interest in.

"Yes, that's why we have to be careful and move quickly," replied Duc, failing to see the irony in the don's response. "But you want me to get some woman out the country. Exporting woman is not a big business here. We bring women in, not out."

"I understand, but I need you to take a certain woman out of here. And I need you to take her somewhere where her life will be hell. Where she will regret what she did to me every day until she dies."

"And what, may I ask, did she do to you?"

"That," said the don, going slightly red in the face, "is irrelevant. I will pay you however much you want if you can promise me that she will suffer."

"OK, OK. You have a picture of her?"

"Yes," replied the don, taking out his iPhone. His fat fingers struggled for a moment to hit the photo icon on the phone, but he got it eventually and showed Duc a picture of Cori-Anne.

Duc whistled. "She is magnificent! I will take her with pleasure. She will sell to a brothel in Laos like this." He clicked his fingers.

"That's not good enough," replied the don. "I told you I want her to suffer."

"I haven't yet told you what this brothel is famous for...."

"Then tell me," said Don Jorge, licking his lips.

After Duc described in detail what went on in the House of Many Screams Brothel in Laos' Golden Triangle, even Don Jorge had to admit that his mind—deranged as it was—couldn't have imagined anything worse. With a little negotiation, they agreed on a price that while high didn't seem overly excessive for what would need to be done. Don Jorge and Nguyen van Duc shook hands, and the don together with his men retreated to the hotel, where they had a nightcap and called up van Tonder.

When van Tonder finally put down his phone after listening to Don Jorge's instructions, he turned to Terre'Blanche, who was sitting on the porch of the farmhouse drinking brandy.

"Man," he said in Afrikaans, confident that Cripps and Ronny, who'd finally gone to bed, wouldn't be able to understand them, "these fucking people are confusing as hell. First, they want us to help those two lunatics kill the yoga instructor and her boyfriend. Then they want us to kill the lunatics after they kill the yoga instructor and her boyfriend. Then they want us to kill the boyfriend and the lunatics, get the yoga instructor to confess something about a condom filled with heroin, then kill her. Now we must kill the lunatics and the boyfriend but keep the yoga instructor alive for that little fucker from Vietnam to take to some brothel in Laos. And, of course, they're all coming here tomorrow to make sure we do what they say."

Terre'Blanche said nothing for a while. He thought about it for a moment and realized he had no rejoinder that would add any semblance of logic. At that moment some of the lions howled in hunger, and he turned to van Tonder. "At least those bleddy lions will have something to eat tomorrow. That's if they can even stomach those horrible bastards. Quite frankly, I wouldn't blame them if they decided to rather die of starvation."

Chapter 18

Hunter's Folly that night

If Eliot was expecting Gosego to be surprised or put-out, possibly taken aback or highly disturbed, maybe even angered at Cori-Anne's revelation of their situation, then he was very much mistaken in his assumption.

"Hmm," said Gosego as he poured each of them a large martini from the stirring jug. "Well, this is not the sort of situation I am accustomed to hear from my guests."

"I'm so sorry," Cori-Anne said, "we shouldn't have told you. It's not your problem. I just blurted it out."

"Please," Gosego said, "these are things that you are experiencing in the real world but not what you should be worrying about while you are here. Here you should be at peace, and it is Bontle's and my job to make sure you are safe. It is also, by the way, not something I am totally unfamiliar with."

"In what way?" asked Eliot.

"My friend Roger Storm, whom I believe you have heard of from his sons, had a very similar experience two years ago when some Laotian hitmen were sent to kidnap him from here.[1] So, now, tell me all about it before the others come, and let's discuss how to keep you safe."

As succinctly and accurately as he could, Eliot explained their situation, leaving out the part about the naked yoga and the heroin. Much to the amusement of Gosego, Cori-Anne filled in those details, and he clapped his enormous hands in apparent glee.

"Hau! You are a remarkable woman." He clinked his glass with hers. But then his expression took a more serious turn. "I suppose I can understand why this Jorge person would be upset, but he is going to extremes to extract his revenge, no?"

"Sending hitmen after us is probably as extreme as you can get," agreed Eliot.

Gosego nodded. "Well, vigilance is what we must practice from this moment on while you are here. I will talk to Bontle after dinner, and I'm sure she will alert her squad to be on the lookout for suspicious people. Let's keep this from the Storm boys and their wives. No need to make them feel uncomfortable."

"Of course," said Eliot.

"Now," continued Gosego. "Two of the guests we have coming—the ones I don't know—are from Germany, both older and retired. The other two are friends of ours from India. He is a top policeman in Delhi, and she is a highly trained army officer and security expert. So, there is no danger from them. In fact, Rohini and her husband Sabhajit Singh may be able to help."

At that moment they were interrupted by the Storm

---

[1] *See Killing Bobby Fatt and other nasty bastards*

party, who were all keen as mustard to try out a martini at the bar named after their father. They were a friendly bunch, and their banter gave Eliot and Cori-Anne a brief respite.

Dinner was a loud and lively affair with excellent wine and a main course of giant prawns cooked Mozambican-style with spicy peri-peri sauce. They drank wine and heard the story of Gosego and Roger Storm's successful attempt to disrupt a Russian oligarch's dastardly plan to genetically modify animals to make them more attractive to trophy hunters.[2] After dinner, Gosego walked Eliot and Cori-Anne back to their tent. He had a powerful flashlight which he used to survey the area surrounding their tent and then inside the tent itself. When he was satisfied that nothing was amiss, he rejoined Cori-Anne and Eliot, who stood huddled on the porch near the plunge pool. He shone the light towards what Eliot thought was a bush but turned out to be a hippo.

"There," said Gosego. "See, I made sure you had someone guarding your tent tonight. No one is going to disturb you with that fat bastard grazing outside. Now, get some sleep because we will wake you early, early. I will talk to Bontle tonight to see if she has any thoughts."

Bontle, as it turned out when Gosego told her the situation, had some very specific thoughts. "I knew it," she said. "I knew the minute that Roger's sons booked their trip that the heavens were going to unleash chaos. Storm by name and Storm by nature."

"But Cori-Anne and Eliot have nothing to do with Roger Storm."

---

[2] See *Killing Valerian Zolotov: and other reprehensible rotters.*

"Maybe not, but the mere presence of his offspring is enough to make the gods angry."

"I think you're being a little dramatic, my love."

"Hmmph," she replied as she undressed. "We'll see about that...but actually I do have one piece of information that may be worth investigating. When Melusi was driving the north boundary track that borders on Groot Witdoosbos, he said he saw some of the boers building what looked like a hunting platform in a Jackalberry tree."

"Not that unusual," replied Gosego, looking at his wife's naked body. "Those bastards will do anything to make the hunting easier for the psychopaths who shoot their lions."

"Maybe you are right, but my gut tells me not. No, something is up...and obviously so are you. You'd better come to bed."

At the time Bontle and Gosego were finished making love and sleeping peacefully, Eliot was lying in bed staring up at the ceiling fan as it turned slowly, pushing down a cooling stream of air that made the mosquito netting dance like a ghost. Cori-Anne was nestled into his side, and he put his hand on her hip more for comfort than anything else. He was desperately trying to analyze the situation and wondering what he could possibly do to change it.

For the first time in his life, he felt totally and utterly stumped. Every scenario he imagined had the same negative outcome. If the cartel and its killers were after them and had followed them to South Africa, then there was no doubt in his mind that they would find him and

Cori-Anne. And if everything he'd seen in shows like *Narcos* and read in books by his favorite author, Don Winslow, were even somewhat true, they wouldn't give up until they'd succeeded, no matter what precautions he and Cori-Anne took. A great sadness came over him, but it didn't last long. Because with the sadness came an even greater determination. He would save Cori-Anne no matter what. He closed his eyes and finally fell into a deep sleep.

While all of this was going on, fate—if indeed there is such a thing as fate, and if the universe is deterministic, and if all these mysterious forces were responsible for this chain of unfortunate incidents in Eliot and Cori-Anne's lives—had also put them in the right place to right their seemingly forlorn situation. For at that moment a strange man was making his way through the bush toward Hunter's Folly, a man whose past and present preoccupation with saving wildlife did not bode well for the current occupants of Groot Witdoosbos Farm and the visitors who were arriving the next day.

Chapter 19

Limpopo Province, the next day

It was still dark when an old man armed with a flashlight and a large grin came to escort Cori-Anne and Eliot up to the main lodge for more bikkies and tea; the real breakfast would be served on their return before their early-morning drive. The promise of a cloudless sky was evident as dawn wriggled reluctantly from behind the lodge, and much to Eliot's delight, any hippos that may have been grazing in the vicinity had moved further afield or gone back into the river.

He checked his messages just before they joined the others. There was one from Thomas telling them to hang in and wait for further news. As they were sipping their tea, Bontle came up and took them aside.

Her expression was kind but serious. "Gosego told me the situation, and I want you to know that we're going to do everything we can to make sure you stay safe. I radioed one of our anti-poaching patrols to keep their eyes open for anything that looks out of place. If there is, they'll know and warn us. We're going to install a camera to monitor your tent to make sure no one sneaks up from the river, and I'm a going to give Kea a rifle to carry in your Land Rover. Just as a precaution, you understand."

Cori-Anne took Bontle's hand and gave it a squeeze. "Thank you. I'm so sorry to put you to this trouble. I just wish—"

Bontle returned the squeeze and smiled. "Do not worry. We cannot always control the things that happen in our lives, and when things go wrong it's all our duties to help. Protection is not our expertise, but it's also not something we are unfamiliar with as I'm sure you heard last night when my husband was talking about his adventures with Roger Storm. This is probably the safest place you can be at this moment. Now it seems as if Kea is ready to roll. I don't know if you heard lions last night, but we believe they are about not too far from here, so hopefully you will find them. Now go and have fun. We will see you at breakfast."

A slightly less-reassuring conversation was taking place on the back porch of the farmhouse at Groot Witdoosbos Farm.

"Kommandant," said van Tonder quietly, dipping a rusk into his coffee mug, "I have been thinking."

"What is it, *boet?*" replied van Tonder, using the Afrikaans word for brother.

"You know you said that after those two bleddy buggers kill the other Americans, we have to kill them?"

"No, I said we have to kill the man, save the woman, and then kill the buggers, or perhaps it's the other way round? All I know is that we have to kill them and have the girl here before the Mexicans and that Vietnamese bastard get here tonight."

"You see, Kommandant, this is tricky and messy and easy to fuck up. That's why I have a proposal."

"Tell me," replied van Tonder, moving closer and giving Terre'Blanche a whiff of his halitosis. "But not too loud. I know they're still sleeping, but that little swine has a nasty habit of creeping up on you."

"Ja, well," replied Terre'Blanche, "we're speaking Afrikaans. They won't understand."

"Pshaw," said van Tonder, or something that sounded similar. "I wouldn't be too sure of that. Cripps speaks in tongues and one of them could be Afrikaans."

Terre'Blanche looked at his boss and shook his head, wondering how a complete moron could be in charge of such a sacred institution.

"No matter. My proposal is very simple and clean, and it removes several steps. We kill Cripps and Rondo and feed them to the lions. Then we capture the two Americans, kill the man, and keep the woman for the Mexican and Vietnamese blokes when they get here this evening. It will save us a lot of time, hassle, and having to talk to those two ever again."

"Ja, no. It's a good idea," replied van Tonder, scratching his beard. "How do you suggest we do it?"

"We take them to see the lions, I shoot the big one in the head, you shoot the small one, and we toss their bodies into the enclosure. Easy, peasy, lemon squeasy."

"What the hell do lemons have to do with this?"

"It's an American expression, Kommandant. It means it will be easy."

"Never heard it before. Sounds stupid, and in my experience, things are never easy or peasy or whatever the hell you said. Especially with that little *bliksem* Cripps. He doesn't let anything get by him." He thought for a moment. "Normally I would say we should follow our orders. But in this case, there is no one giving orders. So, I will give them. We'll have to tell Oom Ebert and Pakkies what we're going to do and make sure the laborers go home for the day. Why don't you go and do that while I wait for Cripps and Rondo to get their arses out of bed? Then I'll text you and we'll meet at the lion enclosure. Make sure you have your nine mil with you. If you're going to shoot the big guy, you're going to need more than one bullet, I think. Two in the chest, one in the head."

While Terre'Blanche went off to speak to Oom Ebert and his sidekick "Pakkies" Potgieter, the two AWB members who managed the farm, van Tonder went into the kitchen to make more coffee and load his Ruger LCR, one of the most compact but nevertheless deadly revolvers. It was small enough to fit in the pocket of his safari jacket, and he practiced drawing it out a few times before he heard the slap-slap-slap of Round Ronny Rundo's giant feet approaching the kitchen in search of food. He was joined by Cripps just moments after.

"What's the damn plan?" asked Cripps without even a cheery good morning. He'd had another awful night, and all he wanted to do was get the hell back to Texas.

"Well, good morning to you, too, Reverend," van Tonder said, handing him a cup of coffee and a rusk. "The plan, ah, yes the plan...."

"Yes, the fuckdangled-goshnageled plan."

"My, my, but you have a unique turn of phrase, Reverend. Anyway. The plan is easy, peasy, lemon squeezy." He looked at Cripps for even a soupçon of acknowledgement at his grasp of the American vernacular but got none. "Your Mexican friends and their Vietnamese colleague will arrive this evening, and so we must accomplish everything before they get here."

"Well fuck me like a fifty-pound sheep," interrupted Cripps, thinking of something he'd once attempted. "Why the hell are they coming here?"

"Look, I don't understand any of you peoples. All I know is what he told me."

"Something stinks," said Cripps, "and it's not just your breath."

Van Tonder looked at the angry little man and made a decision that he'd shoot him in the stomach and let him suffer a bit before tossing him to the lions. How dare he comment on his breath when he himself stunk like a dead aardvark?

"If you're done with the insults, then here's what happens. We know that the targets will be traveling on the road alongside our border fence today. Terre'Blanche has sent the two guys you met last night, Pakkies and Oom Ebert, to set up a little trap. It's a small, anti-personnel mine that will blow out the Land Rover's front tires. We will be watching from the blind in the tree, and as soon as we see the explosion, we will take out the guide and the tracker with two coordinated rifle shots, grab the woman, cut the man's throat, and bring her back here for interrogation. But we must move. So, if you're ready I will text Terre'Blanche to let him know that you agree to the plan. In the meantime, I will give you a quick treat and show you the lions."

"Fine," said Cripps. "But I don't understand why we need to go to the lion enclosure first. I don't need to see them fuckers."

"Ah, please, Reverend Cripps," said Ronny. "I ain't never seen a lion, please...."

"Ja, come on, man," urged van Tonder. "We have time. Put your shoes on and follow me. It's really fun. And then maybe this afternoon when everything's done, you can even shoot one."

Ronny gave a delighted squeak and rubbed his hands together, but Cripps was less enthusiastic. Why had Terre'Blanche said they needed to move quickly yet was now saying they had time? Something was up, and he was suspicious as all hell. No one who liked Cripps—and there must have been someone in his fifty-four years who'd had a somewhat positive feeling towards him—had treated him to anything that could be considered fun. So the idea that someone who didn't like him would offer to do so raised his hackles. He felt in his pocket for the razor he'd retrieved after the baboon dropped it. He pulled it out when van Tonder turned his back and concealed it in his hand so that its length ran up his wrist. Well, he'd go along to see the lions, but at the first sign of anything untoward, he'd slit van Tonder's gizzard like a Sunday chicken.

The lion enclosures on Groot Witdoosbos Farm were no different to those on any of the farms that offered canned lions hunts. Hungry, emaciated, and mangy lions lay in what little shade there was waiting for some trophy hunter to come along and shoot them. Death for most would be a welcome release from the abysmal life they were forced to live so that some emotionally unstable individual could claim to have "bagged" one. But Cripps was immune to suffering, and all he saw was a distraction.

Round Ronny, on the other hand, was like a child going to the zoo for the first time. He put his face up to the wire mesh and made a sound that reminded Terre'Blanche of a goat in heat. Cripps stood to the right of van Tonder. He could see the bulge in the Kommandant's pocket, and he knew it was a gun. Just then van Tonder walked up and gave Terre'Blanche a nod. It was subtle and would have been indiscernible to anyone other than Cripps. Suddenly van Tonder's hand went into his pocket and closed over the grip of his Ruger. At the same time, Terre'Blanche's hand reached round behind his back.

That's when the reverend went into action.

As the few prison inmates who'd survived one of Cripps's shank attacks could testify, when the reverend struck, there was no escape. Before van Tonder's hand clamped over the Ruger, the straight-edge razor severed his femoral artery, causing him to scream and fall to the ground. As van Tonder toppled over, Terre'Blanche pulled his 9mm and fired at Ronny. He made one fatal mistake because for no more than half a second, his eyes flashed towards the fallen van Tonder and, distracted by the scream, he sent the bullet through Ronny's right cheek, where it flipped about destroying his sinuses before it exited out his left eye.

A normal person shot in such a positively horrific

fashion may have fallen to their knees clutching their wound, but not Ronny. He clasped Terre'Blanche's head between his massive hands and began to squeeze while making the sound of a steam train going uphill. Terre'Blanche gasped and tried to raise his weapon, but the reverend cut his hand before he could aim it at Ronny, and the gun fell to the ground along with four of Terre'Blanche's fingers. Terre'Blanche flailed for a second, and then his head vanished between Ronny's hands, and what looked like lava from a failed school-science-project volcano splattered down his shirt. There was a crack like a walnut being crushed with a nutcracker, and Terre'Blanche went limp.

"Don't die on me, boy," said Cripps, grabbing hold of Ronny's arm before he wandered off into a pole. Ronny grunted and then sat down on the ground, his back pressed against the wire enclosure. He looked at Cripps through his remaining eye and gurgled something, which Cripps took to be a positive response. "Good, boy. You can't die yet; we got us work to do. Now stuff this here handkerchief into your eye socket, and let's toss these bodies to the beasts."

Ronny, still gurgling, stood up and grabbed Terre'Blanche by his bloody shirt and began to drag him to the enclosure gate. Cripps opened it and watched in fascination as three lions that had been eyeing them curiously slowly stood up and sauntered over. They sniffed Ronny, who didn't even flinch, and then began to chow down on Terre'Blanche's head, or what was left of it. Ronny walked out and proceeded to drag van Tonder, who much to Cripps' surprise was still alive, toward the lions.

"Don't do this to me," he whined in a pathetic whisper. "I'm begging of you, please."

Cripps aimed a kick at the razor slash on van Tonder's thigh as Ronny pulled him into the enclosure, where two more lions walked up. "Don't do this to me?" mocked Cripps. "God's pizzle makes a barbecue sizzle, you damned nincompoop. Them lions got to eat, and far better you than us. Now, Ronny boy, I believe he still has his revolver in his side pocket. Pull it out and bring it back here."

Cripps watched Ronny carefully as they made their way to the farmhouse. Apart from occasionally wandering in circles and gurgling incoherently (which Cripps preferred to his normal senseless babble), Ronny seemed as strong as ever. Cripps didn't want Ronny to die, or at least not just yet. There was too much to do, and he needed someone for the heavy lifting. As they walked into the house, they heard a radio crackling from a room to the side of the kitchen. Cripps couldn't understand the Afrikaans, but he recognized the voice of Oom Ebert. He clicked on the mic.

"This is the Reverend Cripps. There's been a terrible accident. You and that other fella need to return to the farmhouse immediately."

"What's wrong?" asked Oom Ebert in his broken English. "And you have to say 'over' when you is finished talking...over."

Cripps slammed the mic on the wooden table in frustration. "I said get the fuck back over here."

"There's no need to call Pakkies a 'fuck-back' just 'cause he has a bit of a stoop. Over."

Cripps started to go redder than he normally was. "You and that fella, Pakkies, need to get back to the farmhouse, you dim-witted, dog-balled bastard. Over!"

In the tree-blind overlooking the boundary fence to Hunter's Folly, Oom Ebert turned to Pakkies, who was fiddling with the scope on his rifle. "Good Lord," he said in Afrikaans, "that bloody Yankee has a mouth on him worse than my old grandfather when he'd drunk too much brandy. He called you a fuck-back."

"Cheeky bastard to make fun of someone's affliction."

"Ja, but I think there's been some sort of accident. We need to get back."

"What about the IED?" asked Pakkies.

"Ag, leave the damn thing. Who cares if one of the Hunter's Folly vehicles blows up? Not our problem."

Fifteen minutes later when Oom Ebert and Pakkies walked into the kitchen at Groot Witdoosbos Farm, Cripps shot both of them in the head, and Ronny, who seemed to have got a second wind, carried them to the lion enclosure. The starving lions, still feasting on Terre'Blanche and van Tonder, thought Christmas had come early.

"Now," said Cripps to Ronny when he was back in the kitchen, "this here map shows that the main lodge of Hunter's Folly is no more than a few miles from here. I say we rest up some 'til later this afternoon and then we head off over there and take care of business. We can hide out until dark and then take that evil woman and her boyfriend. You sit here and relax, Ronny. Have some food from the fridge. I'm going to look for some proper guns." He returned less than five minutes later with two large-caliber hunting rifles that he'd found in the gun cabinet.

The Hunter's Folly lions had moved deeper into the bush when the Land Rover carrying Cori-Anne and Eliot arrived at the spot where the pride had killed a zebra the night before. Kea and the tracker walked towards the zebra carcass, which had been picked almost clean by hyaenas and jackals and was only waiting on the vultures that were hovering in a nearby tree to finish up what was left. While the tracker disappeared into the bush, Kea walked back to the Land Rover.

"The lions have moved that way," she said, pointing in the direction where the tracker had vanished. "Normally we don't like to drive off the roads, but in this case, I believe we can do so. Hang on tight and watch out for the thorn bushes." She climbed back in and, putting the vehicle into four-wheel drive, turned off the road. The tracker was no more than ten meters into the bush and as the Land Rover approached, he jumped into the passenger seat and said something to Kea in Tswana.

"Holy shit," yelled Eliot as he and Cori-Anne flew up and down as the Land Rover bounced and scraped its way through the thick undergrowth, avoiding large trees and ploughing over small bushes as if they were daisies.

"You must be quiet," Kea whispered. "The lions, they are not far. Keep your eyes open."

"I have no idea what to look for," Cori-Anne replied. "Unless a lion jumps up in front of us."

"Your bush-eyes will come...look for movement and shadows."

Cori-Anne and Eliot had a hard-enough time staying on the seat and avoiding the long camelthorns that threatened to rip the skin from their arms let alone watching for "movement and shadows." Of course, Kea had no expectations from her rookie guests; she and her tracker knew exactly where they were going. All of a sudden, the tracker held up his hand, and Kea hit the brakes.

"There," she said, pointing to their left. "There they are."

There were two large lionesses lying on a collapsed termite mound and four young males, their manes just beginning to show, lounging in the shade of a leadwood tree.

"Oh, my God," Eliot said, taking photos with his iPhone. "I can't believe this. I've dreamed of this forever." His voice had gone from a gravelly whisper to a delighted squeak.

Cori-Anne gripped his arm in abject terror. "What happens if they jump in the Land Rover?"

"They won't," whispered Kea. "They're used to vehicles like this, and they see them as much bigger than they are, so they won't attack. You are very safe, believe me. Now, quietly, quietly, look there." From behind the mound, three cubs emerged. They were no more than a few months old. "That is their mother, the lioness on the left. The other one is the mother of the four young males under the tree."

They watched the cubs play with each other and their

mother's tail for about twenty minutes until a movement behind the vehicle made Eliot look back over his shoulder. A huge male lion emerged from an acacia bush. He sauntered along the lefthand side of the Land Rover, stopped for a second, and regarded Cori-Anne as if he were considering her (well, that's what Eliot thought) for a potential new wife. Then he walked up to the mound and sniffed at the cubs who froze all play in deference to their dad, gave an almighty yawn, and lay down.

"When a male takes over a pride, he will sometimes kill the cubs if he believes they will be a threat to him," said Kea. "But this old guy, he has fathered all of these cubs, and I don't believe he fears anything. Now come, let us leave them in peace to enjoy their siesta. It is almost time for breakfast back at the lodge, and you do not want to miss that."

Kea managed to maneuver the Land Rover without disturbing the lions or destroying too much of the vegetation until she was pointed back towards the road. She followed the track she'd made through the bush, and when they hit the road she turned right, heading to the camp. If they'd turned left, they'd have triggered the IED, which was buried less than twenty meters away.

Two of the four new guests were sitting in the reception area with Bontle when Cori-Anne and Eliot arrived back at the lodge. Bontle waved them over.

"Cori-Anne van Cleave and Eliot Hart, please meet Rohini and Sabhajit Singh, our old friends from India who are here on their honeymoon."

"Pleased to meet you," said Rohini, shaking Cori-Anne's hand.

"And you," replied Cori-Anne, smiling at the beautiful woman who, like her husband, was dressed in khaki. "And congratulations on your marriage."

"Bontle and Gosego have filled us in on your situation," said Sabhajit, looking every inch a policeman from the tips of his still-highly-polished leather shoes to the top of his maroon turban. He gave his moustache a twirl. "Obviously we will do what we can should anything untoward happen. I shall keep my eyes peeled, and I assure you: not much escapes my notice when my notice is attuned to a situation."

His wife rolled her eyes and smiled. "My husband is, as I'm sure Gosego mentioned and as you can probably deduce from his manner, one of Delhi's highest-ranking police officers."

"Well, we're very grateful, and I'm so sorry you even have to think of this on your honeymoon," Eliot said, totally fascinated by Singh's magnificent moustache.

"A good policeman, like a good doctor, is always on call," Singh said. "But first, breakfast. Let's hope that damned monkey who always seems to steal my food has forsaken that tree in the middle of the dining room."

"Nope," said Bontle, "he's still there waiting for you. Now, if the four of you are willing, perhaps you can share a table at breakfast as you'll be in the same Land Rover on your game drives. Cori-Anne and Eliot, this is Rohini and Sabhajit's second time at Hunter's Folly, so they can fill you in on the place."

They were just in the middle of hearing the Singhs'

account of their involvement in the Valerian Zolotov affair, in which they'd helped to thwart the plans of the Russian oligarch to genetically modify animals to make them more appealing to trophy hunters, when the Storm party got back from their drive. Both Simon and Steven Storm were thrilled to meet two of the people who'd saved their father from a nasty death and been at his wedding to Conchita Palomino. As they stood to greet the Storms, a large monkey dropped to the table and grabbed Sabhajit's croissant, and before anyone could stop him scampered up into the tree.

"What the hell do you think that hairy bastard has against me?" Singh asked, shaking his fist at the monkey enjoying his prize in the branches above. "He could have taken anyone's food, but he seems to favor mine."

"I think he knows you have excellent taste," laughed Rohini.

"Do you know in India," said Sabhajit, "we used to employ monkey policemen to chase away the rotten monkeys?"

"You mean the policemen were actual monkeys?" asked Simon.

"Indeed. They were langurs, which are much bigger monkeys than the bastard in the tree, and they were most effective. But they are endangered, so we cannot use them anymore. Anyway, my love," he said to Rohini, "perhaps we should take a snooze before the afternoon drive. Neither of us got much sleep on the plane last night."

Eliot's email buzzed as he and Cori-Anne entered their tent. Thomas had written to say that there were no new developments other than that the plane carrying Don Jorge Morales had landed in Johannesburg and the South African authorities weren't being overly cooperative in trying to find out any more information. He asked them to email him to say they were safe and to be on the lookout.

"I'm pretty happy that we've got Gosego, Bontle, and the Singhs on our side," Eliot said, lying down on the bed.

"So am I," Cori Ann agreed as she undressed. "Now get off the bed. It's time for some yoga."

"I'm kind of tired," Eliot replied, pulling the pillow over his head.

"Really, too tired for naked yoga? I'll even teach you some tantric yoga, which if done right will allow you to have six variations of orgasm."

Where the morning trip had been incredibly exciting with the lions, the afternoon drive was even more so. About half an hour from the camp they saw a cheetah stalking some impala but missed the actual kill when predator and prey vanished behind a thicket onto the plain beyond.

"We'll catch her on the way back," said Kea. "It's best to leave her at this moment in case we scare her and she loses the kill to some hyenas." They saw more elephants and a couple of white rhinos at a waterhole where they stopped for sundowners and snacks.

"I can't imagine anything more peaceful than this," Cori-Anne said to Rohini. "I'd never ever have thought about going on a safari if Eliot hadn't suggested it."

"It is incredibly peaceful...almost life-changing," Rohini said, taking a sip of wine. "That's why we came back here on our honeymoon. Perhaps when the whole rotten affair with the drug lords is over, you'll consider taking a safari in India."

Cori-Anne smiled and nodded her head. *When it's over,* she thought. What happens if it's never over? What happens if *over* meant she and Eliot were dead?

A tear formed in the corner of her eye, and she turned away from Rohini. Eliot, who'd been eating the *biltong* cut into thin slices unlike the huge strip Ronny had wolfed down at Cape Town Airport, noticed the expression on Cori-Anne's face and walked over. He put his arm around her shoulder but said nothing because he knew what she was thinking. She put her hand up and touched his arm.

"Let's just walk away from everyone for a moment," she said.

"Not too far," Kea shouted when she saw them walking away.

"We're in a pickle, aren't we?" Eliot said, waving an acknowledgement to Kea and pulling Cori-Anne closer. The temperature had dropped, and she was shivering, though whether it was from the cold or fear, Eliot didn't know.

"Yes," she whispered, "and I don't know what we're going to do. I'm really scared and I'm also so sorry, Eliot. I got you into this."

"No. No, you didn't. I got myself into it. And Cori-Anne...." He lifted her head with his fingers. "I'd do the same thing again if it meant being with you."

She kissed him and realized at that moment that she loved him. She knew it was partially driven by their impending death (she'd resigned herself to that), but the sensation which was centered in her stomach was so contrary to anything she'd experienced before. It felt like she'd eaten the most glorious meal imaginable. She was full to the point of bursting but with no hint of regret. In this respect it was very different to how Eliot had come to the realization that he loved her. He had, as mentioned, drifted into love the way he drifted into the slow rhythms of sleep. It was, though he didn't know it at the time, the moment of his transition. The sorites paradox had kicked in.

Without saying a word to each other, they walked back to the Land Rover. Rohini watched them carefully. She'd seen people who were scared out of their minds before. There was certainly that about them. But there was something else, too. The only word that came to mind was *satisfied*. Yes, that was exactly how they looked: totally and utterly *satisfied*.

Chapter 20

Same place but a little later

The two Toyota Land Cruisers carrying Don Jorge Morales and his bodyguards from the airport at Alldays pulled into Groot Witdoosbos Farm just before six o'clock in the evening. Nguyen van Duc, who'd flown in a smaller plane, was able to land on the farm's tiny airstrip. He'd arrived just fifteen minutes before and was standing at the open doorway to the farmhouse.

"Ding-dong," he said with a cheery wave to the don, "there is nobody home."

"Perhaps they've gone to retrieve the woman and her boyfriend," said the don as he walked into the house. The thought of staying in such a spartan though he had to admit neat place for the night did not excite him at all.

"Perhaps you are right," Duc answered, looking somewhat skeptical. "But I have a feeling that not all is right. There is a lot of blood in the kitchen, and when I compare the state of the kitchen to these other rooms, my feeling is that in fact everything is all wrong."

They walked into the kitchen, which as Duc had correctly

observed was a bloody mess. There were pools of blood and what looked like cranial matter spattered on the floor and walls. The fridge was open with half-eaten food mingling with the remains of Pakkies' and Oom Ebert's brains.

A bunch of kitchen towels soaked with blood from Ronny's facial wounds had been tossed on an unrolled map on the kitchen table. Duc flicked the towels off the map and took a look. It appeared to be of the area.

"My God," said a horrified Don Morales, "it looks as if some wild boars have come through here, savaged the owner, and raided the fridge."

"Again, Mr. 'Prostitute Caller,' you may be right. But once again my stomach is telling me that this is not the work of wild boar. This map of the farm and surrounding areas tells me otherwise. Perhaps we should go down to the lion enclosure and see if any of the staff are there. Perhaps they can tell us."

"Good idea," said Don Jorge. "But if you call me 'Prostitute Caller' again, I will personally kill you."

Duc laughed. "Don't be so sensitive. It's only a joke."

"It's not funny at all," replied the don. "And if you think I won't kill you, might I remind you there are six of us and only one of you. If I have to sacrifice Cori-Anne's misery for her quick death, then I will."

Duc laughed and waved the threat off. He wasn't worried in the least.

It was still light enough to see the path to the lion enclosure, and even if it hadn't been, the roar of the now-satiated lions would have made the location obvious. Before they saw the lions or the skeletons of Terre'Blanche and van Tonder, they came across two huge pools of blood just outside the wire fence. At first Don Jorge was certain that the blood must have come from animal carcasses that were about to be tossed to the lions. Then Yuri bent down and picked up two objects which he held up for the don and Duc to examine.

"These look like fingers to me, boss." There was no trace of fear or revulsion in Yuri's voice. He'd held more than his fair share of savagely cropped digits during torture sessions.

"Are you sure?" asked the don, taking a closer look. "They could be centipedes."

"No, boss, they're definitely fingers. Look at the nails."

"Hmm," replied the Don, seeing that they were indeed fingers that in his opinion could have done with manicuring.

"And," shouted Duc from the wire fence, "I think I know who they belong to."

The Mexican group moved over to where Duc was pointing at two mostly chewed skeletons. *Mostly chewed* because the lions had started on the good stuff: intestines, scrotums, fleshy thighs, and buttocks, leaving some of the less appetizing bits for later.

"These must be the South Africans," said the don. "I've never met them in person, but I do know what Cripps and Rundo look like, and these are not them."

"In this case you are 100 percent correct," said Duc. "I can still make out their faces. Well, the one's face at least. The other one's face looks like it was run over by a bus."

Yuri, who'd walked a little further along the enclosure fence, spotted the bodies of Oom Ebert and Pakkies. "Boss," he yelled, "here are two more. You can see these have been shot in the head."

Only a few chunks had been taken out of those bodies, and while Duc thought he'd probably seen the previous occupiers of said bodies on the farm on a previous visit, he wasn't sure.

"My assessment of this peculiar situation," Duc said to Don Jorge, "is that one of two things has happened here. First, and least probable, your targets were captured and escaped, killing the South Africans and taking your American killers hostage."

"Look, Duc," the don said, his voice betraying the intense frustration he was feeling, "that 'assessment' as you call it is ridiculous. We do not have time to waste on this. Every moment the yoga instructor and her boyfriend are either free or alive puts me in more danger."

"Well, Mr. Don, I said that was least probable." Duc didn't like the Mexican one bit. He had no sense of humor and everything about him was unpleasant. What he hadn't mentioned to Don Jorge was that he had six of his own men strategically placed around the farmhouse and that he could at any point give a signal for them to take out the Mexicans with their HK416C assault rifles. So much for six of them and only one of him.

"Well, Mr. Duc," the don replied, trying to sound as sarcastic as possible, "what is the most probable?"

"The most probable is that your assassins killed the South Africans for reasons unknown to me but possibly known to you and are at this moment on their way to the camp at Hunter's Folly to kill the targets. If so, then you have broken the agreement."

"What the hell are you talking about? Do you think I planned for this to happen? I gave specific instructions to the South Africans to capture the woman and kill everyone else—the boyfriend and the two American white-supremacist assassins. As usual nobody listens to my instructions. No doubt they've done exactly the opposite. We'll just have to go back to the farmhouse and wait for their return to see the damage."

"No," replied Duc angrily. "No, no, no. I need this woman alive. I have, since our dinner last night, already sold her to the Many Screams Brothel and I cannot get out of the transaction. The brothel is owned by the most powerful triad gang in Myanmar. Even more deadly than the junta. They'd cut off my head and shove it up your ass. No, we need to go after them and hope it is not too late."

"Well, that is up to you. And for your information, no one's shoving anything up my ass ever again. As far as I'm concerned at this point, I just want her dead. Me and my men are going back to the farmhouse. If you want to go after Cripps and Rundo and retrieve the woman, that is up to you. C'mon Yuri, let's all go back. I'm tired and I need a drink."

Nguyen van Duc stared after Don Jorge as he and his men trudged towards the farmhouse. His initial reaction once their backs were turned was to signal his men to drop them like the swine they were. But there were too many bodies as it was, and once the staff returned to the farm—he assumed they'd all gone home for the night— the don and his men would have more than enough explaining to do and bribes to pay to keep the police at bay. No, he'd follow the two incompetent American assassins who no doubt would have a hard time making their way through the bush at night. He'd kill them, take the girl, kill the boyfriend, and fly out. He called the pilot of his small plane who was sleeping in the cockpit and asked him to fly to the airstrip at Hunter's Folly. No one would hear it from the main lodge or expect anyone to land in the moonlight.

Of the six men in Duc's squad, four were trained killers from Vietnam who'd flown with him from Johannesburg packed like sardines into the plane. The other two were local poachers who not only kept an eye on his business interests in the area but harvested the odd rhino horn when Duc and his friends needed a little boost to their libidos. They were the ones who easily picked up the tracks left by Rundo and Cripps. The tracks went from the farmhouse and into the thick bush to where the dividing fence between Groot Witdoosbos Farm and Hunter's Folly ran. Cripps and Rundo had cut the wire and squeezed through. The poachers, who had powerful flashlights, reckoned the tracks weren't more than an hour or two old. They followed them to the road where they turned left, headed directly towards the main lodge at Hunter's Folly.

In the farmhouse Yuri had found three large jugs of van Tonder's homemade peach brandy in the pantry. He handed one jug to Don Jorge, and he and the other men began to take it in turns to swig from the other two. Much to Don Jorge's surprise, the brandy was remarkably smooth—perhaps not quite in the same league as a decent anejo, but close. After his second glass of the brandy, which unbeknownst to the don was at least 195 proof, he began to have second thoughts about abandoning the capture of Cori-Anne to Duc. This sudden reversal was further emboldened by a yell from one of his nastiest henchmen.. In his search for more brandy, he'd discovered a cache of automatic and semi-automatic rifles in a walk-in closet in one of the bedrooms. The don made his way into the room and picked up one of the assault rifles which Manny had laid on the bed. It was old but in perfect condition. He checked the magazine. It was fully loaded with fifty rounds of 5.56x45mm ammunition, and there was an entire crate of magazines at the back of the closet.

"You know what, Yuri?" slurred the Don.

"No, boss, I don't," Yuri replied.

"Of course you don't, you idiot," said Don Jorge. "That was a rhetorical question. I didn't expect you to have an answer."

"Oh, I see. OK, boss, then I do know what."

"No, no," screamed the don. "You don't. You're missing the point, Yuri. Just shut up and listen."

Yuri shrugged his large shoulders. Don Jorge was a hard man to understand at times.

"Here's what we're going to do. We're going to get in the cars and drive to the main road until we get to the gate at Hunter's Folly. Then we're going to drive to the main lodge and kill everyone but the girl."

"Uh, then what, boss?" Even to Yuri this sounded like the worst plan he'd ever heard. The brandy was making him decidedly sleepy.

"Then what? Well, Yuri, then we're going to drive back to Alldays and get in the plane and fly back to Sinaloa."

"What about Cripps and Rundo and Duc?"

"Fuck Duc and fuck those two white supremacists. I

looked at the map. If we drive on the main road, we'll get there first. Then we wait for them to attack. They'll be coming from here while we're coming from...I don't know, it doesn't matter. While the Hunter's Folly people are fighting them, we simply come in from behind and...boom!" He pointed the rifle at the ceiling and pulled the trigger. The gun blew a hole in the ceiling, showering the entire group with dust and plaster. No one said a word for a moment. Then they all laughed. Then the don smiled. "Sorry, I didn't mean to do that. Anyway, at least we know they work. This is going to be easy."

Yuri had his doubts. He respected Don Jorge, and there was nothing in the world he wouldn't do for him. But it sounded like the plan of someone who'd had too much to drink. Which of course it was.

Chapter 21

Hunter's Folly late than night and early the next morning

The mysterious man who'd been making his way through the bush towards Hunter's Folly paused for a moment. The sound he'd heard wasn't made by an animal unless Gosego had trained some baboons to talk with an American accent, and a southern one at that.

Ishea Payamps[3]—half-Puerto Rican, half-Lakota Sioux, ex-special forces, mercenary, and currently wildlife activist—was on his way back from a mission in Botswana, where he'd taken out three French trophy hunters who'd already killed two fully grown elephants and a baby. They'd been part of an advance party of hunters who'd obtained the first licenses to kill now that Botswana had begun to allow elephant hunting. Ishea and the people who supported him believed the only deterrent to these psychopaths was to make it clear that they'd never be safe and that *legal* was not an excuse for

---

[3] See the Roger Storm books

immoral. Ishea often ended up at Hunter's Folly after one of his operations, and both Gosego and Bontle welcomed him, though of course they could never acknowledge him openly.

Like Cripps and Rundo, Ishea had been following the road. It was not only easier, but at night he felt it was safer if animals could see you clearly. The only weapon Ishea carried was a knife designed for him by Yoshikazu Ikeda, the famed Japanese blacksmith. It was sixteen inches long, made from white steel, and could split a small log and slice through a human neck with hardly any effort. Ishea twisted his right arm over his left shoulder and slowly drew the long knife from its leather scabbard that was strapped to his back.

He pulled into the shadow of an acacia bush and watched the strange pair stomping their way along the hardened dirt road. The larger of the two men seemed to be struggling more than the smaller one, and as they passed Ishea he saw that the big one had severe head wounds. His feet were dragging, and his back bent under the two big-bore hunting rifles slung over his shoulder.

"What the hell is up with you, boy?" said the smaller one. "If you don't pick up your goddammed pace, we won't be at the lodge before dawn. Now step it up, boy, you hear me?"

The big man mumbled something incoherent and tried to lift his feet, but it was clear he was out of steam. The little man turned around and regarded his partner angrily. The big man took one more step and then fell forward. He made a valiant effort to get up, but the best he could manage was to turn over and stare up at the sky.

The little man walked up and kicked him in the ribs.

"Jesus-H-fucking-Christ-on-a-cracker, you useless sack of horseshit," the small man said, giving him another solid kick in the ribs. "Once again it appears that I have to do everything myself. Well, as far as I'm concerned you can just lay here and die. Now, give me my rifle." The large man gave a moan that reminded Ishea of a buffalo trapped in the mud and then began to sob loudly.

"Cryin' ain't worth shit to me, you big ape." The little man knelt down next to the big one and pulled what looked like a straight razor from his pocket. Then in one swift move he cut his throat. The big man didn't even gurgle.

Ishea, who generally had neither the time nor the empathy for his fellow humans that he displayed for animals, almost felt sorry for the big man, who now lay silent on the road. He watched as the little man picked up one of the hunting rifles and walked off down the road. There was no point checking to see if the big man was actually dead; that much was obvious to Ishea, who'd seen the dead and dying more often than he'd had hot breakfasts. However, he didn't want to leave the corpse in the middle of the road for a group of unsuspecting tourists to come upon on their morning drive. So, after checking pockets for any form of identification, of which there was none, he took the rifle and dragged the corpse off the road into the bush, where he was sure hyaenas and jackals would take care of it. He slung the remaining rifle across his back.

The little man intrigued him. He had absolutely no clue as to who he was or what he could possibly be doing at

Hunter's Folly. All he knew is that he was up to no good, and so he decided to follow and confront him. The *follow* part worked for less than two minutes when Ishea became aware of more sounds. Not voices this time, but the slow, steady sounds of people moving along the road behind him. He heard them stop at the point where Cripps had killed Ronny and the low murmur of voices discussing what had happened.

He'd kept off the road since moving the corpse, but he had no doubt any poacher—and he assumed the people behind him were poachers—would pick up his tracks. His best bet, he decided, was to cross the road, leaving no tracks on the hard surface in the middle, and then double back. If by chance they found his tracks leading to the road, they'd assume he was moving forward. He needn't have worried. The group were tracking someone, but it wasn't him.

When the trackers found Rundo's body no more than minutes after they discovered the pool of blood in the road, they called over to Duc, who took a long look.

"It appears," he said to his four associates, who'd gathered round the corpse, "that one of the assassins has been eliminated, and no doubt by the other for whatever reason. I think it is more imperative than ever that we move quickly to take the remaining assassin before he screws this whole thing up." He turned to one of the trackers. "How far ahead is he?"

"Maybe ten minutes, but he is moving slowly."

"Then we must move quickly," replied Duc. "I want him dead before we get to the lodge."

Ishea, who didn't understand the first part where Duc

spoke to his team in Vietnamese, did understand when Duc spoke to the trackers. *Eight people,* he thought. *If they eliminate one, then that leaves me seven. The trackers won't fight, so that means I need to take out five people. But five people armed with compact assault rifles and very little cover. I can probably take out two from behind but then....*

There was only one course of action. He'd have to get to Hunter's Folly before the Vietnamese and warn Gosego. He had one rifle, and he remembered there were a few at the lodge and that Gosego and Bontle knew how to use them. But he'd have to hurry.

To his dismay and shame, Nguyen van Duc totally underestimated the Reverend Clayton Calvin Cripps' ability to survive. After all, someone who's endured an abusive father, an even more abusive juvenile detention center, and a prison system that made the previous two abusive situations seem like a church summer camp (the non-abusive ones) doesn't suddenly become an easy target.

The results of the underestimation happened a minute later when two shots rang out and both his trackers went down.

Chapter 22

Hunter's Folly, that same night and early the next morning

Eliot couldn't sleep. He picked up his phone and for the umpteenth time looked at the clock. It was two-thirty, ten minutes later than the last time he'd looked at it. He got out of bed slowly so as not to disturb Cori-Anne, who was lying on her back snoring gently. Once again, he thought of the predicament that he and Cori-Anne were in, and he tried his best to analyze it. If there was a logical way out other than an unpleasant death, he couldn't think of it. Perhaps a short walk would help clear his head. Bontle had advised against it, and while the old Eliot would have heeded that sage council, the new Eliot did not.

He had on a pair of athletic shorts and a grey t-shirt that he'd worn to bed, and his sneakers were on a bench on the deck. As quietly as he could, he unzipped the flap and tiptoed onto the wooden deck. He put on his sneakers and took a look to see if there were any hippos grazing on the lawn. The moonlight cast an eerie silver glow over the camp, but the only shapes he could discern were bushes and trees and two of the other tents. Eliot stuck to the path as he made his way up to the main lodge to see if there were still some bikkies in the big glass jar on the coffee table. He certainly didn't need a snack, but he always believed his brain worked better with something in his stomach. Halfway to the lodge he saw a shadowy figure moving in front of him.

He gave a silent squeak and narrowed his eyes, trying to work out if it was a man or an animal. Much to his relief it appeared to be a man, and he was just about to offer a friendly "hullo" when he realized the man had a rifle slung over his back. He froze in horror, and myriad thoughts began to buzz around his brain like an angry swarm of bees. Was this one of the killers? If so, where was the other or others? Should he run back to his tent to protect Cori-Anne or follow the shadow and try to tackle him? He looked back at their tent, but there were no nasty shadows creeping about, and so he made a decision to follow the mysterious man. He looked around for a weapon, a branch or a stick or a stone, but could see nothing. The shadowy figure made its way to the main lodge and then round the side to what Eliot believed to be Gosego and Bontle's living quarters.

Suddenly what sounded to Eliot like two shots rang out in the distance. The shadow turned around and pulled a small sword from a scabbard on his back next to the rifle. He ran towards Eliot, whose legs refused to obey the frantic commands issued by his brain. The shadow, which turned out to be a huge man, grabbed Eliot's neck and the point of the blade pricked his skin just under his left eye.

"Who are you?" whispered the man.

I'm Eliot," replied Eliot, trying not to throw up. "I'm just on my way to get a bikkie."

"What the hell are you talking about?" The man pulled the tip of his knife away from under Eliot's eye.

"Are you the assassin?"

Before the man could reply, the door to Gosego and Bontle's quarters opened, and Gosego appeared brandishing a pistol and a powerful flashlight.

"Ishea!" he yelled. "Why are you harassing the guests?"

It was clear to Eliot that Ishea, as Gosego called him without bothering with introductions, was a highly disciplined soldier. He let Eliot go and explained the situation to Gosego and Bontle in a calm and concise manner that conveyed utmost urgency without a hint of panic. Eliot was surprised that Ishea had an American accent, but he quickly decided that this was not an opportune time to discuss the good old US of A. What happened in the next few minutes was what Eliot imagined a special forces operation would look if most of the soldiers were in nightgowns and boxer shorts.

Bontle and Gosego were on their phones calling up the game rangers and Black Mambas anti-poaching squad, who met them in the office where the gun safe was. There were six rifles in the safe, which meant together with the one Ishea had taken off Ronny Rundo and Gosego's pistol, eight of the force were armed. Bontle sent two of the Mambas to round up the guests and bring them to the lodge. Eliot wanted to go with her to get Cori-Anne, but Gosego told him to stay in the main lodge and that her tent would be the first they visited. Ishea positioned the armed rangers strategically so that they covered both the road to the lodge and the surrounding bush.

"Those two shots we heard," he said, "those were rifle shots, which means they came from the assassin, not the Vietnamese. They didn't fire back, which means we have to assume that there are a minimum of five automatic weapons and possibly one rifle, and on whose side the rifle is at this moment I can't tell. That means we have at least six armed assailants, five with automatic weapons. You won't get a second shot, so make your first count. Now turn off all the lights."

Eliot was beginning to panic. He had no idea what the hell was going on. He was relieved to see the two Mambas shepherding the guests onto the porch of the lodge. He looked desperately for Cori-Anne, but he couldn't see her. Then one of the Mambas went over to Bontle and said something to her in Tswana. Bontle looked over at Eliot and his heart sank.

"What's the matter?" he shouted to Bontle. "Where's Cori-Anne?"

Bontle walked over to Eliot and put her hand on his shoulder. "She's not in the tent."

"What do you mean? She was sleeping...."

"There are signs of a struggle but no blood. Someone's taken her, Eliot. But we need to look at the footage from the camera."

"Oh, Jesus," Elliot yelled. "No time for the camera footage...I have to find her." He turned around and began to run. And that's when all hell broke loose.

There was a burst of automatic fire, and plaster flew off the wall above Eliot's head. One of the guests screamed. Gosego, who had walked over to try to stop Eliot, pushed him down hard onto the concrete.

"Stay down—just wait," demanded Gosego. But Eliot didn't want to wait, and he struggled to get up until Gosego put a large foot on his back. "It's you they're trying to kill, dammit. Stay the fuck down."

From where he lay Eliot could see Bontle as she aimed her rifle, though he couldn't see what she was aiming at. She pulled the trigger, and he heard a scream followed by more automatic fire, more screams, flashes, grunts. He saw one of the rangers clutch his arm and drop his rifle. Then Rohini Singh picked it up and began to fire. Eliot felt as if his head would burst. Tears of frustration and fear filled his eyes, and he knew he had to do something. Someone shouted that there were two other vehicles approaching, and Gosego swore and pulled his foot off Eliot's back. Eliot sprung up and began to run towards the path leading to his and Cori-Anne's tent. He heard what sounded like an angry hornet and he felt a searing pain just above his right eye and then...just darkness.

The arrival of the Mexicans changed everything. While Bontle's shot had taken out one of the Vietnamese gunmen, the Hunter's Folly defenders—despite the fact that Gosego, Ishea, and both Singhs were trained soldiers—were outmatched and outgunned. Their attackers knew this, and though their intended targets were Eliot and Cori-Anne, they had no compunction taking on the defenders.

It was Nguyen van Duc's bullet that sent Eliot spinning to the ground. He looked through his night-vision scope at the huddled guests hiding as best they could behind the large couches, but he couldn't see the woman. His men had seen the pictures of her, and they knew not to shoot her on pain of death. One of his men was down, shot by the tall black woman, but there were still four of them including him. He drew a bead on one of the rangers who was trying unsuccessfully to hide behind one of the wooden pillars, but his shot was interrupted by the sudden arrival of two Land Cruisers filled with the Mexicans.

The Land Cruiser headlamps illuminated the four remaining Vietnamese, and the Mexicans rolled out and began to fire at whatever they could see. Two of the Vietnamese gunmen went down immediately. The other two returned fire, killing or severely wounding three of the Mexicans. Then Ishea struck. He'd given his rifle to Sabhajit, gone out the back of the lodge, and crept through the shadows until he was behind the combatants. He knew he'd have to get close enough to use his knife, and the arrival of the Mexicans had given him exactly what he needed.

He sprung forward and drove the fifteen-inch blade through the throat of one of the two remaining Vietnamese. He turned to the other, a white-haired man, who on seeing death in the eyes of the enormous man moved back with his rifle pointed at Ishea until he was level with one of the Land Cruisers. Then he jumped into the vehicle, which was still running. To Ishea's amazement, the two remaining Mexicans, seeing that it was over, jumped into the same Land Cruiser and sped off out of the camp along the same road Duc and his men had taken from Groot Witdoosbos Farm.

Duc hadn't expected Don Jorge and Yuri's company.

He'd have shot them as they got in, but he'd thrown his rifle onto the back seat. The don, who'd partially sobered up, stuck the barrel of his rifle in Duc's ear.

"Great job," said Don Jorge. "You really fucked that up."

"Oh, really? We were doing just fine until you arrived on the scene unexpectedly. You told me you weren't coming."

"Yes, well, I didn't have faith in your abilities."

"Is that so? Well, I killed that man, Eliot, and we were about to take the woman—"

"But you didn't, and she is the one that we need. I should shoot you right now."

"First, we'd crash, and second, I have a plane that can get us out of here. I just need to call the pilot to go back to the farm."

"Did you kill those two gringo assassins?" the don asked when Duc had made the call. The alcohol had worn off and he sounded tired.

"No. The little one must have killed the big one. We found his body just off the road, and then the little one shot my two trackers. I don't know what happened to him."

The don just shook his head and gave a deep sigh. An overpowering sense of maudlin filled his entire body.

"Why does nothing go right? You know, Duc, I find that no one listens anymore. You ask someone to do something your way, and of course they have a better way because you're old. Young people today have no respect for the wisdom and experience of their elders."

"I respect you, boss," said Yuri, placing a reassuring hand on the don's shoulder. He actually didn't respect

Don Jorge at all, but he felt he needed a hug at this time more than a rebuke for getting them into this situation and losing the men, most of whom were Yuri's friends.

"I know, Yuri. You're a loyal and good man. But everyone else...it's been an absolute nightmare."

"Well," replied Duc, "as it happens, I know what you mean. I have a similar issue with younger people in my own organization. Always think they know better. You have no idea how many of them I've had to kill just to get respect. Now, look carefully because the hole in the fence where we came through from the lion farm should be very close."

They missed it but not the IED that Oom Ebert and Pakkies Potgieter had buried in the road in the original plan to take the Hunter's Folly Land Rover out of commission. IEDs do not discriminate between Land Rovers and Land Cruisers, so when the front left-hand wheel of the Land Cruiser carrying Duc, Don Jorge, and Yuri went over the pressure plate, it delivered what it was designed to do and then some. The pressure plate connected to the detonator and initiated the explosion sequence.

Once again, adding more credence to the woeful lamentations of both Don Jorge and Duc that people do not listen anymore, Pakkies had placed a lot more explosives into the IED than would have been necessary to disable the Hunter's Folly vehicle. The Land Cruiser rose into the air on a ball of flame and high-pressure shockwaves and landed with an awful crunch of bent metal and hard clay. The explosion killed Yuri, ripped the head off Don Jorge, and severely disabled Duc, who somehow managed to crawl from the burning wreck. There was a six-inch piece of steel from the engine block in his thigh, and all he could do was pull himself with his hands to the side of the road.

He was bleeding profusely from the wound, and he knew that he probably wasn't going to make it. He felt in his pants pocket for his phone, but when he tried to pull it out, he realized that the metal spike in his thigh had gone right through it. He wondered if the people from Hunter's Folly, who must have heard the explosion, would get to him before he croaked. He hoped not. This was his time to die.

He managed to roll over on his back and stare up at the sky. The moonlight had blurred out many of the stars, but those he could see were beautiful, and he wondered why he'd never taken the time to really look at them before. He could hear lions roaring from somewhere. Perhaps they were the ones on the farm giving thanks to the gods that their tormentors were suffering as much as they had. Then the stars began to dim as Nguyen van Duc faded alongside them into the vast universe from where he came.

Chapter 23

Hunter's Folly, that same morning

The explosion, though it was at least five kilometers from the main lodge, echoed through the last of the darkness as the first pale light of the morning began its slow march over the bushveld.

"What the hell was that?" asked Sabhajit as he and Rohini stood on the porch watching the rangers and Mambas dragging the dead Vietnamese and Mexicans to the side of the lodge. Everyone stopped when they heard the noise.

"Sounds like an IED," his wife replied. "Must be the Land Cruiser."

"I hate making assumptions in the field," Ishea said as he and Gosego walked up to them, "but we need to assume that was either the Land Cruiser or an elephant triggering the explosives. If it was the Land Cruiser, then the three people in it are either disabled or dead. That only leaves the other assassin. And from what we saw on the camera footage, he's the one who took Cori-Anne. The question is: where will he take her?"

"The explosion looks to be very close to the boundary fence between our place and the lion breeding farm," Gosego said. "And I don't believe it was an elephant. There are none in that area. But it does mean that is where the attackers were heading, and I would think that the assassin would be heading there, too. I do know that the *boers* use the Vietnamese to take the lion bones out the country. So maybe the Mexicans are connected to that somehow. There are tracks from Eliot's tent heading back into the bush. Two people...let's go."

The pain from the gash in Eliot's forehead where Duc's bullet had grazed him was nothing compared to the pain he felt about the disappearance of Cori-Anne.

"She must have been in the Land Cruiser," he said to Bontle, who was cleaning his head wound.

"No," she replied, "Ishea said there were only three people: the white-haired Vietnamese and two of the Mexicans."

"Then she's still out there. I have to find her. There must have been someone else who took her."

"I understand," said Bontle, trying to sound gentle but firm. "My Mambas and the rangers are going to go out with Gosego and Ishea. They'll find her, Eliot. I promise you, they're the best. They'll track her and the assassin, and they can move a lot quicker than someone who doesn't know the bush."

"You don't understand, Bontle. I left her alone. It's my fault. I couldn't live with myself if something happened to her."

"Eliot," Bontle said, "you're not thinking rationally. What happened is not your fault. And if you'd been in the room, you probably would have been killed. You can't go with them. You'll slow them down, so sit here and drink some hot tea."

But hot tea wasn't going to cut it, and Eliot sat with his head in his hands staring down at the floor. He was an idiot. A damned fool who'd overthought everything. Even things that didn't need thinking about. So why had he started making quick—and most probably idiotic—decisions so suddenly? Why had he booked a safari to the other side of the world in less time than it normally took him to peruse a menu at a fast-food restaurant? What in God's name made him decide to take a walk last night when another two seconds of thought would have convinced him it was a foolish idea?

Then it hit him. At some point over the past few days, he'd crossed into the realm of underthinking. He'd become the sorites paradox in reverse.

Rohini and Sabhajit watched Eliot as he sat staring at the floor. "I feel so bad for him," said Rohini.

Her husband gave a dismissive grunt and went into full police inspector mode. "Well, these sorts of things don't happen on their own. They happen to people who never consider the consequences of their actions. It's simple cause and effect. And the effect is considerable in this instance."

"Spoken like the consummate policeman."

"I shall take that as a compliment, my dear."

"Well, it's not meant to be in this case. The man's suffering, and I don't think any of this is his fault. We need to do something, and I have an idea."

Bontle didn't like Rohini's idea any more than Sabhajit did. But she understood the psychology, and so she asked Kea, who was helping some of the others who hadn't gone out with Gosego and Ishea, to serve breakfast to the German couple and Storm party so they could borrow her vehicle. Five minutes later Kea's Land Rover was travelling slowly along the road towards Groot Witdoosbos Farm.

Chapter 24

Hunter's Folly, earlier that morning and a little later

The Reverend Clayton Calvin Cripps had ditched the heavy hunting rifle shortly after he'd shot the two trackers. He still had van Tonder's compact revolver in his pocket together with the straight razor. His preferred method of dispatch was slitting, but he wasn't averse to shooting if needs dictated it. Both weapons would serve his purpose adequately.

Killing the trackers had bought him at least ten minutes, he reckoned. He was a little confused as to whom precisely he'd shot at. Two of them had obviously been locals, but the others looked Asian, and he made the assumption that they were most probably the Vietnamese that van Tonder had mentioned. But why they were on the road was anyone's guess. He put the thought out his mind and doubled his pace. He'd need the extra time to discover Eliot and Cori-Anne's tent before the mayhem began.

The layout of Hunter's Folly camp was clearly marked on the map in the farmhouse, and he knew there were five tents spaced far enough apart to ensure privacy. He estimated at least a minute's walk between each tent and so he began to do a peculiar half-walk-half-run movement until he sensed someone or something ahead of him on the road. He stopped for a second and listened. Whatever it was, it was moving even quicker than he was. All of a sudden the road twisted, and he saw a clearing to his right with the main lodge in the center.

The tents were further off towards where he could hear the river beyond the dark trees. There was no sign of whatever it was that had been ahead of him, and so he moved off as stealthily as he could in the direction of the tents. He stood for a moment wondering just how he'd possibly be able to find Cori-Anne and Eliot without waking the other guests when to his surprise he noticed a figure using the flashlight on his phone emerge from the furthest tent. He crept closer and then offered a prayer of thanks to Der Furher. Eliot Hart, that sneaky hog-balled bastard, was taking a stroll. He considered running up and cutting Eliot's throat with the razor, but he wasn't sure he could get close enough before Eliot heard him and shouted a warning. In any case Cori-Anne was the key. He'd grab her and while the Vietnamese were attacking the camp, he'd take her back to the farm where he assumed Don Jorge was waiting.

Cori-Anne was still on her back snoring softly when Cripps unzipped the flaps to the tent. He had the pistol in one hand and the razor in the other as he lifted the mosquito netting. Cori-Anne stirred and she put her arm out as if looking for Eliot. She opened her eyes slowly and then sat up. Instead of Eliot she saw a shape that could well have been a large baboon until the shape hissed a warning.

"Be very quiet, girlie, or I'll slit yer throat like a Christmas turkey."

Cori-Anne gave a low, uncontrollable moan, and Cripps hit her on the side of the head with the gun. It was hard enough to stun her but not to do much damage.

"Listen up and listen good, girlie," said Cripps, waving the razor in front of her face. "Git your ass outta bed and put on some clothes and shoes because you're coming with me."

Cori-Anne put her hand up to her head where the pistol had hit. She could feel a gash and blood beginning to seep out. It hurt but not too badly.

"Who are you?" she asked in a low whisper. "And where's Eliot?"

"I said shut yer goddamned mouth and hurry up. I ain't got time for questions. Now if you don't hurry, I'll cut yer cheeks open with this here razor."

Cori-Anne had little doubt that he'd do it, and so she stood up slowly and reached for her jeans and top that she'd put out for the morning drive. She could feel Cripps' beady little eyes watching her intensely as she pulled on her clothes, and she felt the bile rise to her throat.

"Now," he said, cutting two strips from the sheet, "I'm gonna gag you and tie yer pretty little hands, and then you and me, we're marching out of here. And if you expect someone to come to your rescue, you'll be wrong. In about two minutes, fire and lead will be reigning down on this place."

He'd barely finished the sentence before the firefight

began. He looked out through the flaps and saw that it was concentrated around the main lodge. Rangers were spreading out towards the tent where the sleepy guests, awakened by gun fire, huddled in front of their tents. Then Cripps saw a ranger with a rifle running towards the tent where he held Cori-Anne captive.

"Quickly now, girlie," Cripps said, pushing the barrel of his pistol into Cori-Anne's spine, "walk out real slow towards the bushes by the river, and don't make a sound or I'll cripple you." Even if she wanted to cry out—and she did—she couldn't have. The gag held her tongue firmly in her lower jaw, and all she could get out was a soft moan. Cripps gave her another shove, and she began to walk as steadily as she could towards the riverine forest. Before the ranger reached their tent, she and Cripps had vanished into the trees. Their progress was slow, but they eventually came out of the bush onto the road that Cripps had taken from the lion farm.

Cripps was wiry and strong, but he'd already walked five kilometers, and the cushioning soles on his Adidas sneakers were starting to lose their springiness. After a kilometer or two down the road, his feet began to drag.

"I need to sit down for a moment, but don't git any damn ideas that you can skedaddle into the bush. I'll drop you like a Texas persimmon with one shot."

Cori-Anne stopped and looked at the little man sitting on a termite mound wiggling his feet as if he were trying to restore circulation. She took a deep breath and let it out one nostril as she'd been taught at the ashram in California. Minutes after Cripps had pushed her out of the tent, she'd used the exercise known as *pranayama* to regulate her breathing and clear her mind of the horror of her abduction. Even then she couldn't stop the palpitations and choking feeling she got when she looked at the hobgoblin-like creature who'd threatened her with such excruciating things. The sounds of shots intensified, and she wondered if Eliot was safe. The thought of losing him brought tears to her eyes.

Cripps, too, turned his head in the direction of the fighting, and for the first time he began to question his situation. As far as he knew, the Mexicans were still at the lion farm waiting for him to bring the woman. But what if they took her and then killed him? He had no idea how many were at the farm, but if there were more than two, the odds of him doing the killing and not being killed slimmed down considerably. If they weren't there, how would he get back to Texas?

He had a few hundred dollars in his wallet, but all the travel arrangements had been made by Rodolfo, and he hadn't heard from the bastard since they'd landed in Cape Town. Then again, his father had impressed upon him that the Cripps did not give up. True, his father had said that when his parishioners had signed a petition to get him to cease the consumption of alcohol, but they were words that Clayton Calvin Cripps had never forgotten. "We Cripps ain't quitters," his dad had said, slamming him on the side of the head with his Bible for no apparent reason other than he was a horrible bastard. This admonition had gotten Cripps through foster care, juvenile detention, and prison. Even when beaten bloody by another inmate or guard, he'd never cowed or begged for mercy. "It's as if he feels no pain," said a brutal prison guard named Perkins to the warden. "Even shoving a cattle prod up his ass had him laughing like a demented hyena and sporting an impressive erection for such a small guy. My suggestion, warden, is that we parole him. He'll be less of a problem out in some godforsaken corner of the Texas panhandle than he'll be in here."

"And," said the warden, nodding in agreement, "he'll be someone else's problem, not ours. Good thinking, Perkins." Fifteen minutes later the warden signed and stamped Cripps' parole papers, and Cripps found himself standing outside the main gates of the prison. His only regret was that he'd miss lunch, when he was planning to shank a prisoner who'd called him a "mother-fuckin' cracker midget."

At this moment, though, cattle prods and prison guards were not the issue. What to do with Cori-Anne was. Should he just kill her now and sneak back to the lion farm at his own pace? He'd cut off her hand and present it to Don Jorge as proof, then demand the rest of his money and his ticket home. Or he could ungag her, record her confession on his phone, and then kill her. He weighed the options and decided on the confession, which he'd then sell to other cartel leaders as planned with Rodolfo. He put the razor in his pocket, took out his phone, tried to find a recording button , and then realized he didn't have a clue how to do it. Even if he had, his ten-dollar flip phone didn't have a recording app or any other app for that matter. In any case his battery was dead.

His mind whirred for a few seconds and settled back on killing Cori-Anne and taking his chances on his own. He pulled the razor from his pocket and grabbed her hair, but he was distracted by the sound of a vehicle approaching. He pulled Cori-Anne off the road behind a large fever tree and watched in confusion as a Land Cruiser driven by the old Vietnamese man who was talking rapidly to Don Jorge and Yuri shot by.

"Dadgummit," yelled Cripps, closing his straight razor, "now I got to take you back to the farm. That little yellow bastard wants you alive. So, git a move on or I'll cut you real bad."

Cori-Anne moaned in terror (the yoga breathing technique having called it quits several threats ago) and began to edge forward. Cripps gave her a shove and they set off down the road again. Cori-Anne was as worried about being eaten by a predator or stomped on by an elephant as she was about Cripps' razor.

The gunfire from the lodge had stopped, and an eerie silence descended on the bush. She thought of Eliot again and started sobbing. Her nose began to run in sympathy with her eyes, and she sniffed loudly.

"Stop yer snorting," said Cripps. "We need to move in silence."

Cori-Anne stopped for a moment, sagged her shoulders as if she'd given up, and then began to run as fast as she could, zig-zagging from one side of the road to the other. She had no idea why she did it. All she knew was that she had to get away from the monster. If the old Eliot was in her place, he'd have weighed up the risks and decided that the possibility of death or maiming outweighed the potential of escape and safety by 96 percent and resigned himself to his fate. Cori-Anne, on the other hand, had neither interest in nor time to do the calculations. As it happened, fortune held her in its favor and allowed her to take advantage of the 4 percent opening.

Cripps was startled for no more than a moment. He yelled for her to stop running and then fired three shots at the serpentining yoga instructor who'd disappeared into a clump of trees. Not only did he miss each time, but the sounds of his shots were dwarfed by the boom of a massive explosion from somewhere ahead. This was fortunate for Cripps because neither Gosego nor Ishea nor the Mambas, who were all headed on various trails from the camp to the lion farm, heard the shots, or they'd have moved faster and caught him before he found Cori-Anne.

Chapter 25

Hunter's Folly very early that morning

Cori-Anne hadn't gone very far. In providing the opening for her escape, Fortune showed itself to be sympathetic. But as Cori-Anne soon discovered, it was not merciful. The bushes at the side of the road—especially given that she was running in blind panic and hindered by hands bound behind her back—were too thick and thorny for navigation. Huge camelthorns ripped at her arms and legs, and roots and termite mounds tripped her up until she fell right in the path of an old male leopard who was desperate to eat anything he could find.

The science of fear is well understood. Deep in your brain, the amygdala sets off an alarm bell. This triggers the hypothalamus, which gives you an instantaneous burst of adrenaline, which causes your heart to pump blood to your muscles. At that moment of the process, fright turns to flight. Of course, whoever came up with that explanation had not been in the path of a 165-pound killing machine with its mouth open, displaying teeth that—in their day—had ripped apart a giant eland. Cori-Anne froze in terror.

The leopard liked the look and smell of the human who lay in front of him doing her best to scream but making a sound that reminded the old cat of a mewling cub. What the leopard did not like the look of was the upright human waving his arms and yelling at him. Cripps, who'd had his share of google-eyed idolators in prison, was more accustomed to being demonized by those who feared him, and he read fear in the leopard's eyes. The leopard gave a low growl and then retreated into the bush.

Whether Cripps saved Cori-Anne from a fate worse than death or for a fate worse than death was yet to be determined. "You filthy whore-spawn," he shrieked, kicking her in the ribs. "Try one more trick like that and I'll cut yer hamstrings and drag you back by yer hair."

To prove he meant business, he waved the razor in front of her face, grabbed a handful of her hair, and pulled her into a standing position. He gave her a shove and they set off once more.

Cripps had no idea what caused the explosion nor what had exploded. He'd completely forgotten about the IED that Pakkies and Oom Ebert had buried in the road up ahead. With the revolver pushed into her spine and her ribs aching from where Cripps had kicked her, Cori-Anne moved ahead, hoping her bladder would hold up. She tried once again to practice *pranayama* and achieved a modicum of success. She had a strong feeling that Eliot was alive and that he'd come for her. She had no idea why she felt this, only that she did.

As the sun rose the shadows began to dissolve, and for the first time Cori-Anne saw that they were walking close to the fence of the reserve. Neither she nor Cripps could see what had exploded up ahead, but they could smell burning, and when Cori-Anne nearly tripped on the severed head of Don Jorge, she threw up into her gag and almost choked.

The Land Rover carrying Eliot and Rohini and Sabhajit Singh sped along the main road from the reserve towards the entrance to Groot Witdoosbos Farm. Rohini was driving with her husband and Eliot, hanging on for dear life as the vehicle fishtailed on the gravel.

"Good God," exclaimed Sabhajit, holding on to his turban, "you're going to kill us."

"Relax, my dear," replied Rohini, going into a four-wheel drift. "I was going twice as fast in the South Sudan trying to escape a truck filled with Janjaweed militias. Here, this must be the entrance."

The gates were open, and a broken chain dangled from one of the links. Rohini slowed the Land Rover as they made their way down the heavily corrugated road that led to the main farmhouse and lion enclosures. Eliot thought he heard a lion roar, but other than that the farm was enshrouded in an almost oppressive silence. Even the birds that should have been chirping away in what ornithologists call the "dawn chorus" were oddly silent. As far as they could determine, the place was deserted.

Rohini pulled up behind a large knob thorn tree and held up her hand. Eliot immediately stood up and began to climb out the Land Rover. He was quickly stopped by

Sabhajit, who grabbed his arm and pulled him back in.

"Now," said Sabhajit, firmly though not unkindly, "this is where you must listen to us. The wrong action can result in severe consequences. I cannot stress this point enough. I am, as you may know, a highly decorated police officer and Rohini a trained soldier with a fearsome reputation. You will allow us to assess the situation before we permit you to approach."

Sabhajit's tone was so peremptory that Eliot sat down. He stared at the policeman for a moment, his mouth open, as if to protest. Then he shut it and let out a sigh.

"OK, I'll wait, but please—"

"Of course," said Rohini, knowing exactly what Eliot wanted to say. "The second we see or hear anything, we'll come back to get you." She grabbed her rifle and followed her husband towards the farmhouse. Eliot sat in the Land Rover and watched as Rohini and Sabhajit crept along the side of the house looking in the windows. They turned the corner, and he lost sight of them. He got out the Land Rover and walked a short distance to see if he could catch sight of the couple.

Then his whole body went rigid.

The Reverend Clayton Calvin Cripps, looking like some demented gremlin, shoved Cori-Anne through a hole in the fence, and Cori-Anne stumbled, falling onto her face in the brush.

"Git up, yer sow-teeted bitch," shrieked Cripps, pulling the straight razor from his pocket and flicking it open. But Cori-Anne didn't move. Cripps kicked her and yelled at her to get up. He grabbed her hair, jerked her head up, and put the razor to her exposed throat.

"I've had enough of you, girlie. Let's see how long you last after I open yer windpipe." The razor touched her throat and then flew into the air as Cripps was sent barreling back onto the fence as Eliot's head slammed into his body.

Florida man saves naked-yoga instructor from Nazi hitman by chewing off his ear was the headline somewhere towards the back of the New York Post a few months later. All of it was true except for the fact that Eliot hadn't yet established residence in Florida.

Eliot's impromptu reaction may have been triggered by a subliminal image of a move performed by a wrestler in the only match Eliot had ever watched on TV when he was a small boy. The time elapsed from the moment he left his hiding place behind the Land Rover and launched himself into the air could have been measured in nanoseconds. There was no strategy behind it, no hastily—if ill-conceived—plan; only action.

His skull on a trajectory that would have delighted Werner von Braun, the scientist behind the V1 and V2 rockets and coincidently also a Nazi, missed Cori-Anne's upturned head and hit Cripps just below his chin.

The impact that would have incapacitated most people did little more than dislodge Cripps from Cori-Anne. He fell backwards onto the fence and rebounded into a standing position.

"Son-of-a-bitch," he yelled, scrambling for his razor and then leaping onto Eliot, who hadn't managed to get to his feet. He held the razor under Eliot's nose. "Well, ain't this perfect. I get to slash and gash both of you, just like the butcher ordered."

Eliot, whose head had taken a number of beatings over the past few days starting with the one outside Cori-Anne's studio in Miami, was dazed from the impact. Up until that moment he'd only seen Cripps from a distance, but the close-up version was unbearable. Cripps lowered his face until his ear was just over Eliot's mouth.

"I want to hear you scream, boy. I want to hear yer very last breath ooze out yer split neck like slime from a frog pond."

Eliot felt the razor glide across his neck as if Cripps were making a practice run before the real event, and so he did the only thing he could. He opened his mouth, sucked in Cripps' ear like an oyster, and then bit down as hard as he could. Cripps screamed and tried to pull away, but Eliot—mad with fear, his mouth full of blood—bit down harder and held on. Then Cripps leaped up, howling in pain and cursing as he clutched the side of his head where his ear—which now dangled from Eliot's mouth—used to be.

"Heil Hitler!" he yelled and sprang forward at Eliot. Rohini's shot took him just below his eye. Cripps fell to his knees, said something unintelligible, and toppled over quite dead. Eliot spat out the ear and fainted.

When he came to—and it was probably no more than a few minutes later— he was propped up against the side of the Land Rover with Cori-Anne beside him. Cori-Anne looked over and handed Eliot the bottle of water she'd been sipping. Her voice was hoarse from the gag, but she managed a "thank you" and then took Eliot's hand and kissed it.

"I thought I'd lost you," he said, putting his arm around

her and pulling her closer. "I couldn't have stood that." Pain and dizziness prevented any further restorative groping.

"That was a very brave thing you did," said Rohini, looking up from where she and her husband were examining Cripps' corpse.

"And without doubt an act of extreme stupidity," added Sabhajit, sounding very much like the police officer he was.

"I didn't think—" began Eliot.

"Most people don't when they embark on behavior that is both precarious and foolhardy."

"You don't understand," laughed Eliot. "I didn't think... I didn't think."

"That's the second time Eliot's saved my life," Cori-Anne blurted out. "So don't you dare call him a fool."

"I was referring to his actions, not his motivation," replied Singh indignantly. "Though I fail to see his apparent joy in 'not thinking.'"

Eliot started to explain, but Singh had already walked off to greet Ishea, Gosego, and the trackers who'd arrived at the farm. He stood up slowly and made his way to the opposite side of the Jeep, where Rohini was examining the cut on Cori-Anne's head from Cripps' pistol. When Rohini saw the look on Eliot's face, she sensed her presence was not required at that moment and moved off to join Gosego and the others.

They were both in pain, but the need to hold each other overcame any physical discomfort for thirty seconds when Cori-Anne's bruised ribs decided they'd had enough.

"Yeow, that hurts," she said, pulling back. "Look at

us—we're a mess. There's blood from where that little...I don't know what to call him...cut your neck, and my ribs feel like someone hit me with a baseball bat. It hurts to love you Eliot Hart, but I do."

"So do I," he said. "I mean I love you too, not me—"

Cori-Anne silenced him with a finger to his lips.

Chapter 26

Hunter's Folly that night.

P re-dinner cocktails at Hunter's Folly that night were more raucous than usual. The guides and trackers who normally retired to their own quarters at the end of the day for an early night were celebrating what Gosego called the "Battle of the Bushveld."

"Personally, I believe a more somber tone should have been adopted," said Sabhajit, taking a sip of his martini. "If this had happened in India, I'd have shut the entire operation down until we had examined every facet, every detail of what transpired to ascertain precisely what happened and why."

"Aren't you glad we're in Africa, then?" replied his wife, giving him a playful shove. "In any case, what other facts were there to examine? The local police were satisfied that two rival gangs of international animal traffickers who worked with the owners of that lion farm had a shoot-out."

"What you need to understand, Sabhajit," said Bontle, who'd walked over to the two honeymooners, "is that we take the protection of our wildlife heritage very seriously. With the exception of the so-called canned lion-hunting industry, which we are trying to get stopped, no one here is inclined to waste resources on criminals like the Vietnamese and the Mexican traffickers when a bullet will do the trick. It's doubtful that their respective governments will intercede. Incidents like this are best buried for everyone's convenience."

"Well, it's highly irregular," said the policeman. "But you're right, my dear." He gave his wife a squeeze. "We're not in India and I'm not on duty and we're on honeymoon… and quite frankly I'm all for shooting poachers and animal smugglers."

"Good," said Bontle. "Then why don't the two of you come over and meet some old friends. Conchita and Roger arrived about half an hour ago, and they're about to join us for dinner."

The elderly German guests decided to dine on the deck of their tent rather than mingle with a group of people they considered certifiably insane, but Eliot and Cori-Anne were invited to join the party.

After a local doctor had treated their wounds and declared them to be non-life threatening but advised them to stay away from any strenuous physical activity for a week—Eliot interpreted his admonition as yoga and Cori-Anne as sex—they put in a call to Thomas Mortimer Jones in Miami.

"I was tying up a few loose ends on the case," said the district attorney, "before calling you. But I just put the phone down with my contact in the Mexican Police anti-narcotics unit—one of the few that hasn't been corrupted—

and he tells me you're off the hook with the cartel. Apparently, Don Jorge's uncles are thrilled he's dead and according to my contact would like to reward you, but—"

"How much?" Cori-Anne asked.

"Whoa," Thomas laughed. "You can't actually take a reward, you know. It's illegal drug money, but—and don't interrupt me—we've taken possession of the Ram-Dann Anubis Hard Core Yoga and Pilates studio, which I've been tasked with informing you that you can buy from the DEA for $1."

"Thanks, but no thanks," replied Cori-Anne, giving what sounded like a sniff. "I don't need it. I'm happy with my old place and it's where my students feel most comfortable. So, if it's all the same, I'll just go back to what I was doing before."

Eliot cleared his throat, "Uhm, what about me?"

"What about you?" she asked. And then before he could put into words all the angst his face betrayed, she said, "Do you honestly believe I'd do anything without you?" Her lips found his, effectively shutting down his brain. After a minute of watching impatiently for the snogging to end, Thomas Mortimer Jones ended the call.

The dinner turned out to be an old friends and family reunion. With the exception of Eliot and Cori-Anne and the younger Storms, everyone knew each other. Simon and Steven hadn't seen their father for four years, and they'd not met his wife, Conchita Palomino, whose initial apprehension at meeting her new family quickly vanished with laughter and hugs. Eliot and Cori-Anne sat in the middle of the long table with Rohini next to Eliot and Gosego on the other side of Cori-Anne.

The big—and still mysterious—man, Ishea Payamps, hadn't said more than a few words to Roger and Cori-Anne after their ordeal and, judging by his grumpy expression each time Eliot tried to engage him in conversation during dinner, had no intention of remedying that. He sat opposite Rohini and was soon engrossed in an intense conversation about the state of India's game preserves.

Eliot tried to listen, but his mind was elsewhere. He found himself staring at Conchita, trying to determine just who she was and why someone who managed to be strikingly beautiful yet strangely terrifying at the same time could be in love with a shlumpy fellow like Roger Storm. There was no question in Eliot's mind that they were infatuated with each other. Roger, who Eliot thought looked more like an aging academic than a person hardened by the bush, held his wife's hand and kissed it every time she drew a reaction from his sons. She in turn smiled at him when he touched her hand to his lips, and her dark blue eyes seemed to flash with pleasure. Roger caught Eliot staring, but he gave him a cheerful wave and returned to squeezing Conchita's hand.

Suddenly Eliot felt embarrassed. Who was he to question Roger and Conchita's relationship when he couldn't quite understand what it was that made Cori-Anne love him? If anything, he was ever-so-slightly shlumpier than Roger. He glanced at Roger again and found that Roger was looking back at him. Before Eliot could turn his head, Roger gave him a thumbs up. People of a less vulnerable disposition may have interpreted

Roger's signal as a bromidic gesture of "all's good." Eliot did not. He saw it—and it was confirmed with Roger a year or so later—as a conspiratorial indication from a fellow shlump that "we both hit the jackpot." He grinned at Roger, who nodded his head in acknowledgment, and all of a sudden Eliot knew what he needed to do.

As soon as dinner was over and they were certain that their presence wouldn't be missed, Cori-Anne and Eliot retired to their tent, where they fell asleep holding hands. It was a deep, untroubled sleep—the first they'd had since they'd met in Miami—uninterrupted by visions of mayhem and murderers. A doctor may have concluded that it was brought on by painkillers and exhaustion, but the smile on Eliot's face said something different.

Just before he'd fallen asleep, he'd asked Cori-Anne to marry him. It was a rash decision, one that the old Eliot couldn't possibly have made in under a month. It had taken him less than ten seconds to decide to pop the question, and Cori-Anne even less to agree.

If indeed, as the poets say, the best kind of love is one we fall into accidently, without knowing it, without ceremony or effort, then it was clear to anyone they met that Eliot and Cori-Anne were utterly and undeniably in love. It was a love that neither increases nor lessens with time, and unlike the heap of rice in the sorites paradox, it needed no additional commitment. There was nothing that would have made it any stronger nor left it stranded like an ebbing tide on a moonlit beach. For the first time Eliot knew that the transformation that had begun the moment he laid eyes on Cori-Anne was complete.

Epilogue

Eliot moved to Miami two days after the account of *Florida Man bites off Nazi's ear...* ran in the newspaper. They were married the following weekend by Coachella De Ville, who'd bought the online Universal Life Minister Premium Wedding Package for $59.99. All of Cori-Anne's students—except for Leo Goldberg, who'd died a few days earlier before his new teeth had arrived— attended, and Shelly Gotlieb and Tina Constantinedes acted as bridesmaids. Thomas Mortimer Jones was Eliot's best man. Cori-Anne's mother declined the invitation when she heard that Jesus would not be present at the ceremony. She deeply appreciated the $100,000 that Eliot sent her, though she gave almost all of it away to the leader of her church group, who told her that the Lord had instructed him to buy a new Range Rover.

Eliot finished his paper on the sorites paradox, which was rejected by Princeton. He threw it in the garbage, went snorkeling in Biscayne National Park, and began to plan his and Cori-Anne's trip to Rwanda to visit the mountain gorillas. Since their return from South Africa, both had decided they wanted to see as much of the world's wildlife before it vanished forever. Just as he finished making the arrangements with Jodie from &Beyond, he received an email from Bontle to say that the lions they'd rescued from the canned hunting farm had been successfully relocated to a nearby animal rescue sanctuary, and the $250,000 Eliot had sent would see them and other animals taken care of for the rest of their lives.

The End

Also by Jonathan Harries

The Roger Storm Books

Roger Storm, drinking heavily and contemplating suicide after his divorce and unceremonious firing from a high-powered job, gets the shock of his life when he meets his childhood friend, Freddy Blank, years after his supposed death. Roger soon finds himself dragged kicking and screaming into an adventure where a mysterious international organization is taking out poachers and trophy hunters in precisely the same ways they take out animals. Don't miss this hugely inventive, action-packed, hilarious debut novel from Jonathan Harries!

Roger Storm is back in this thrilling second book in the series! The bucolic peace of Hunter's Folly Private Game Reserve is shattered by the discovery of a noseless hunter next to a hornless rhino carcass, sending Roger on another mad adventure helping his

254

friends to take down one of the most vicious animal trafficking rings in the world—and helping the animals to fight back!

On a remote hunting preserve in Namibia, a brilliant Indian geneticist is facing a rather nasty end unless he can find a way for elephants to grow longer tusks, rhinos bigger horns, and lions thicker manes. Behind this dastardly scheme is the notorious Russian oligarch Valerian Zolotov and members of *Bratva*, the Russian mafia. But there's an equally dangerous group determined to save the geneticist and put a permanent stop to these rotters.

Tales of the Sica

I had absolutely no intention of getting into the family business. As I told my father the night he enlightened me on what my ancestors had been up to for over a thousand years, "Sticking a curved dagger into someone's liver ain't quite my cup of tea." As it turned out, I had no choice. When your family's been assassinating reprobates and other loathsome individuals for seventy generations, you have a certain obligation.

THE CARPET SALESMAN FROM BAGHDAD
ANOTHER TALE OF THE SICA
BY JONATHAN HARRIES

Can you blame a chap for wanting to turn his otherwise humdrum family into a bunch of assassins? It turns out you can. I found this out soon after my novel The Tailor of Riga was published, and I received a bunch of beastly emails and threats from incensed family members horrified that I'd portrayed them as the descendants of bloodthirsty hitmen. Then, out of the blue, a package arrived from a long-lost cousin in Argentina that changed everything.

THE BODYGUARD OF SARAWAK
ANOTHER TALE OF THE SICA
BY JONATHAN HARRIES

When the British Secret Service Bureau commissioned my great-uncle Leon to whack a Russian Count aboard the SS Gwalior on its way from Cape Town to Mombasa, he had no idea the size of the maelstrom into which he was about to plunge. After tossing out bodies to the lions of Tsavo in Kenya, graduating with honors from a school specializing in sexual techniques in Singapore, avoiding headhunters in the sweltering jungles of Sarawak, to becoming bodyguard to his highness Charles Brooke, the 2nd Rajah of Sarawak, Leon carves a magnificent swath of death and seduction as the 68th generation in our family assassination business. Read now!

THE CORRESPONDENT OF PETROGRAD

It's the spring of 1912 and my great-uncle Leon, freshly returned to London after his assignments for the British Secret Service Bureau in Africa and Asia—including a crash course in sexual technique at the Heavenly Abode of the Crimson Lotus—is ready to settle down. Against overwhelming odds and with the assistance of the mysterious Mata Hari, Leon takes out a double agent in Vienna, dispatches a Turkish brothel-owning spy in Hamburg, and ends up in Petrograd, where his hitherto unknown involvement in the death of Rasputin is finally revealed. Read now!

THE MERCENARY OF URGA

Great-uncle Leon, the most successful assassin in our family's 2000-year-old history, is back. When a battalion of British soldiers is shanghaied by a diabolical Baltic baron hellbent on conquering Mongolia and backed by an international organization of fascists, Sir Mansfield Smith-Cumming, head of the SIS, sends his number-one assassin to take care of business. From London and Paris to the Crimea, Georgia and war-ravaged China and Mongolia, Leon and his accomplice, the beautiful Countess Catherine von Merenberg, are plunged headfirst into a maelstrom of horror to rescue the British troops and stop the reign of the Bloody White Baron.

Acknowledgements

I like the "writing" part of my job. It's everything else that goes into finally completing a novel that causes my bowels to contract most painfully. Staring at a blank screen wondering just what the heck my characters are supposed to do next. Deciding I need a break when I took one ten minutes ago. Wondering if I'm going to be sued by someone in real life I used an inspiration for one of my nastier characters. What I'm going to eat for lunch, and should I go to the store now so that I can have the rest of the day free to write. In fact, anything to avoid actually writing.

Then there's the part that I wouldn't have the foggiest idea how to do. Which is basically everything else it takes to finally get a book into print. For that I can only begin to thank my friend, agent, and editor, Melissa Mazzeo. Her patience, her insights, and her kindness are so deeply appreciated. I cannot thank my old colleague and friend Luis Silva Dias enough for always coming up with yet another brilliant cover. He is a wonderful designer and an inspiring creative mind whom I've known for years and was the backbone of some of the best advertising campaigns done at my old advertising agency, FCB.

To my family, especially my sons, Simon and Steven, and their wonderful wives, thanks for always being so supportive. To everyone else who reads and hopefully likes my books, thank you so much. Everything you fork out goes to different animal and environmental causes. Finally, to trophy hunters and. animal traffickers, I hope one day you get everything you deserve.

About the Author

I grew up in Namibia, an extraordinarily beautiful and wild country where the desert meets the sea, with not a blade of grass in between. In my early teens we moved to South Africa where, after completing the perfunctory exercises necessary for entering adulthood, I began a career in advertising. While my love and fascination with wildlife began in Namibia, it grew into a passion in South Africa, and I spent every chance I got going to Botswana and other places where you could—and luckily still can—see animals in their natural habitat.

I moved to the US in 1986 because it didn't seem as if apartheid would ever end, and I've lived here ever since. I retired just over a year ago as Chairman of FCB, a global advertising agency, and published my first book, *Killing Harry Bones*. Both my sons are passionate about animals; my elder son, Simon, moved back to South Africa for a few years to become a safari guide. My wife and I go on safari as often as possible and have had some incredible trips into the bush, bringing back memories rather than trophies.

—Jonathan

www.ingramcontent.com/pod-product-compliance
Lightning Source LLC
Chambersburg PA
CBHW031614240626
47153CB00002B/751